CHASING JUSTICE

DANIELLE STEWART

RANDOM ACTS PUBLISHING

Cover Design by Gin's Book Designs (http://ginsbookdesigns.com/)
Image used under license from Shutterstock.com / ver0nicka

ISBN-13: 978-1492283218

ISBN-10: 1492283215

❀ Created with Vellum

To my husband who frequently reminds me to breathe, and my son who always takes my breath away.

Thank you to my sisters, Jennipher and Nichole, for all they've added to this book and my life. Gratitude to Emily and Karen for your honest and invaluable feedback. And a special thank you to Becky, for her incredible support, and her vast knowledge of proper comma placement. I'd be nothing without your red pen.

CHASING JUSTICE

Piper Anderson has been given a fresh start in the picturesque town of Edenville, North Carolina. But her plans of settling into a normal life are derailed when she witnesses a prominent judge in her community committing a violent assault. Running from her own past and fueled by a passion to make the judge answer for his crimes, Piper is forced to decide if she'll play by the rules or achieve justice in her own way.

Complicating things further, Piper finds herself fighting a powerful attraction to rookie cop, Bobby Wright. Although she's increasingly enamored with Bobby, his staunch belief in the justice system is in stark contrast to her own. She may not share his opinions about the effectiveness of the law, but she certainly can't deny how safe she feels when she's in his arms or how every kiss leaves her desperate for more.

For Piper, the idea of finally living an ordinary life with a man to love is tempting. However, fate keeps placing the judge, quite literally, in her path. Will she decide the only way to win is to be as wicked as the judge, but with righteous intentions? And more importantly, will Bobby choose to let her go, or follow her as she crosses the line and takes justice into her own hands?

PROLOGUE

The world is full of terrible people. I'm sure you've heard that before, maybe even said it yourself. But when you say the "world" you don't mean *your* world. You're not thinking about your supermarket, your children's school, the place you work. You're thinking about those big cities with those big problems, not your neighborhood.

This kind of talk makes me sound paranoid, and maybe I am. But I'm also right. I know the pedophile blurs into the role of coach. The violent sex offenders deliver your mail or bag your groceries. So often we find out too late the laws that are meant to protect the innocent instead shield the offenders. There was a small window of time in my life when I thought I could be one of the "good guys," and I use the term lightly as I happen to be a woman. I believed I could follow the letter of the law and still take part in cleaning this world up a little. But I was wrong. You can't do things the right way and still win when the villains have no code. The only way to get anything done is to be just as wicked, but with righteous intentions.

My ideals aren't something I've formed half-heartedly. They've been forged like steel, burned in a fiery pit and then hammered relentlessly. I've been hurt. I've faced death. I've made many mistakes. My spirit was broken and I believed the only way I could repair myself was to knock a little piece of evil off this planet.

One afternoon, as I stared outside, I came face to face with my opportunity. I had left my window slightly open so the breeze could balance the stale, recycled feeling of the air conditioner. Late summer in North Carolina was usually humid and stagnant, but I remember on that day the wind was moving nicely through the trees. I had hoped it would blow new life into me.

The rear of my townhouse faced an alley where an Italian restaurant backed up to the bank. Out the back door of the restaurant stepped a man familiar enough for me to take notice, but not so much that I could place him. From behind him came a girl, who even from the distance, I could see was half woman and half child. She was dressed in mismatched clothing not suited for her age.

The two looked like a peculiar pair. They were clearly not father and daughter, not student and teacher. There was something about their demeanor, the way the man was moving with force and the girl creeping behind him timidly, that made my skin break out in goose bumps. Something was not right.

Suddenly the man turned on his heels to face the girl. He cocked back his fist and before she could even raise her hands to protect herself he struck her hard across the face. The girl stifled a yelp as her hands rushed to her nose which had instantly begun bleeding. She slouched forward, and the man straightened her by grabbing the loose ponytail on the back of her head. He leaned in close and hissed into her face. "You don't get to talk to me here. You don't get to *know* me here. This is my real life and you are a whore who I screw when I feel like it. If you ever approach me in public again I will end you, and there isn't a soul in this world who would even know you were gone. No one misses a fourteen-year-old hooker." He tugged again at her hair to make sure she understood, and she nodded through the pain. In a moment of clarity I suppose, the man looked over his shoulder to see if anyone had been within earshot. I ducked back behind my curtains. As he turned again toward her I realized where I had seen the salt and pepper in his hair, the lines on his red doughy face, the roundness of his bulbous nose.

He looked different without his black robe but there was no doubt—he was a judge whose courtroom I had sat in while shadowing a lawyer a few weeks earlier. There he was standing in an alley beating an underage prostitute who had the unfortunate judgment of addressing him outside the confines of whatever seedy motel they usually frequented. This man of stature and prominence in our community was a sex offender.

Any reasonable person would stop what she was doing and immediately call the police. But I believed I could do something about this on my own. To understand why, you would need to know what makes me different from the general population. You would have to understand what brought me to North Carolina in the first place. No, I'm not an assassin who spent her childhood being groomed by monks in the art of ancient jiu jitsu.

As a matter of fact, even if my life depended on it, I'd be hard pressed to do a chin-up. I'm about as graceful as a seasick flamingo. My overall endurance makes me pretty sure I'm one of those people who is thin on the outside and fat on the inside. I don't have a weapon, I don't have any allies, and I don't really have a plan.

I have no particularly impressive skills besides perhaps valuing my own life so little that I'm willing to risk it even when the odds are stacked against me. I'm delusional and I'm damaged, but I'm brave. That's really all I have right now.

So how did I get here, how did I get to a point where I thought I could take justice into my own hands? I arrived in North Carolina two years before I had witnessed the judge's assault. The life that lay before me was blank. I was given a clean slate; clean to a degree that many people would envy considering the circumstances that led me there. Yet to me, the void stretching before me was suffocating rather than liberating. I was adrift in a new town, a new world. I was twenty-three years old and essentially born again, burdened with the ignorance of a child and the expectations of an adult.

My "relocation," as I have come to internally label it, had afforded me a small place to live. It was paid outright, and it was mine. I had a sum of money that, in my naïve, unworldly experience, seemed like a small fortune. In truth, it was just enough to be swallowed up by the reality of existing on my own. As it turns out, barricading myself in my townhouse and ordering delivery pizza couldn't be a long-term solution. It was as bad for my mental health as it was for my desire to fit into my skinny jeans.

I was the warden in my own prison. That realization hit me on a Tuesday and by the following Monday, I had enrolled in college. It was something I had never allowed myself to consider in the past. I was breaking free of the chains, and embracing my new life.

It made perfect sense to me that I should major in criminal justice. I had the unfortunate experience of seeing the system up close and personal from a very young age. The first year was thrilling in its fairy-tale-like explanation of our justice system. I was slightly older than many of the other students who were fresh out of high school, but no one seemed to notice. The excitement of the large lecture halls with stadium seating like I had seen on television made muddling through my general requirement courses a little more bearable. It was text books and study groups. It was me practicing my new life, my new name.

Because I had more time than the average student I enrolled in a few classes that would have normally been reserved for the following year. I was completely captivated by the curriculum in my criminal profiling and theories of crime classes.

The philosophies I learned were idealistic and stirred something within me. I had a newfound feeling of empowerment and pride. My entire life had been so turbulent, such a mess, but now here I was in college dreaming of something better. It seems ridiculous looking back on it now, but I believed I could change the world. Maybe I couldn't do anything about my own past, but someone else's future could be shaped by my actions, my hard-line belief in the system.

During my second year it was time to plot out the direction of my career. How would I apply this degree? So I went out into the world. I ventured into the streets of this new town I had been dropped in—Edenville, North Carolina. Its population was just over fifteen thousand, but it had pockets of small town charm, and I lived right in the middle of one of those communities. This place was so different than the world in which I had grown up. There were times I felt like I had been transported to Mayberry.

To get started, I set up appointments at the courthouse to shadow criminal attorneys and police officers. I toured the prison two towns over and visited the child protection agency. I was enamored with the thought of making a difference. Then, slowly, reality began to set in. People, bad people, were let back into society because of clerical errors or loopholes.

I observed eight cases, and as far as I was concerned, six of them were completely disheartening. I saw children torn away from caring and loving foster homes and placed back with drug-addicted parents, all in the name of "keeping a family together." I saw a rape victim being persecuted for the low-rise cut of her jeans and the long line of boyfriends she had leading up to the attack. There were drug dealers who walked free because the police made several errors bringing the case to trial.

The picture slowly became very clear to me. A trial is a game where the truth is of secondary importance and each side aims to win regardless of the collateral damage.

My naïve exuberance turned quickly to disdain. These were the people who failed me; they were no different.

So the moment I saw the judge punching the young girl behind my house I found my purpose. It made me realize that just because I could not arrest or prosecute someone for a crime didn't mean I couldn't punish him. And just like that, I dropped out of school. I tossed my books in the trash and ignored emails from my professors.

I, Piper Anderson, was unwilling to accept the world through the eyes of a defeatist. My life up until that point had been wasted. I wasn't going to spend another minute watching the system fail people. The time I had spent in school showed me that a man like that judge would never be held accountable for his crimes. I'd need to find a way to do it myself. There had to be a place in this world for my idea of justice, and if there wasn't I was damn sure going to do everything I could to make room for it.

CHAPTER 1

Short of grabbing tights and a cape, Piper had to think long and hard about what channels she would follow in order to right the wrong she had witnessed that day. She was a *no one* in this town and the judge was certainly a *someone*. He made decisions and had important friends, many of whom would probably defend his character out of obligation. Would she depend on finding some diligent assistant district attorney who would believe her? Perhaps she'd contact the FBI, though they didn't seem to have a toll-free number floating around.

Piper knew Edenville's size would make it all the more challenging to poke around and go unnoticed. It was an insulated suburb on the fringe of Durham, North Carolina.

This place was so different than the world in which she had grown up. Brooklyn, her hometown, was a place where anonymity was as easy as losing yourself in the crowd of morning commuters. That wouldn't be an option here in sleepy Edenville where everyone was a familiar face.

There seemed to be no limit to the number of times you might run into the same person day after day. The courthouse, the bank, the post office, and town hall were all housed in drafty old brick buildings with Main Street addresses. The mainstays of downtown dining included the diner, the deli, and the general store. At lunchtime you'd find the same people ordering the same meal at the same time every day, and folks seemed quite content to be known as regulars in any of the establishments. The rest of Main Street was made up of florists, hobby stores, and consignment shops. There were banners advertising an upcoming festival celebrating Edenville's textile mill heritage. It had the quintessential small town façade, but now Piper knew it hid big city secrets.

The one thing that worked to Piper's advantage was her ability to be insignificant and overlooked. She found this to be ironic since she had spent the majority of her life attempting to draw the attention of men, regardless of whether that attention was good or bad. Before she moved to Edenville, getting a man to look her way, to engage her in some flirty banter, was a hobby of hers.

Before she came here Piper had kept her hair long, well past her shoulders. She would highlight it with blonde streaks that would catch any man's eye. Now it was shorter and she kept it her natural dark chocolate color. It was average and forgettable.

To further her attempt to go unnoticed, her covered skin to exposed skin ratio had dramatically swung the other way. Now even on warm days she found herself in long pants instead of the minuscule shorts of her past.

However, even with the changes to her hair and clothing, Piper hadn't quite perfected the technique of ambiguity yet. There were still a few distinct features she hadn't been able to camouflage. Her brown eyes had the depth of an old soul and frequently drew compliments from people. When the light caught them, they had a sparkle that no amount of work on her part could extinguish. They were framed by long lashes and, although she had stopped covering them with mascara, they still seemed glamorously exotic. Her skin was a glowing caramel that needed next to no maintenance in order to remain flawless. And her smile, though it rarely made an appearance, had frequently been called stunning. She had perfectly honed the use of her impish innocent face to appeal to men. Now, as she tried to fade into the walls of Edenville, she realized getting people to remember you was a lot easier than getting them to forget you.

In spite of the added challenge of a small town, Piper took to following the *Honorable* Judge Randall A. Lions. He ate regularly in the diner, and this became the best way to learn more about him. The wait staff was straight out of a movie, with their pale blue polyester uniforms and frilly white aprons. One waitress in particular always captivated Piper. Her name tag read "Betty" and Piper overheard her say that she had worked there for over ten years. Doing a job like that for so long had given Betty a very acute sense of people.

After two weeks of what Piper was calling surveillance, she felt as though she had learned a lot. The judge seemed to be well-liked by those who frequented the diner, but he only noticed the people who came right up to greet him. If you stayed in his peripheral and acted as though he was not there then he would ignore you. To Piper it seemed like your run-of-the-mill above-the-law narcissism. Another nausea inducing quality of the judge was the way he ate eggs sloppily; it never failed to turn Piper's stomach. On occasion she would catch Betty's eye and they would both realize they were wearing the same expression of disgust. They'd smirk and turn their gazes quickly in opposite directions.

The judge was regimented about his time which, thankfully, made following him relatively easy. He frequented the diner, the bank, the Italian restaurant, the back door of the Blue Fox Motel on Tuesdays, and, of course, the courthouse. The rest of his time was spent at home. His house was beautifully landscaped, and about seven blocks from Piper's. This was where she was most apprehensive about watching him because she struggled to blend into the scenery of his quiet neighborhood. She had taken to posing as a jogger, which, even though she was thin, was clearly a stretch. Her stamina left a lot to be desired. But the exhaustion proved worth it when she caught a glimpse of the judge's wife one morning. She was a stunning woman with dark black hair, exotic features, and an amazing figure. Piper assumed she was somewhere around fifty, but could easily pass for thirty-five. The judge, she had learned from public records, was sixty-six. Seeing Mrs. Lions infuriated Piper. She could never understand why men cheat, but especially why they cheat on beautiful women.

While jotting some notes about the judge's schedule in her tattered black notebook, Piper heard the bell over the door of the diner jingle as a man entered. He was someone she hadn't seen during her weeks at the diner, and she found herself intrigued. After a couple days perched in one seat you tended to see the same people, so a stranger was interesting.

The man was tall and too thin for Piper's taste, though, to be honest, she didn't think she had a taste in men. Her past had made men as a whole seem rather repulsive. He looked like someone recovering from the flu in need of rest and food. Outside of that, he was beguiling enough in his own way to pique her curiosity, and she continued to watch him. His hair was dark, almost black, and cut short in a military style. He had great posture, and Piper thought perhaps he was a soldier who had mastered standing at attention. There didn't seem to be anything extraordinary about this man, but for some reason Piper was captivated by him. She watched him the way you might watch a child who's been accidently separated from his parents in a crowd—watching to make sure he found his way. This man seemed lost in some way, and Piper stared, waiting to see if he'd find what he was looking for.

Betty jumped up from the stool where she sat counting her tips when she saw him enter. "Bobby you look like you've been running all over hell's half acre." For a moment Betty looked like she might throw her arms around him, but instead she slapped him across the shoulder.

"Oh come on Betty, don't give me any shit. I've been laying low for a while, waiting for this whole thing to blow over. Can I get something to eat or what?" Bobby scanned the diner as if to make sure whoever he was avoiding while laying low wasn't present.

"You have nothing to feel bad about. It could have happened to any cop on the force. Two week suspension is malarkey. I'd've gone right in there and given that captain a piece of my mind if I didn't think those crooked bastards would be in here shutting the diner down the very next day. You keep your chin up, and I'll get you the usual." Betty was halfway in the kitchen as she finished her sentence and Bobby had no time to retort. His face was flush with embarrassment, and he sulked over to the corner booth where Piper was sitting.

He didn't notice Piper until he was almost ready to sit across from her. There were plenty of other empty booths, so she looked annoyed as she said, "Excuse me." The man seemed to wake from a dream and shot back an equally irritated and confused look.

"This is my booth. You're in my booth." He stood waiting for the girl to gather her things and move. When no attempt was made, he backed away more aggravated.

"I've been sitting here for the last couple weeks," she croaked at him. Piper thought to herself, *what kind of weirdo has his own booth and expects people to get up when he comes in?*

"That's because I haven't been here for the last couple weeks, but for five years I've been sitting here every morning for breakfast. So yeah, it's my booth. But whatever, I don't need this today." He slinked into the adjacent booth as Betty re-emerged from the kitchen and immediately read the scene.

"Oh Bobby, get over it. It's just a seat and this young lady has been a loyal customer, as loyal as you or Judge Lions. Like clockwork." At the sound of these words Piper's cheeks pinked. Had she been so obvious with her attempts at surveillance that a waitress could spot her motives?

"Fine," Bobby mumbled. "I just want to get my life back to normal as soon as possible. My suspension is over, and I'm back on duty this morning. I was hoping that two weeks of being gone wouldn't mean my whole life would be upside down." He peppered the eggs Betty had brought him and moved them around his plate like a pouting child.

Betty smiled at him and squeezed his shoulder. "Well you weren't suspended from the diner, and in the words of a wise man 'move your feet, lose your seat.'" She leaned in and whispered loud enough for Piper to hear. "It's going to be all right Bobby, and if it means that much to you, go sit with her." He rolled his eyes up at Betty and put his hand over hers that rested now on his shoulder. He let the firmness in his jaw relax slightly but stopped short of smiling.

For no apparent reason, and without much thought, Piper was intrigued enough to chat with this man. "So what did you do? You know, what got you suspended?" Initiating a conversation with a stranger was completely out of character for Piper. She hated small talk. Why, she wondered, was she even bothering to talk to this guy?

"Who the hell are you?" he barked, and Piper shrank back, not expecting that degree of harshness from a man with such warm brown eyes. If this had been two years ago, if she had been back home still living her own life, then this man would have been in for the tongue-lashing of the century. She would have gone up one side of him and down the other, spouting expletives he probably had never heard before. But things were different now. Just like she had worked hard to lose her accent, she had worked hard to control her temper. Where she was from it was a weapon that proved necessary, but here all it would do was turn heads her way.

"Nobody," she whispered. "You can have your seat back." She was painfully aware of how drawing attention would undermine what she was doing here in the first place. She grabbed her things, left money on the table for Betty and hustled past him. He called something out, but Piper was already under the jingling bell of the door.

Bobby reluctantly peeled himself from the booth and jogged out to catch her.

"Wait," he called out to the girl as she crossed the street. He saw her turn and look back toward him and then increase her pace slightly. He was a high school track star and one of the fastest men in his class at the police academy. There was no way she was going to out run him. He hadn't been a perfect gentleman, but he wasn't so rude that she needed to run away. This all seemed a little extreme to him.

As he jogged up behind her she stopped abruptly, looking completely frazzled by his presence.

"What?" she asked, clutching her notebook tightly to her chest. She worried that perhaps he had glimpsed her notes or maybe Betty had tipped him off to her peculiar behavior.

Bobby ran his hands over the bristly stubble that covered his cheek and sighed loudly, looking utterly overwhelmed. "I'm sorry I was short with you. I'm not having a great couple of weeks." Piper caught a glimpse of his flexed bicep and felt herself drawn to it, staring for a moment. He stood nearly a foot taller than she was but, unlike some men of that size, he was warm not intimidating. He was the kind of man that made you feel safer when he was around. It was clear the blustery rudeness he had just exhibited was not his normal temperament. His face was tired but too gentle for that to be true. Still, Piper wasn't interested in his apology.

"All right," she snapped curtly, and began to turn away from him.

"That's it? That's all you have to say? I'm trying to apologize here." He may have chased after her partially out of guilt but also because she was captivating. Not gorgeous, not exotic, but there was something fascinating about her. His curiosity, however, was waning as her rudeness seemed to grow. He had thought that he might be able to redeem himself by the over-the-top gesture of running after her and apologizing. He was wrong. Much like the rest of his life right now, things weren't going as he had imagined.

He watched her impatiently tuck her silky brown hair behind her ear and he realized that maybe he had misread her. Back in the diner he thought her murky dark-brown eyes had been calling out to him in a haunting way. She seemed to have a depth that he had struggled to find in anyone lately. Maybe at first she seemed like something beautiful that had been knocked down and was waiting to be picked up and dusted off. Now standing on the sidewalk, with no words passing between them, he felt silly.

"Well, I guess that's it then," he said awkwardly, turning on his heels. It wasn't usually hard for Piper to watch anyone walk away from her. She normally found herself relieved to be alone. This felt different. She had to stifle a little tug at her heart as she watched this man leave, and all that did was annoy her. She didn't need butterflies in her stomach; she needed ice in her veins.

Piper didn't like the way he looked at her penetratingly, like he could see something that others couldn't—the heaviness she carried. Starting right now he would be someone she'd need to avoid.

CHAPTER 2

"Betty." Bobby waved her over before she could head back to the kitchen. "What's that girl's name, and, for that matter, what's her story?" At that question Betty lit up like a Christmas tree and plopped herself down in his booth, his real booth, the booth he moved to the moment he came back to the diner.

"I have no idea. The girl doesn't say a peep. Polite as pie, easily pleased, but she is closed up tight as a clam. I haven't pried much, but you know how most people love to come in here and gush about themselves? Well she sits, reads, writes, and watches." Betty's hands were moving frantically, as they usually did when she gossiped. Bobby often wondered if she would know what to say if she couldn't flail her hands around when she spoke.

"Watches what?" Bobby asked, losing more interest in the story by the minute. After Betty's animated response he was more convinced than ever that the girl was probably only taking in the sights of a lackluster town and dreaming up some soap opera to write an English paper about. That was the problem with living so close to a college. You often found yourself dealing with entitled students.

"Everything. The girl seems like a private eye. She watches

everything, and everybody. To tell you the truth, she's got my antennas up. You know how I have that sixth sense about people? Well my radar is going off like crazy with her. She's got something going on. I just haven't asked the right questions." Betty's excitement over the whole thing had sealed the deal for Bobby. A nosy waitress hoping a boring customer will turn out to be something more than she is.

"I've got to get to work." Bobby laid his money on the table for Betty and kissed her lightly on the cheek. The woman was a bit cracked but she'd been better to him than his own family at times, and something about her always made him feel good.

God knows he needed a reason to feel better. There were moments in everyone's life that could be considered tipping points—events that became large black lines forever separating the before from the after. Bobby's came two weeks ago, and it certainly changed his life, career, and plans.

Sam Manton. Just thinking his name put a brick in Bobby's stomach. He'd spent four months of this year, his rookie year, building a case against this creep. Manton was pretty widely known for importing dope of all kinds into Edenville and the surrounding areas. No one in the department showed much interest, which still puzzled him.

Taking Manton down seemed like a no-brainer. Sure, maybe it was only water cooler chatter but the rumors of Manton's deals had become enough to convince Bobby it was worth the department's effort. It was at least worth investing some time into checking him out a little more.

Bobby remembered thinking that he signed on to this job to make a difference. He wasn't interested in sitting around the donut shop on lazy afternoons with the rest of the beat cops comparing stories about the couple of times in their years of service they actually saw some action. He had heard the story of Donny Lee foiling a bank robbery so many times that he felt like he'd been there making a deposit himself that day. In reality, it was a transient guy passing through town who handed a note to the teller. She pressed the silent alarm, and Donny peeled himself off his diner stool, crossed the street, and strolled down to the bank when he heard it go over the radio. The guy was walking out with the money when Donny was walking in. He drew his gun, said, "Freeze," and that was that. But now whenever the opportunity arose he told the story like a scene out of Point Break.

So one day Bobby decided he would spend his free time watching Sam Manton. He would do a little freelance P.I. work and see if the story would start to come together. The problem was it didn't take much work on his end to see what was happening. Manton had been running guns into town and then selling them to drug dealers in nearby cities. His drug trades were fairly easy to spot as well but didn't seem to be his main focus. The guns must have been where the money was because that's what he was moving and moving them fast. It took some snooping, some eavesdropping, and some patience, but nailing him was not quite the insurmountable task Bobby feared it would be. There were moments Manton seemed to parade his deals down Main Street.

Bobby considered himself lucky. He would be the rookie who would make a name for himself through the takedown of a sloppy arms and drug dealer who had become too cocky. Bobby detailed reports and had documented everything he gathered in hopes of bringing the information to his captain. He assumed Captain Baines would congratulate him and form a task force to take down Manton with the information Bobby collected.

Baines was a brash, overweight, stocky man with a short temper. He didn't tolerate anything that resulted in having to listen to static from the mayor. If a cop in his department did something to draw negative attention or acted a fool, he'd be in for a quick and fierce punishment from the captain. Bobby had tried to stay out of his way until this point. He had ignored the smell of whiskey on Baines's breath as well as the bags under his tired eyes. There was a chain of command for a reason. It was Bobby's job to take orders, not ask questions.

Much to Bobby's surprise, Baines assigned Officer Rylie to assist him on the bust. He was told that the fewer people who knew about something this important, the better. Aaron Rylie was an old school cop who had been on the job for over twenty years. He kept himself fit, unlike many of the other cops his age, and Bobby appreciated that about him. He seemed to take his job seriously and didn't let his many years of service become an excuse for taking a more lax approach to his duties. Bobby knew Officer Rylie was from the Irish crew of cops that had been part of some really impressive busts over the years. His reddish-brown hair had started to grey, and his skin was leathery from so many days out walking the beat. He was a man of few words but seemed very interested in what Bobby had been able to find out about Manton.

Bobby's information suggested that the guns would be following the delivery schedule of a fake transport business Manton had created. This deal was especially important because it involved Manton being present to receive the shipment and meet a person who Bobby deduced was the supplier. He hadn't managed to pinpoint who that was exactly.

The morning came and Bobby readied himself for what he assumed would be a career-changing moment. Little did he know how right he was. It certainly changed the trajectory of his life, but not for the better. Going in with only two cops seemed light when dealing with a serious case like this, but he ignored his gut and trusted his superiors as he had been taught to do in the academy. After all, they knew best.

Bobby and Officer Rylie arrived on the scene and the rest was a blur. The delivery had already been made. The new supplier, who Bobby assumed would be collateral damage and turn into another historical collar for him, had left. Perhaps they had been tipped off, or maybe Bobby had gotten his information wrong.

Officer Rylie nodded for Bobby to climb the chain link fence that separated them from Manton and two of his cronies who were hastily moving the crates into a truck for transport. Bobby landed and steadied himself after hopping the fence. He drew his weapon, announced himself and told them to put their hands up where he could see them. One man reached for what Bobby's training had taught him to assume was a weapon tucked into the back of the man's belt. When the perp saw Officer Rylie, he relaxed and moved his hands back to his sides. Bobby assumed the presence of another officer led the man to believe he was surrounded or outnumbered and it would be unwise to pull a weapon.

Manton gave a curious look over Bobby's shoulder to Officer Rylie. He seemed puzzled rather than scared. It wasn't the reaction Bobby anticipated, but hell, it was his first real action as a cop. Who was he to assume how anyone would act in this type of situation?

Bobby approached the man who had reached for a weapon first and pulled the gun from behind his back, tucking it into his own belt and reaching for his cuffs. Officer Rylie was cuffing Manton and seemed to be speaking to him more than one would think necessary for a collar like this. Manton never spoke. Bobby was out of earshot, but whatever Rylie said had Manton nodding his head in agreement.

The process was going smoothly and Bobby's confidence was growing with each passing minute. Bobby approached the third man, his service weapon now holstered, and read the scene as contained. He reached for his zip ties since his other cuffs were being used, and in that moment felt a wall of pain hit his face. He fell backward to the ground, stunned and unaware of what exactly had happened. There was a kick to his stomach and chest, then a stomp on his back as he attempted to roll away. He reached for his weapon and wondered for a brief second what Officer Rylie was doing. Finally Rylie was there, gun drawn and pointed directly at the man, telling him to back the hell up before he blew his head off.

Bobby lay there, gathering himself while Rylie cuffed the third man and called for backup.

When other squad cars began to arrive Bobby managed to stand and knock most of the dust off his uniform. But the skin over his cheekbone had split where the man's gaudy gold ring had made contact. An ambulance pulled up and, as much as he had attempted to wave them off, Rylie had insisted Bobby go in and get checked out.

Ten hours later, when he had expected to be collecting the accolades for a job well done, Bobby was being suspended and gun dealers were being released back onto the street. The explanation he was given was that since this was Bobby's bust he was the point person, even though Rylie had tenure. Rylie had mentioned this to him that morning, but Bobby was too insecure to ask him to elaborate on exactly what their roles would be. He didn't want to sound green, so he clammed up and nodded his head in agreement. Because he was distracted by the boxing match he was having with assailant number three, none of the men had been read their rights. The officers who came to the scene to transport had assumed Bobby had done so, and proceeded to book them. Their lawyers, who were obviously the kings of technicalities, had been made aware of the minor detail and had their clients walking free in no time.

Bobby shook off the memory as he pulled up at the station. He wasn't sure what his first day back would involve. Would his fellow officers slap him on the back and tell him not to sweat it, or would his locker be plastered with printed copies of the Miranda rights? He pulled his duffle bag from the trunk of his car and drew in a deep breath. No matter what was in store for him, the first day back would be a long one.

CHAPTER 3

The following day Piper walked hesitantly into the diner. Yesterday's commotion had done more than just piss her off; it reminded her that she wasn't invisible. A scene like that could be enough to draw the attention of the judge, attention she was trying to avoid.

Sitting on the opposite side of the diner wasn't an option considering she needed to be outside the direct view of the judge in order to watch and listen to him. During the last couple weeks she had managed to overhear a few interesting conversations that the arrogant judge assumed were spoken in a code that no common person could decipher. She didn't want her run-in with this guy Bobby to undermine her real goal. With that in mind she chose the booth adjacent to the one in which she had previously perched.

Betty sauntered up with her pad in hand and a smile across her wrinkled face. Something about her expression gave Piper a glimmer of joy. Betty's bliss was as contagious as the flu. It was impossible to keep from smiling when she was shining her bright eyes at you.

"I'm so glad Bobby didn't run you out of here. I was afraid he scared you off before I had a chance to find out more about you." Betty's heavy southern drawl was sweet delight, and the tone of her voice was as warm and welcoming as fresh-baked cookies. Piper had grown fond of her unique turn of phrase over the last couple of weeks.

"It takes more than a little fuss to keep me away," Piper smirked wryly. She glanced over the menu, though she and Betty both knew that she'd be ordering the same thing she had for the last two weeks—a bowl of oatmeal with strawberries and syrup. It was the closest thing on the menu to the pouches of instant oatmeal she had grown accustomed to making herself as a child. Piper's eating habits were so full of prepackaged food that she now found it hard to eat meals that didn't come from a box.

"He isn't a bad guy really. He's a nice guy having some bad luck and taking it out on anyone who has the misfortune to get in his path." Betty, to Piper's surprise, sat down across from her in the booth. Apparently, the occasional unannounced break wasn't frowned upon in this particular diner.

"In my experience when someone says, 'I'm not a jerk once you get to know me' what he really means is, 'I'm a real ass but you'll get used to it after a while,'" Piper said, thinking back to all the people she knew who fell into this category.

Betty let out a howl of a laugh and slapped her knee. "Isn't that the truth? Well usually, but I can tell you that don't apply to Bobby. You got my word." Betty drew a cross over her heart with her finger as she continued, "So, I've been dying to know more about you. What's your name? I've been meaning to ask you for some time but you always seem so focused." Betty tucked her pencil behind her ear in true diner-waitress fashion. She dropped her pad on the table as if to indicate she had no plans for writing down any orders until she heard some answers.

Piper hesitated, separating in her head her old life from this new one. Remember the right name, remember the right details, she told herself before speaking. No matter how much time passed, when you were told never to speak your real name again, it always felt like it was dancing at the back of your throat, about to jump out.

"Piper Anderson," she said, stumbling a little. She was convinced it didn't sound natural, and she felt her face flush slightly.

"Oh my word, what a sweet name that is," Betty said in her singsong voice and Piper felt her shoulders relax. "Are you a student? You look like a student."

"I was in school, but I quit. And I know how dumb that sounds, but I can assure you it wasn't because I drank too much or slept through my classes or anything." Piper had begun anticipating people's disappointment upon hearing her status as a college dropout, and she felt it easier to head-off that conversation early.

"Oh you won't get any lecture out of me, that's for sure. If I had a nickel for everything I've ever quit I wouldn't be serving eggs to assholes every morning at five a.m." Piper appreciated the way Betty didn't clean up her language for her sake. A few good curse words were pretty refreshing. "What were you going to school for anyway?" She tucked her hand inquisitively under her chin and glanced at Piper over the rim of her eyeglasses sitting low on her nose.

"I was going to school for criminal justice," Piper said, waiting for her to respond. But Betty's strategically placed silence worked perfectly, making Piper feel obligated to continue. "The first year was all about the idea of justice and how lucky we were to live in a society like ours. The second year was reality, which is how lucky *criminals* are to live in a society like ours. Once I saw a handful of really repulsive people rejoin the general population because of one loophole or another, I realized I'd better save my time and money." Piper let the words flow from her mouth easily rather than catching them at the back of her throat and scanning them for any slip-up or misstep as she usually did when speaking to people. Betty seemed to put her at ease. She made her want to talk, which was not an easy task.

"Well that's not something you need to explain to me, especially not in this shady town. My husband was a cop for sixteen years, the entire length of our marriage. He started two weeks after our wedding day." She pursed her lips in what Piper read as anger.

"Are you divorced?" The question was forward but Betty didn't seem to mind a direct question. She certainly didn't mind asking them.

"Widowed, he died on the job." Betty swallowed hard. "That's why I started working here. I couldn't stay in the house anymore and carry all that grief. All my mind did was work through the conspiracy theories."

"Conspiracy theories? What do you mean?" Piper thought Betty to be eccentric but not an alien-chasing kind of crazy.

"Nothing they ever told me about his death made any sense. He was meticulous about how he did his job, how he took care of his weapons. It'll be eleven years this fall and I swear there isn't a day that goes by that I don't wonder what really happened to my husband. My Stan was a good cop and a smart man. He wouldn't have walked into a situation without proper backup or with a dirty weapon that would jam. I should have known by the way he had been acting the few months leading up to it that something wasn't right, but I tried to mind my own business. I don't trust a single cop in this town besides Bobby, and especially the ones Stan thought were his friends. Not one of them came by the house to see how Julie and I were doing. I mean, she was only fifteen years old and burying her father. If it weren't for Bobby I'm not sure how she would have made it through." Betty seemed lost in thought as she trailed off.

"Are you and Bobby related?" Piper asked, genuinely interested in the answer. Piper had overheard enough of Betty's conversations to realize there was always something worth hearing.

"He grew up next door to us, which in these parts practically makes you kin. His father is a businessman and wasn't around too much, a cat's-in-the-cradle type thing. So Stan took to spending time with him. He coached his baseball team and such. Bobby took it real hard when Stan died, but even at fifteen he was a great support to my Julie. They were thick as thieves since they were about ten years old. They rode out all their growing pains together, and if you'd have asked me a couple years ago I'd've told you they'd be married by now." Betty was lost in a sweet memory for a moment.

"But as Bobby got older it became clear he was determined to join the force. It was all he talked about. Julie couldn't deal with it. She wasn't willing to put herself through the risk of losing someone she loved again, and they've never been the same since. She went off and married this moron. I don't use the term moron lightly either. The boy doesn't know whether to check his ass or scratch his watch. She and Scott met one week after Bobby left for the academy. For the life of me, I could not see what she found appealing in this lump of a man. They dated for about six weeks and Jules was acting like a lovestruck puppy. I finally called her out on it and she told me that Scott was all she ever wanted. He was simple, which I thought to be the understatement of the century. He had a good safe job and wanted a normal life. What I started to realize was that my daughter was trying to be with someone she didn't love who had a very low-risk job. She was looking for the complete opposite of Bobby, and I give her credit. If nothing else Scott was certainly that. I told myself I'd let her get this out of her system and when Bobby came back from the academy, he'd help me set all this right. But then that spiteful little hothead went and eloped the night before Bobby was set to come home. It was a nightmare. I didn't like Bobby joining the force either, but I never expected Jules to go out and do something so impulsive and frankly dumb. To be honest, I couldn't forgive Bobby myself for a while until I realized how proud Stan would've been of him for becoming a cop. That made it all a little easier. But listen to me ramble on about my old, dusty history. I just wanted you to know that I got it when you said the system wasn't all it's cracked up to be. I think I'll go to my grave not knowing what happened to Stan." Betty's voice was barely above a whisper and she frequently looked over her shoulder, checking to see who might be listening.

"I'm sorry to hear all that, Betty, and I hope you do find out someday." Empathy didn't come easily to Piper, but she had watched enough television in her day to be able to fake it.

"And now?" Betty let the words drag out, saying them slowly and inquisitively. The question seemed to strike Piper unexpectedly, as though the air leaving her lungs was being pulled by a vacuum. Filling the void in conversation, Betty thought she should frame up that vague question a little. "Do you have a job or are you independently wealthy or something?" She leaned in closely and whispered slyly, "Old family money?" She winked as if to say, your secret is safe with me. Which Piper doubted it would be.

"No, don't I wish. I'm looking for a job. I haven't found anything that suits me quite yet." Piper tucked the loose hair that had fallen toward her face behind her ears. She always thought it made her look mousy and studious with it pulled back but she couldn't stand to have it in her eyes.

"We're always looking for some help on the graveyard shift here. It pays crap and is boring as hell but you can't screw it up." Betty leaned back and raised an eyebrow at Piper, goading her to take her up on the offer.

"That sounds like a challenge, because, trust me, I could certainly screw it up. I'd be a terrible waitress. Frankly, I don't like people all that much, and I have the patience of a two year old. I appreciate the offer, but it's not something I would be any good at." The thought of working in a diner, wearing that hideous getup and pulling her hair into a bun was enough to make Piper queasy. She'd rather rob a bank and live on the run than come home with a pocket full of loose change and smelling like bacon.

"Is there anything you're good at?" Betty asked, seemingly disappointed to not have Piper signed on as the newest addition at the diner.

"Not particularly. I've always liked computers. I'm pretty savvy with technology I guess. But without a degree I'm sure there isn't much work out there for me," Piper said, shrugging it off.

"Well, not so fast. My moron of a son-in-law happens to work for the cable company. Since no one seems to be able to live without cable now I know his place is always hiring. That's all that computer and technology junk right? You could get a job there." Betty's face was lit again with the spark of excitement. It was clear the thought of being a part of something, being a help to someone made joy rise within her.

As Piper began to decline, Betty cut in with something interesting. This could be something that would again open a door, quite literally, for Piper and her greater plan. "You know everyone lets the cable company in their house. Think of how many dirty little secrets you'll be finding out, and you can come back here and gossip until we're blue in the face about it. Who's ordering dirty movies, whose house is a disaster? You know, all that good stuff."

Dirty little secrets? Piper thought. Betty was right; everyone lets the cable company in. It would be easy access to someone's home. She might be on to something.

"Betty, that sounds like a really nice offer, but I couldn't put you out like that." Betty cut into Piper's words with the waving of her hands.

"That boy owes me so many favors I can't even dream up

enough ways to collect on them. The biggest of all is the fact that I let the idiot live after he married my daughter. I'm telling you, he's usually as useful as a screen door on a submarine so trust me, if there is something he can actually do to help, then he should."

"But you don't owe me anything, so why would you help me?" Piper furrowed her brow, for the first time letting her skeptical nature shine through.

"I consider myself a pretty sharp judge of character, and you, my girl, seem like a good kid. I haven't quite gotten you all figured out, but I've seen enough to know I like what I see. Now come on over to my house tomorrow for dinner, and I'll have my daughter and my son-in-law over. We can talk details. I have to get back to work, so I'll just see you tomorrow." Betty patted Piper's hand and stood. She pulled her pencil from behind her ear and jotted an address on her order pad, ripped it skillfully, and handed it to Piper.

"That sounds good but…" Piper said sheepishly.

"Oh Piper, it's no trouble. I guess you're one of those people who don't like to take help from anyone… but, it's nothing." Her hands were perched on her hips and had a "not taking no for an answer" kind of look.

"I was just going to say I was hungry. I haven't eaten yet." The two broke out into a laugh as Betty slapped her hand across her forehead. "Coming right up," she called as she hustled into the kitchen.

CHAPTER 4

The average person might take for granted how much an upbringing prepares one for adulthood. By the time most people hit their mid-twenties they are, at a bare minimum, equipped to attend a casual dinner at the home of an acquaintance. But, of course, most folks don't have the paralyzing social ineptitude that comes from being raised by criminals.

Piper sat in front of her computer staring at the void line of a ready and waiting search engine. She wasn't quite sure how to word her inquiry, and it had her eyes practically crossing as she tried to focus on the screen.

Finally she typed in "How to act at a dinner party" and hit enter. Much to her surprise she was met with over seven hundred thousand results. Perhaps she wasn't the only person in the world not given the tools to succeed. And, like so many times before, the vast information floating around the Internet had saved the day.

She browsed over each link and settled for the blog including five easy steps of dinner party etiquette. She figured she couldn't possibly go wrong with five easy steps. She pulled out her notebook and proceeded to jot them down. She always seemed to retain more information when she was writing it for herself.

Step 1: Always bring a gift or dish for the host and hostess.

Step 2: Unfold your napkin and place it across your lap. When your meal is finished place the napkin neatly back on the table.

Step 3: Wait your turn for food. It is traditional to serve the most senior lady at the table, then the other ladies in descending order of rank (usually equating to age unless you have royalty staying), and lastly the gentlemen. *Never* start eating until the hostess begins to eat.

Step 4: With many different sets of cutlery beside the plate, start at the outside and work in. If in doubt, look at what the other guests are using.

Step 5: Make polite conversation with those guests around you. Dinner parties are not just about the food; they are intended to be a sociable occasion.

Piper closed her notebook feeling like those were pretty manageable rules to follow. Now she just had to pick something to wear and which dish she would bring for Betty, considering her plates were all pretty plain.

As Piper approached the house at the address Betty had given her, she felt tightness in her chest. Social endeavors of any kind were something she avoided. She continued to remind herself this would all be worth it when she was working at the cable company and coming and going out of people's houses without having to put breaking and entering onto her record.

Betty's home was fairly unassuming and old-fashioned. Parts of it teetered on being in disrepair in Piper's opinion. The clapboard siding was faded with the paint chipping and peeling. The bones of the house seemed tired but the attempts at keeping it fresh were easy to see. The garden was full of fresh blossoms and the hedges that hugged the outside of the house were well-kept and blooming beautifully. The windows were sparkling, and white cotton sheer curtains were blowing in and out of them with the breeze. The front porch had an old style hanging swing with floral cushions that Piper immediately found inviting. She imagined how relaxing it would be to waste away an afternoon there.

It was farther outside of town than Piper expected. She didn't realize Betty had a twenty-minute drive to work each day and that the house would be tucked so far from the road. The long dirt driveway was lined with trees and an old stone wall that had seen better days. It was quieter here than any place Piper had ever been. The only real noises she heard were the idling of her own car engine and the birds chirping in the trees.

As Piper parked her car she saw Betty's rusted blue sedan and a shiny, red antique pick-up truck parked ahead of her. She reached into the back to get her purse and the plain blue empty plate she had brought. And finally it hit her. The article she read didn't mean to bring your hostess an empty plate; it meant a *dish,* like peas or salad! "What an idiot," she thought to herself, feeling grateful that she hadn't brought the stupid plate in with her. She rummaged through her glove box to see if she had something that would qualify as a gift for her hostess. Nothing. Well, rule number one had been broken.

Piper walked toward the house and heard the swinging of a screen door as Betty stepped out onto the porch to greet her. Betty's smile wasn't a cosmetically pretty one, but the way it spread across her whole face made it striking.

"I'm so glad you found the house. We're so excited to have you, and I hope you're hungry. I know you're not from down South, so I made you some good ol' fashioned country food for you to try out." Betty hardly took a breath as she spoke, and Piper only had time to nod and follow her obediently into the house.

"I've got some more work to do in the kitchen so you go on into the sitting room, it's two doors down that hall. I'll get the rest of the meal all finished up." She pulled her apron back up over her head and around her neck. Before Piper could ask if there was anything she could help with, Betty was gone.

Piper intended to make some polite conversation with Julie and Scott and do her best to not sound like a fool until Betty came back. As she entered the sitting room she was surprised to see Bobby lounging comfortably on the couch reading a car magazine.

"What are you doing here?" Piper asked without the slightest attempt to cover her disappointment at his presence.

Bobby did a slightly better job at hiding his surprise. He had years of experience at dealing with Betty's meddling ways. He kept his face unaffected as she spoke. "I come here every Wednesday night for dinner, but I would have made the exception and skipped tonight had I known I'd be in mixed company." He barely spared her a glance over the top of his magazine before nonchalantly returning to his reading.

At the sight of this man lounging confidently and flinging insults her way, Piper felt her fight or flight mechanism kick in. Running out of the room seemed slightly ruder than engaging him in some hostile banter, so fight would have to do right now. "Do you have some sort of mental disorder or something? Because it seems like you do a lot of the same things at the same time in the same place every week. You might want to have that checked out. I'm going to give Betty a hand in the kitchen." Piper turned to leave as Bobby stood up. She was still taken aback by his height and the width of his shoulders, but more so by the way he carried his size. He was so much larger than her but not the least bit intimidating.

"No, don't go into the kitchen. Then Betty will think I was rude to you, and I'll catch hell for it. Sit down and I promise not to bother you." He caught her elbow gently and she felt a shock go through her body. Its intensity was unfamiliar and scary. She didn't think she liked the way Bobby's touch rocked her. He pointed to the wingback chair across from the couch.

Piper looked closely at the chair, peeking on either side of it and behind it.

"What are you looking for?" Bobby asked, thinking this girl might be crazy.

"I'm trying to make sure your name isn't on this chair anywhere. I'd hate to take a seat that belongs to you again. I've learned my lesson." Piper kept her face intentionally serious even though she felt like a wry smirk would fit the moment better. Bobby rolled his eyes and flopped back to his seat heavily. He pulled the magazine up in front of his face and she felt slightly victorious as she caught a glimpse of the corners of his mouth rising in a reluctant smile.

The screen door squeaked open and slammed shut as someone else entered the house. A younger version of Betty stood in the doorway of the sitting room. She had all of Betty's features: the small pointed nose, almond shaped eyes, and feminine jaw line. But they were all in a form that had not been weathered by half a lifetime of worry. Her hair, however, was crimson red—not at all like Betty's dark caramel tresses that were now streaked with gray. Everything about this girl seemed perfectly proportioned and delicate. Her nails were artfully polished, her hair bright and voluminous. Her lips were a soft pink and freshly glossed contrasting her pale complexion which was dotted with endearing little freckles. It would have been easy to tell which attributes came from her mother and which from her father, even without ever meeting him.

"Hi, you must be Piper. I'm Jules." She reached her hand out and Piper shook it firmly. Piper meant to say that it was nice to meet her as well, that she was grateful to Betty for having her over for dinner and helping her to get a job. Instead all that came out was a timid "hello" and then it was too late, the conversation moved on without her. Piper hated how the events in her life over the past few years had changed her so greatly and how weak she must look to people. She missed being labeled as a firecracker and partaking in clever banter. She felt constantly confined by her new identity and her responsibility to maintain its credibility.

"So you don't even say hello anymore, Bobby? Have you been as rude to poor Piper here as you've been to the rest of us lately?" Jules's hand rested on her hip, and she stood on tippy-toes to catch Bobby's eye over the top of his magazine.

"Hello Jules. Where's Scott, or have you wised up and left him?" He raised his magazine higher as a shield from her frosty stare.

"You're such an ass. Actually he's stuck on a job. He'll be here when he's finished." She crossed the small room and sat beside him on the couch. She was just about to turn the conversation back to Piper when Bobby spoke.

"Some big cable company emergency? Boy they sure are lucky to have a dedicated guy like Scott there when HBO is on the fritz. I'm sure he's up for a medal or something by now." He threw his magazine to the coffee table and readied himself for Jules to fire back. Piper was having a hard time telling if they were both enjoying themselves or genuinely couldn't stand each other. Regardless, she was slightly envious of the chemistry between them. This was the dynamic she had missed since moving here.

"You know what Bobby? His job is important, and he's good at it. What's the point of having some big job like yours if you're just going to screw it up in the first place?" Piper cringed with the direct hit that Bobby had just taken to his ego.

"Whatever, I'm going in the kitchen to see if Betty needs any more help with dinner. The sooner it's ready the sooner I can get out of here." He went to stand and Jules grabbed his sleeve and pulled him back to the couch.

"No way, if you go in there she'll know I am giving you a hard time and she'll give me hell for it," Jules stammered.

With that, Bobby's eyes met Piper's and they both did their best to stifle a laugh.

"Supper's ready," Betty called from the kitchen. It was still strange to Piper to hear the last meal of the day referred to as supper, rather than dinner. There were certainly things down South she felt she'd never get accustomed to.

Piper felt her palms begin to sweat as she ran through the rules of etiquette once more in her mind. She waited for everyone to take what she assumed were customary seats. Betty pointed to the open chair by Bobby, and Piper cringed inside at the thought of having to apply rule number five regarding polite conversation to him. She was still beating herself up about blowing it on rule number one, but was relieved to see a paper towel in place of a napkin sitting across her plate. She still laid it over her lap, but at least it wasn't a beautifully folded cloth napkin to contend with. She also noticed that there was no endless line of different shaped cutlery at either side of her plate, just a fork and knife.

"So Piper, this meal is about as country as it gets, and I won't be offended it you don't like it. I know we all tend to like what we grew up on. You eat what you like; no feelings will be hurt here. What was your favorite dish growing up, dear?" Betty asked as she served herself a heaping spoon of mashed potatoes and passed the bowl over to Bobby. Piper noticed no one at the table seemed to have read the same article she had regarding etiquette.

"Um… we ate a lot of takeout when I was growing up. Pizza, fast food, not a lot of home cooking, but this all looks amazing, I'm sure I'll love it. Are these your own recipes or something from a cookbook?" Piper had become incredibly astute at redirecting a conversation away from her. She had found people generally enjoyed talking about themselves more than listening anyway.

Betty proceeded to go into elaborate detail about how the fried chicken recipe had been handed down through many generations of her family. She talked at length of how it was her mother who had started adding sour cream to the mashed potatoes, her great-grandmother who had first fried the okra, and how the biscuits were a family secret.

Piper, who had no appreciation for cooking, or food for that matter, was astonished by the pride Betty associated with the simple act of mixing up some ingredients. It was another reminder there was no shortage of things that separated Piper from the rest of the world.

The screen door swung open and slammed shut again, and in walked a stocky bald man wearing the navy button-down shirt of the cable company. This must be Scott, thought Piper. He was as dull looking as Betty had implied. Piper thought she recalled Jules mentioning that Scott was twenty-eight, but he could easily pass for forty. His eyes were slightly vacant and droopy like those of a basset hound. His round face was flush and sweaty from working outdoors. Piper thought if you put a hard hat and tool belt on this guy he could be the poster child for blue-collar work in the South.

"Hi Scott," Jules squeaked. "This is Piper; remember Mom was telling you about her? She's interested in a job at ComCable with you. Remember?" It was as if Jules was willing him to not say something dumb or to admit that he didn't remember who the hell Piper was or why she was there.

"Oh, yeah we'll get you a job." He smiled, flashing the small gap between his front teeth. "I mean, a hot chick like you they'll hire in a minute. I was afraid you were going to be some cow with a unibrow, and I'd have to find some nice way to tell you no dice on the job. But any of the guys would be all right with you on the crew." Scott clearly couldn't see the icy stare of his wife or the enormous, gloating grin plastered across Bobby's face. Scott just continued to check out Piper's goods and assess her *qualifications* for the job.

Piper coughed as the water she was drinking lodged slightly in her throat. There was really nothing left to the imagination when it came to why Bobby had been so snarky about the love of his young life marrying a dumbass. No wonder Betty was disappointed in her daughter's choice for a husband, especially when there was a man like Bobby in the running. Scott was exactly as Piper had imagined him, maybe slightly worse, but he was going to get her a job and access to what she needed. That was really all that should matter to her. For some reason however, a small part of her ached for everyone in that room, excluding Scott.

"Thanks Scott. For the job and the self-esteem boost. I was feeling a little bovine-esque lately." Piper knew she was speaking to only one person in the room. That was Bobby. She knew her comment would fly over Scott's head, sting Jules and maybe even Betty, but Bobby would appreciate it, and she found herself wanting to put a point in his column for some reason. It worked, because as she glanced over at Bobby she saw him smiling. Her remark may have been funny, but her timing was terrible, as he too coughed back a sip of his drink.

Bobby shot Piper a grateful look and she felt herself blush slightly.

"Oh good," Scott said obliviously. "Can we get to eating now? I'm so hungry my belly thinks my throat's been cut." He reached his large arm across Jules's plate and began to serve himself.

Getting the dinner back on track quickly became Betty's number one objective. They all ate sheepishly. They knew any amount of fooling around would result in some form of scolding from Betty.

The remainder of the meal was uneventful but delicious. They kept the conversation limited to the unusually warm weather they were having. Normally by September in North Carolina you could count on a break in the humidity and the evenings would be cool enough for a sweater at times. Each of them took turns commenting on how the extended heat had them all anxious for winter. It seemed to be the only common ground they could find.

Piper had barely left room for dessert but decided it would be rude not to partake in Betty's peach cobbler. She looked around the table, and, although the tension was still palpable, she found herself envious that all these people would be back here next week. The bickering and jabbing that might have seemed annoying to all of them was charming to Piper. No one here was throwing things; no one was threatening anyone's life or slamming a door. They were simply disagreeing without being overly disagreeable. It was such a stark contrast to all Piper had ever known, and she wished it didn't have to end after just one night.

Jules rose abruptly from the table after Scott had taken the final bite of his second helping of cobbler.

"Ma, I'll help you clear the table, but I've got a big day at work tomorrow and we'd better get going." Jules physically lifted Scott upward by hooking him under his arm. He clearly had not gotten the message that she was anxious to go. As far as Piper could tell, he was completely oblivious to any tension circling the table. As a matter of fact, it seemed like there was no shortage of things to which he was oblivious.

"Don't you touch a dish. I know there's a lot going on in your office. It seems like every time I drive by, there is a line practically out the door. That's what happens in a growing town like ours. I guess everyone needs something from town hall. Permits, licenses, records. In a small place like Edenville they expect you guys to do it all."

Betty turned toward Piper and said with pride lighting her face, "My Julie is in charge of the whole town hall. Well pretty much." Piper loved how Betty seemed to be the only one who called her daughter by her full name. She wondered when it had morphed into Jules for everyone else and why Betty had decided that just wouldn't do for her.

"Not quite, Ma. It's too bad you quit school Piper. If you ever go back we'd be seeing a lot of each other. All the courthouse documents are housed in my archives. The lawyers, detectives, and such are always pawing through and leaving it a mess." Jules was still trying to shuffle Scott away from the table as she spoke.

"It was really nice to meet you Piper, I'm glad Ma had you over and that Scott will be able to help you get a job." She leaned in and whispered to Piper. "He means well, you just have to get to know him better." She smiled through the embarrassment of having to plead her case for compassion for her husband. She pulled Piper in for a hug and continued their private conversation. "And keep your eye on Bobby for me. He's on a slippery slope. He could use a friend right now."

"We're not really friends. He's been kind of rude actually. All we've done is argue with each other," Piper whispered, with a confused look on her face as they broke their embrace.

"Well that's how most epic love stories begin," Jules insisted, as she turned away from Piper and toward her husband who had his fork back in the serving dish of peach cobbler. "Are you kidding? Let's go already Scott." She yanked on his arm and he finally moved in the direction of the door.

"Come down to the office tomorrow, Pepper. I'll have everything set up for you," Scott mumbled, his mouth full of cobbler.

"It's Piper, Scott. I swear you have the memory of a gold fish." Jules physically shoved him the rest of the way through the door and toward the porch. "Bye Ma," she called out behind her.

Betty walked out behind them and waved from the porch until they were out of sight. Bobby and Piper had begun clearing the table, and she quickly hustled back into the dining room to stop them.

"You put those dishes down and get on out of here. Go sit out on the porch, and I'll bring out some tea. Dishes keep, good company doesn't." She shooed them out the screen door, and they found themselves standing there awkwardly, not sure exactly what had just happened or how they ended up alone again, something neither of them wanted.

"I should actually get going," Piper said just louder than a whisper. "It's getting dark and I don't know these roads very well. It's taking me a while to get accustomed to things down South, especially no street lights on these country roads." She fished in her pocket for her car key and looked through the screen door, hoping to see Betty on her way back out.

"I know, moving down South takes a little while to get used to. I was young when we moved here from New Jersey, but it took me years to get accustomed to things like chicken fried steak and grits. Listen, you might as well have a seat. Dark or not, Betty won't let you go without a little time on the porch, it's what we do on Wednesday nights. She's been letting Jules off the hook, but I think that's only so she doesn't have to listen to Scott snoring after he falls asleep on the swing. If you want I'll follow you home, make sure you get there safely." Bobby flopped down on the squeaky swing whose chains groaned under his weight.

Piper forced herself to brush past his offer. She pushed out of her mind the thoughts of him getting her home safely, and the even more dangerous thought of him getting her to her bed safely. She did not like how she felt in Bobby's presence, how caught up in him she was getting. He was taking up far too much space in her head. Instead she went right for the other interesting part of his statement. "You're from New Jersey?" Piper asked, intrigued enough to sit down next to him without thinking of how boorish he had been toward her.

"I knew you weren't charming enough to have been born here. You lack the innate warmth of a southerner. I mean you have that endearing little drawl and the *yes ma'am* thing going on, but I knew you were too brash to be a good ol' boy. Northerners are a different breed. We're skeptical and hotheaded. I could tell you had a little of that in you. I blame it on the cold winters. There is something about dredging through icy puddles before the sun comes up that makes it impossible to love thy neighbor the way people do down here." She poked his chest accusingly with her finger. It was firm and muscular and bent her finger back slightly.

"I guess that's one way to look at it. I like to think I have more than a yes ma'am and a drawl. I learned the exaggerated wink, and I'm practically a professional chitchatter in the supermarket. You've got the wrong idea about me. If you had met me a month ago, you'd think I was the poster child for southern gentlemen. You, on the other hand, are clearly from the north. Which frosty New England town do you hail from?" Bobby asked, starting to realize Piper hadn't said much at all about herself in their few encounters. She had clearly tried to drop her accent but it still lingered enough for him to hear it occasionally.

Piper wasn't sure how she had let this conversation get away from her. This is what happened when she let little pieces of her former self show through, people always wanted to dig deeper. If she hadn't been lost for a minute in the majesty of the setting sun falling behind the tree line, then she would have been more effective in guiding the conversation.

"We moved around a lot. But this is as far south as I've ever been, and sometimes I feel like I'm on a different planet. What's this whole sweet tea thing about? They know it tastes terrible, right? I can't tell you how many glasses I've had to choke down since I moved here just to be nice." Piper hoped a little commiserating about the *swill of the south,* as she liked to call it, would have them focusing on something other than her mysterious past.

Betty pushed the screen door open with her elbow while balancing a tray of empty glasses, a bowl of ice, and pitcher on her forearm. "Who's ready for some sweet tea?" Betty sang with an enormous grin. Piper had made the idiotic assumption that Betty was inside brewing some hot tea and coffee for an after-dinner treat. But obviously she was inside mixing up the simple syrup and black tea bags to pour over large glasses of ice.

Bobby's face was bright red as he tried half-heartedly to stifle his laughter. Piper plastered a gigantic smile across her face and said with as much conviction as she could muster, "Yum." At that, Bobby let loose his poorly contained amusement. His body shook as tears began to roll down his cheeks, and soon Piper followed suit. The two couldn't catch their breath long enough to give some explanation to Betty, not that they would have told her the truth anyway.

"Are you two on drugs? I mean it's nice to see you getting on so well but someone's going to pull a muscle." The two had begun to gather their composure, sit upright again, and wipe the wetness from their eyes. "Well that's better," Betty sang, grabbing the handle of the pitcher she had placed on the small outdoor table. "Now we can have our tea." Piper and Bobby erupted once more in irrepressible laughter.

CHAPTER 5

Piper found the cable company to be a relatively good fit in her life. She had made it easily through her training as well as her thirty day probation period. She was ready to get started on her unaccompanied installations and repairs. The work was repetitive but gave her time to think, and she appreciated that.

For the last month she had continued to join Bobby, Scott, and Jules for dinner at Betty's every Wednesday night. Because of her rotating schedule she didn't have the ability to tail the judge as well as she had before. It also meant fewer breakfasts at the diner with Betty, which was disappointing.

These new friends and a new job were beginning to lull her into complacency. The world was looking a little shinier and brighter these days, and the memory of the judge's assault was becoming fuzzy. Her nights were spent dealing with long, internal battles between what she thought was right and what she currently *felt* was right in her life. She had spent so much of her adolescence immersed in turmoil that for the first time she was feeling a sense of normalcy. Who in their right mind, she wondered, would give that up for the sake of traveling the moral high ground? There were days when she was convinced she had the righteous fortitude to continue chasing down information. Then there were other days she could easily picture herself being quite content swinging on the front porch and counting the lightning bugs after a home-cooked meal at Betty's house.

Piper wasn't inclined to believe much in fate, but it seemed hard to deny as she pulled her white cable van into the driveway two doors down from the judge's house. She sat for a moment staring over at his door. She told herself if a sign of some sort presented itself then she'd let it reignite the spark that had seemed to be burning so brightly a month ago.

Piper's attention was drawn from the judge's door to the entry of the house she was parked in front of. A tall, voluptuous blonde woman stood waving and practically bouncing out of her much-too-tight clothes. This woman looked as though she was greeting a ship coming home on military leave rather than a stranger from the cable company. Piper liked playing a new game she called "What would Betty say?" Betty would probably describe this woman's clothes as being tight enough to see her religion. She loved Betty's unique colloquialisms and found many of them stuck in her head.

"I'm so glad you're here," she called to Piper as she stepped out of her van. "Oh, you're a woman? Well I wish I had known that, I wouldn't have gotten all gussied up for nothing." The overwhelming excitement that had seemed to fill the woman left her body all at once.

"Sorry, Mrs. Jenkins, right? I got a call that you're having problems with your cable connection." Piper looked down at her clipboard and read through the brief notes left by the dispatcher.

"Yes, I'm Mrs. Jenkins. The box thingy won't come on. I didn't realize they let women do this kind of work now. I was hoping I'd get one of those tall, handsome men with a baseball hat. Are you one of those lesbians or something? It's okay if you are. I'm no bigot or anything, not like Mr. Avery down the block. If you tried to fix his cable he'd be standing behind you quoting the

Bible to you like he was performing an exorcism or something. But I applaud you people really, bless your heart." The woman clasped her hands together and tilted her head in a look made up of pity and encouragement.

"I'm not a lesbian," Piper said flatly, completely puzzled by how the conversation had turned from a faulty cable connection to her sexual orientation.

"Oh, thank Jesus. I didn't think so because you're so pretty, it really would be a shame," the woman said as she showed Piper into the house.

Piper considered starting a long conversation about how assuming that the outward appearance of someone somehow contributed to her sexual orientation did, in fact, make this woman a bigot. But she had to remember that this was a customer, and pissing her off certainly wouldn't help her in the long run.

The entryway and formal living room were massive. Piper had never been in such a stunningly decorated home in her life. There were multiple bouquets of fresh flowers adorning every available nook and mantle. Beautiful artwork was hung thoughtfully around every corner. Either Mrs. Jenkins was a designing genius or she had an amazing interior decorator. Considering how hideously and inappropriately Mrs. Jenkins was dressed, Piper assumed it was the latter.

"You have a beautiful home, Mrs. Jenkins. Now which television is giving you the problem?" With her frighteningly long candy apple red fingernails, Mrs. Jenkins pointed to the spacious media room that had more audio equipment than the local cinema. Piper said a silent prayer that the problem would be something minor and she wouldn't need to call for any assistance. She wasn't sure she could stomach one of her coworkers pawing at Mrs. Jenkins and belittling Piper for not being able to do the job.

In the center of the room, sitting crossed-legged on the floor in front of the coffee table was a girl. She had dark brown hair cut in a short pixie style that suited her sharp-edged features. She had three large textbooks open in front of her as she tapped her pencil to the beat of whatever pop song was playing through her iPod. She looked up at Piper and Mrs. Jenkins and rolled her green eyes that were covered in far too much pink eye shadow and black eyeliner.

"Are they finally here to fix the cable? It's about time. I told you to tell them to hurry up, Mom," she huffed loudly in the way only a teenager could.

"Nikki, what are you still doing here? You're supposed to be over at Judge Lion's house already. Get your things and go," Mrs. Jenkins spoke in a hardline voice significantly different than the bubbly exuberance she had shown Piper—well, prior to insulting a whole subset of the population by announcing that Piper was too pretty to be a lesbian.

Upon hearing the judge's name Piper stumbled and knocked over the tool bag she had just placed on the side of the cable box. Had she really just heard Mrs. Jenkins tell her daughter to go to Judge Lion's house?

She quickly tried to gather up her loose tools from the hardwood, praying one of them hadn't scratched it and the commotion wouldn't push the conversation into another room.

"Mom, I told you I didn't want to go there anymore. It's boring. All we ever do is talk about old court cases and look through stupid photo albums of people I've never heard of. I wrote one paper on the guy because I figured it would get me a good grade, and now he thinks he's my mentor. I'm over it." Nikki's argument didn't seem to faze her mother, who had begun closing her books and shoving them into her backpack.

"You are going. Having a man like Judge Lions take an interest in you is an honor, and you aren't going to blow it because you think it's boring. The man is very important in this community, and if he sees potential in you then you should take it seriously.

Do you want to end up working at the cable company like this poor girl? She has people thinking she's a lesbian all day, and do you know what? She isn't. Do you want that to be you? Do you want to wear that unflattering shirt and khakis, crouching down behind people's televisions all day?" Mrs. Jenkins continued to gesture over at Piper as though she were an exhibit at a museum rather than a person with feelings who might take exception to the insults being hurled in her direction.

"No, I don't want that. Fine, I'll go." Nikki snatched her backpack from her mother's hands and stomped heavily out the door.

"Kids—they think by thirteen they have it all figured out," Mrs. Jenkins sang to Piper, seemingly unaware of how wounding her little speech may have been. "Just let me know when you have it fixed," she said, sauntering out of the room.

Piper went from her crouched position behind the television to sitting with her back up against the wall. She thought if she didn't lean on something she might just fall over. Her mind swirled with thoughts.

Was Judge Lions so brazen that he would groom his neighbor's daughter for some kind of sick purpose under the guise of mentorship? Was that the real reason Nikki didn't want to go there? It was infuriating to think that he had this community so blinded by his prominence that people were begging to send their daughters to him.

Maybe it wasn't like that with Nikki. She seemed very strong-minded and self-confident. She didn't seem like someone who would carry that weight around with her, even under the pressure of her mother. Either way, regardless of Nikki's situation, the thought of Judge Lions being allowed in the presence of a young girl was sickening to Piper. Here was her sign; the flame inside her that had dimmed over the last few weeks was officially reignited.

The image of the powerless girl in the alley, bleeding and petrified, was once again as clear as it had been the day she had witnessed it. The nights she spent parked outside the motel watching the judge exit the back door and arrogantly pull away in his black Mercedes were now all she could think of. She had assumed her sign would come in the way of seeing the judge. Instead, the possibility of another victim was enough to remind Piper why she started this endeavor in the first place.

CHAPTER 6

Her time at the Jenkins home had Piper's mind wandering through the different possibilities of proceeding with her plan. She knew the judge was a lofty target, she knew following the regular law enforcement channels wouldn't work, but she also knew he needed to be stopped. She had thought about going to Bobby and telling him what she had seen that day. But after he had shared with her what had gotten him suspended, she realized he didn't need any more attention. She put herself back in a dark place, one she worked hard to stay out of. She asked herself a question she hated, *How would my father have handled this?*

The question may have terrified her, but it did offer a solution. Her father wouldn't have turned the judge in, because he knew that wouldn't result in the outcome he needed. The judge was well-connected and would likely be protected. Her father would realize when a man is well-insulated by people, then the only way to make him vulnerable is to turn his protection against him. So the key for Piper would be to learn about the people with whom the judge had frequent dealings. Who was making it possible for him to regularly meet with prostitutes, yet never get caught? Would people protect him in return for judicial rulings in their favor or some sort of "you scratch my back and I'll scratch yours?" There was very little Piper would admit she had learned from her father, but in this case she knew it was advantageous to have had such a dysfunctional family. Her father had taught her that no man attempting to live two separate lives could maintain such a lifestyle autonomously. Someone, maybe multiple people, must be helping him to continue his charade. Finding out who would be the key. That led her to an old acquaintance she actually found herself happy to see again. He had been one of the first people she connected with when exploring her criminal justice career in Edenville.

"Piper Anderson, I thought you had fallen off the face of the earth. I haven't heard from you in over two months," said the absolutely statuesque Michael Cooper. He stood in the waiting room of his upscale office, ready to escort Piper in. Michael's hair was sandy blond and a little longer than Piper usually liked on a man, but he kept it styled perfectly with a litany of salon products. "I was so happy to hear you had made an appointment with my office. I hope you weren't waiting long."

"Good to see you as well, Michael. No, I wasn't waiting long at all, thank you." Piper took a seat in the large leather chair that Michael had gestured toward. She loved being in his presence. She felt like a different person when she was with him, very much her old self.

He brought back the unshakable confidence she thought she had lost. When they had spent time together in the past Piper found herself becoming bolder with each encounter. Being with Michael was easy. He was self-absorbed enough not to really notice that Piper never mentioned her past. He never asked her deep questions, and never seemed to need an explanation for anything. When they were together, they lived in the here and now, and something about that made Piper feel completely at ease. In her entire time in Edenville, he had been the only person to have that effect. When she was with Michael, she almost felt like she had an alter ego. Or maybe she simply allowed herself to fall back into being the dynamic, vibrant person she used to be. Everything that had been taken from her seemed to come back when she was with him.

"I was secretly hoping you had reconsidered my invitation to dinner. I know I'm at least ten years older than you, but I really felt a connection. You are one of the most passionate students I've had shadow me in all the years I've been doing this. You're really something special. So it had me thinking we should get to know each other a little better." Michael lounged back in his plush leather office chair and laced his fingers behind his head. If Piper hadn't had the pleasure of seeing his bleeding heart in action on three pro bono cases she might find him to be another slimy prosecutor. She had watched him work tirelessly for people and things he believed in only to be let down by the very rules he was fighting to uphold. He may have wanted to seem arrogant, but he couldn't convince her.

Piper fought a smile as she spoke. "It's awkward for me to have to be the one to break this to you, but you know you're gorgeous right?" She leaned in toward him and waited for his response. They'd had their share of playful spats over the course of their brief time together, so she knew he would be game.

"I'm not really sure how to answer that without sounding completely self-absorbed. Thank goodness I'm not under oath." He sat up from his lounging position, readying for her quips.

Piper continued in a mock serious manner. "You're gorgeous. You have blond hair and those mesmerizing emerald green eyes. Chiseled movie star features. You're over six feet tall right? You've got to be in the gym at least five times a week to have a body like that." She gestured at his chest. "You wear perfectly tailored thousand dollar suits. I'm sure you have a really expensive car and only eat at the finest restaurants. Let's face it, you smell amazing. I have a hard time sitting next to you without becoming completely intoxicated by that cologne. And Michael," she continued coyly, "that smile... you could be in a toothbrush commercial with that smile. You pretty much have what every woman wants."

"I thought you were making a case for why you didn't want to have dinner with me," he said, raising his eyebrow skeptically, unwilling to accept the compliments until he knew her angle.

"Well, you see, you're single. Any man with all those qualities who's still single has one of two problems. Maybe his standards are far too high, and if I don't meet them my self-esteem will be shattered, and I'll develop an eating disorder or get addicted to plastic surgery." She smiled wryly at him and shrugged her shoulders.

Michael loved every second of this banter. Too often women tried hard to be accommodating to his ego, so it was nice to have a woman willing to shut him down. "Well, I think we both know there isn't a man in this world who could put a dent in your self-esteem," he countered.

Piper found this hilarious. If Michael could only see how fragile she really was he'd be stunned.

"You have no shortage of confidence. And you said two problems. That was only one problem."

"Maybe you have some fundamental personality flaw that has women running from your house screaming once they discover it. You speak in the third person during sex, or you have an inappropriate bond with your mom or something," Piper said, fighting hard to keep her face serious.

"Wait, women don't like those things?" Michael asked with a look of shock as he pretended to write down what she was saying. "Hold on let me take notes since you seem to have this all figured out."

"Seriously, Michael, there would be absolutely no hope of anything ever panning out with us, and I happen to like what we have right now," she said with a more serious tone in her voice.

"What exactly do we have right now? You stopped calling

months ago. Then I hear from you out of the blue and still don't know why. Did you kill someone?" Michael tried to let the blow to his pride from her rejection go, and turn the mood back to a light one.

"No, I didn't kill anyone. You'll be glad to know I do need your help though. I know men like you really enjoy chivalry. So, no, I won't have dinner with you, but I do *need* you." She pulled a notebook and pen from her bag and placed it on her lap.

Michael was intrigued now. He was born with that unfortunate gene that made it impossible not to help a beautiful woman. "I guess I can settle for being your hero and buying you a drink. What exactly do you need?"

"I'll definitely take a raincheck on the drink, maybe next week? Today I need some information. I'm writing a paper for school on judicial ethics," Piper lied. "I need some real world examples to be able to get my head in the right place for this assignment. Since I sat in on some of your cases I thought we could use things that I can relate to. Do you think you can help?" She did her best to look pathetically desperate, and it seemed to be working.

"I guess so. But it's important you know, I barely even talk to my mom, and I only refer to myself in third person when I'm getting ready in the morning. It helps me get pumped up for the day." Joking with Piper was like being on vacation, and he would help her write ten papers if it meant she'd stay in his office a little longer. Being a lawyer wasn't nearly as exciting as he thought it would be. So when a woman like Piper walked in, with a jagged sense of humor and the ability to keep up intellectually, he took notice.

"Great! Now what was that judge's name for that drug case you lost? The older guy with the big nose?" Piper put her pen to her lips and pretended to rack her brain.

"Judge Lions? I've tried a bunch of cases in front of him. We can use him as an example, but you can't cite any names in this paper. Not mine and not his, understood?" The joking had clearly ceased for a minute while Michael made his point.

"No, of course not, I'm trying to get a few real life scenarios so I can make this paper feel authentic. Now let me ask you, have you ever felt like Judge Lions was being biased or unethical?" She put her pen to the paper, ready to write.

"I can't answer that question. You're asking me to say if I think a judge who I stand before regularly is doing his job appropriately. I'm sorry, kiddo, that's not going to happen," Michael insisted, shaking his head.

"No, that's not at all what I'm asking you to do. I'm wondering if there have been cases where you feel like the judge is leaning in favor of the defendant for personal reasons. Come on Michael, I promise I won't bring you into this—or the judge for that matter. I want to be able to look through the eyes of your years of experience. Please, I need your help." She hated to play that card, but with a man like Michael, who always wanted to lend a hand, she knew he would cave.

Michael gritted his teeth and his nostrils flared. This damn girl was driving him crazy. "Fine, here's what I'll tell you. Every judge has a life outside of the courtroom. Each grew up a certain way, had a whole existence before becoming a judge, and there are times when I think that can make a difference in how they rule, even though it's not supposed to. I don't really care for Judge Lions myself. I have tried about nine cases in front of him and seven were lost because he either suppressed evidence or ruled some testimony to be stricken for one reason or another. He never did anything illegal in my eyes, but I've felt sour about those cases. That comes with the territory. Do I think there are crooked judges out there? Yes. Do I know if Judge Lions is one? No. Writing a paper about judicial ethics is a slippery slope, Piper. You can't go calling people out and trying to break the next big story. If I were ever to accuse a judge because I thought he was ruling on something based on personal bias and I was wrong, my career would be over. That means all the people I plan to help for the rest of my career are out of luck. In this business you help who you can, and you play by the rules. I know it doesn't sound like we're all following our moral compass here, and maybe it's disheartening for someone starting out, but it's the truth. I can win a lot of small battles but the odds are I can't win the war. If you want to continue down this path then you're going to have to come to terms with that."

Michael never liked to be the one to break it to people that sometimes there was a whole lot of grey in this profession, not nearly as much black and white as they led you to believe in school.

Piper was unimpressed and annoyed. "That's kind of bullshit. You're telling me that if you thought the judge was, let's say taking money from someone and then making decisions in their favor, you wouldn't do anything?" Her voice was a few octaves higher than she meant it to be, but it was becoming clear Michael wasn't going to give up much helpful information without perhaps being argued into doing so.

"That isn't what I said. If that were the case I would bring any information I had to my superiors and push to have him removed if there was enough evidence." Defensive tones didn't sound as good as playful banter.

"Oh sure, and when your boss is on the take too, you find yourself careening off the side of a mountain because someone cut your brake line in an effort to keep you quiet," she said with true conviction on her face.

"You've been watching way too many movies. Are there some rumors and grumbling from prosecutors who feel Judge Lions might be more lenient to the defendants in some cases? Sure. But mostly that's because, as you never fail to point out, prosecutors have giant egos, and when we are bruised we go looking for a reason for why we lost." Michael hoped this explanation would be enough to redirect Piper's focus away from a conspiracy within the judicial system.

"Which group do you think he is more lenient toward? Is there a specific subset of people that he tends to favor?" Piper was not stupid. She saw her window of opportunity closing quickly, and dancing around her questions wouldn't serve her very well with Michael.

"That's all you took away from that?" Michael asked, clearly exasperated. "Listen Piper, I don't know what this is all about, but you are heading down a path with far greater repercussions than you can imagine. I know what it's like to be starting out and to feel like there has to be more you can do to take the bad guys off the street, but trust me, being a good prosecutor is the best thing I can do. Whether this is a paper or an investigation, leave it alone." Michael paused and ran his fingers through his hair trying not to get too wound up. "Even as I say it, I know you aren't listening, so rather than have you go poking around and asking someone else, I'll tell you that all cases are public records. You can see the players, the verdicts, and the evidence all down at town hall in the records department. Go do the math and draw your own conclusions. But I need you to promise me two things." Michael leaned forward across his desk and put his hand on Piper's. There was electricity when he touched her. It was enough to get her attention, but in paled in comparison to the feeling that shot through her when Bobby sat close enough to her for their arms to touch.

She looked directly into his green eyes and nodded her head as he continued.

"Promise me that I'm your only contact for this. You don't go running around asking any lawyer who will listen what he thinks of a sitting judge. You can trust me, but you got lucky. Next time you might be asking the wrong person." He released her hand and sat back in his chair.

"I promise, I won't go asking these kinds of questions

anywhere else. You said to promise you two things. What was the other?" Piper had hoped it was something lighthearted and back to being about dinner plans.

"Promise me that if you get in over your head, with anything, you'll call me. I'd like to hope that after leaving this conversation you'll go home and run a search on your computer for judicial ethics, piece together some fluff paper, and put all this behind you. But I'm not getting that impression. So in light of that, if you get yourself in a tough spot, promise you'll give me a call." Michael had no idea what was so magnetic about Piper. She was beautiful and came across as incredibly confident, but at the same time she seemed very broken. Maybe it was those big brown doe eyes with lashes that seemed to go on forever. Something about her made him think she was a walking contradiction. She managed to be both a headstrong woman and damsel in distress. It was hard to put his finger on but something about her always left Michael wanting more.

He was physically attracted to her, but if he was honest with himself, at the end of the day it was more that he wanted to know her, and to know she was all right. She had never volunteered much information about herself and it wasn't in Michael's personality to go digging for it. At work that was all he seemed to do, search for the truth. In his personal life he preferred to leave his connections with people fun and light. That's why things worked so well with Piper. She didn't spend all her time gushing over her last terrible boyfriend or her daddy issues. There were times, however, when he considered using his prosecuting skills to find out more about her, but he always reconsidered. Some territories are better left unexplored.

"I will, and thank you, Michael." She tucked her pen and notebook back into her bag and stood up.

"Don't thank me for that information. I'm sure I've done you more harm than good." Michael stood as well, although he was sorry to see her going.

"I'm not thanking you for that. I'm thanking you for being exactly the guy I hoped you were. I'm not sure why I knew I could come to you, but I did, and you proved me right. There are a lot of disappointing people in the world, and today you weren't one of them." She smiled at him gratefully.

"Should we hug? I feel like we should hug." Michael walked around his desk with his arms stretched out, ready to embrace her.

"Why on earth would we hug?" Piper asked, stepping back from him and laughing.

"I was hoping if I could press you up against me, get you close enough to smell my cologne and touch my rock hard muscles, then you'd be so overcome with my charm that you would reconsider my dinner offer." He stepped in closer to her.

"Then we should definitely hug, because there is no chance of that happening," she replied, with a deadpan look on her face as she let him wrap his arms around her.

He put his lips to her ear and whispered through her hair, "Is it working?"

"Not even a little bit," she said, and he let her go as they laughed. She threw her bag over her shoulder, and he opened his office door for her.

"Be smart, Piper," Michael called out, as he watched her walk back through the waiting area. She turned and smiled, mouthing the words "thank you" as she passed through the glass doors and back toward the elevator.

CHAPTER 7

As Piper walked the eight blocks from her apartment to town hall she tried to internalize the warning Michael had given her. She wasn't entirely sure this endeavor was something that could exist in reality. She reminded herself that there would be a point in time when it would be too late to turn back. She still had time to change course and mind her own business, get on with the new uncomplicated life that lay in front of her. She ran Michael's words through her head over and over, but it didn't seem to matter. She was committed to this now, and no amount of admonition would be enough to deter her.

She was lost in her own thoughts when she suddenly found herself knocked backward. She had run right into someone and she, being the smaller of the two, had toppled back onto the sidewalk. She felt a cold liquid spread across her chest and stomach. As she regained her bearings she heard a familiar voice over her.

"Oh my," shouted Judge Lions. "My dear I am so sorry. Are you hurt?" He reached his hand down to lift Piper back to her feet, but shock kept her from taking his assistance. "I spilled my sweet tea all over you. You poor girl." He crouched down next to her and with his large hands and sausage-like fingers began trying to wipe at Piper's shirt.

"I'm fine," Piper grunted, brushing his hand away. She wanted to shove his hand back and ask what kind of man uses the guise of a spilled drink to fondle a stranger, but she held her composure. This needed to be a relatively quick event with no lasting memory for the judge. She didn't want to be on his radar in any way, especially as the woman shouting at him for groping her.

As hard as it was at that moment, Piper smiled at him. "I'm so sorry, I wasn't looking where I was going, and I'm not hurt. Thank you for trying to help, but I'm on my way to an appointment and have to run." Now standing, she was close enough to smell his dated musky cologne and to see the large black hairs in his nose and ears. She couldn't be sure if it was her knowledge of his deviant ways that made him so repulsive or if he truly was a disgusting looking man. Either way, from this close proximity, her stomach turned at the sight of him.

"Are you sure? I've ruined your shirt." He reached out and touched Piper's shirt just over her belly button and it took an enormous amount of self-control for her to not physically strike him.

"I can pay you for dry cleaning costs if you like. Or we can go right into that shop there and I'll get you a new one, whatever one you'd like. We'd probably get it for free. I'm a judge, you see, and I've helped Martha with a few speeding tickets, she drives like a lunatic. I'm sure she'd be delighted to return the favor." He pointed to the shop across the street that read "Martha's Boutique and Fine Jewelry."

Piper winced as the judge's breath, tainted heavily with the smell of onions, blew across her face. She supposed when you paid people to like you, or even to have sex with you, there was very little grooming required.

She took a few steps back then pointed over her shoulder. "That is such a nice offer, but I really have to get going. I appreciate it." She let her words trail off as she turned and quickly walked away from him.

She climbed the large cement stairs outside of town hall practically in a run, skipping two at a time. She stepped into the revolving door and pushed it quickly around, pressing herself against the glass and willing it to move faster.

Once inside the lobby, she braced herself with her hands on her knees, trying to catch her breath. Her hair had become wild, knocked out of its barrette when she fell. She felt jittery and blood was pumping quickly through her veins, but she didn't realize how tousled she really looked.

"Piper?" She heard someone calling her name, but couldn't register it without more oxygen making its way to her brain. "What happened to you?" Piper squinted and looked hard, trying to make out the blurry figure standing in front of her. It was Jules, and she was staring at Piper as if she had seen a ghost, a very out of breath ghost covered in sweet tea. She took Piper by the arm and led her into an office, shut the door and offered her a chair.

"I'm fine. I bumped into someone on my way here and took a little fall. He accidently spilled his drink on me. It's nothing really." Piper wiped at the front of her shirt, not realizing until right then how much of the drink had actually landed on her, and how transparent her white T-shirt had become.

"Well here, you can wear my sweater." Jules pulled her red sweater off and handed it to Piper. "I always wear layers when I'm here. You never know if the old air conditioner in this building will be blowing hot or cold air. It has a mind of its own." Jules look suspiciously at Piper. "Are you sure you're okay?"

"I'm positive. It was my fault really. I was distracted and I slammed right into the guy. I landed on my butt, and I was a little embarrassed I guess. I wanted to get out of there as quickly as possible." Piper smiled as convincingly as she could, and Jules's worry seemed to diminish.

"Give me that shirt and I'll go wash it out in the bathroom and run it under the hand dryer. I spill so much coffee on myself here I'm like an expert with that thing." Sitting in wet clothes in the drafty building had given her a chill and she was grateful for the sweater.

Piper slipped her wet shirt over her head. She hadn't heard another soul around the office since she had sat down. But of course that changed the moment she tossed her shirt over to Jules.

A quick knock before the door swung open sent Piper nearly jumping out of her skin and standing up abruptly. The sweater fell between the wall and the chair, out of her reach.

"Hey Jules, your mom asked me to stop by and see if you..." Bobby was halfway in the door before seeing Piper, standing shirtless, with a deer-in-the-headlights expression. The moment seemed to last forever. It was long enough for him to catch a glimpse of the subtle lace of her bra contrasting against the crimson red of her skin, flush with embarrassment.

"Bobby, get out," Jules shouted, shoving him backward and slamming the door nearly on his head. "I'm so sorry, Piper. I didn't know he was coming. He always just comes right in like that. I should have locked the door." Jules hustled over to her and reached down under the chair for the sweater. Piper was still standing motionless. Then a small smile broke across her face. Jules wasn't sure exactly what to make of it. "Why are you smiling?"

"I'm trying to imagine what he's thinking in the hallway. Like what kind of scenario is he's envisioning that would have me in your office half dressed in the middle of the day? This is pretty embarrassing for me, but I'm betting he is dying out there." Piper slipped the sweater on and sat back in the chair.

"Should we let him sweat it out a little, wondering what the hell we're doing in here?" Jules was so grateful that Piper had taken a lighthearted approach to this uncomfortable situation.

Having Piper around had helped alleviate some of the tension that had grown between her and Bobby since Scott came along.

"No, let's let him off the hook. It's not like he came running into the ladies' room or anything. This is an office, I should have known better. I guess we're lucky it was him and not some stranger looking for directions to the bathrooms," Piper said, gesturing toward the door.

"All right, Bobby, it's safe to come in now," Jules said as she opened the office door and waved him into the room. He slinked back through the door, trying hard to avoid eye contact with Piper.

"I'm sorry about that Piper, I really didn't see anything. I've come in this office a thousand times and there have never been any half dressed women before. I can assure you if there were I'd be by more often." He regretted his joke the moment he said it. He fixed his gaze on a colorful framed picture on the wall.

"It's not your fault. I had a little accident on my way here, and someone spilled his drink all over me and knocked me on my butt. Jules was nice enough to offer me her sweater, and I wasn't thinking when I started to change. Let's forget it ever happened. And like you said, you didn't really see anything anyway. Now someone change the subject please," Piper said, looking expectantly at Jules.

"Oh, all right, well why are you here, Piper? Did you need something or was it a friendly visit? I've got to get back up front to help out, so I can't stay back here too long," Jules said, amused by Bobby's red face.

"Actually, I need some time down in the courthouse archives. An attorney friend of mine needs a hand with some research, and I told him I'd help out. I need you to point me in the right direction." Piper stood, and was ready to get back on course, the one she had been on before Judge Lions physically knocked her off it.

A page rang out over the old intercom system calling Jules to the front to assist. She rolled her eyes and headed for the door. "I swear they can't last five minutes without me up there. If you want to hang on for a bit, I can come back and help you out. It's a little confusing down there. It takes a while to find what you're looking for unless you've already used our system." The static and cracking of the intercom rang out again, calling for Jules to come to the front.

Bobby, looking for a way to make this situation right, cut in with an offer."I can give you a hand. I know my way around the system pretty well, and we can probably figure out the rest together until Jules gets a free couple of minutes." Bobby was still not looking directly at Piper for fear his eyes would be drawn back to her chest out of some uncontrollable magnetic curiosity.

"Great," Jules called as she headed out of the office. "When I get a few minutes I'll join you guys." She walked swiftly toward the front of the building as the intercom rang out a third time.

"Bobby, I know you're busy. I appreciate the offer, but I don't want to put you out." Piper was confident that she could have researched the cases she needed with the help of Jules without raising any suspicion, but Bobby was a different story. In the last few weeks that they had spent time together she had found him to be very perceptive. He, in true police officer fashion, asked piercing questions and seemed to retain information exceptionally well.

That troubled Piper. Most people preferred to talk about themselves and rarely remembered details she shared with them about her past. This was helpful as the particulars were all fabricated and, at times, difficult for her to keep straight. It was why, whenever possible, she redirected the conversation away from herself. But this had stopped working with Bobby.

"I know that was kind of awkward, me walking in and seeing you without a shirt, but I don't want it to make things weird for us. I've really enjoyed hanging out over the last few weeks, and I hope this doesn't mess that up. Before you came along, Jules and I were on a pretty destructive path. You've helped offset that dynamic a little, and I don't want what happened today to wreck things." Bobby finally found the courage to look back in Piper's direction as he spoke.

It amazed Piper how much he had changed in the last month compared to the first day she saw him in the diner. It wasn't limited to the fact that he was much more considerate and soft-spoken than he had been during their first few meetings, but he actually looked different now, too. In the diner he was pale, unshaven, and thin. During the past month he seemed to have gained a much-needed ten pounds, and the color had returned to his cheeks. With his shy smile and his face clean-shaven, Piper found him almost unrecognizable from her first impression.

He was not the same kind of handsome as Michael. He and Michael were polar opposites in many ways. Michael kept his fingernails perfectly groomed and shining, whereas Bobby tended to have painfully short nails often imbedded with grease from the work he had been doing on his truck. Michael had piercing green eyes and Bobby's were a swirling espresso flecked with gold. Michael was like a performer; he walked with an air of confidence, almost a stage presence. Bobby stood like a soldier, back straight and arms by his side. They were both tall, but Michael had maybe an inch or two over Bobby.

It struck Piper as odd how she could find two men with completely contrasting features and builds both incredibly attractive. And yet she didn't consider dating either one of them. Any other woman in her place would be pouring her time and energy into gaining the affection of one or the other, or maybe both. The fact that she wasn't doing this only reminded her of how damaged she truly was.

"I guess you can get me started, but I don't want to keep you here all afternoon. I know you'll be having dinner at Betty's tonight, and you need lots of time to prepare funny digs about Scott to drive Jules crazy," Piper teased, poking an elbow into Bobby's ribs as she passed him. She might not be actively pursuing his affection, but it sure was nice to find reasons to touch him every now and then.

"Do you think I do too much of that? Maybe it's to the point where I need to be supportive of her. She's married now and I'm her best friend. Best friends don't act the way I've been acting." A look of worry filled Bobby's face as he thought about how terrible he had been lately. He gestured down the dark hall where the court records were kept, and she joined him in that direction.

"Jules is lucky to have you as a friend. You love her, and sometimes it's hard to watch people we love do things that aren't in their best interest. It's a lot like how she probably felt when you became a cop. You're both watching each other make these choices, and then acting like idiots because you're worried. You had your reasons for becoming a cop, and Jules had her reasons for marrying Scott. But what you need to decide is if you'd both be willing to give up those things to be together." Every now and again Piper surprised herself with how insightful she could be. Maybe she didn't know the proper etiquette for everyday social settings, but she understood the idea of love.

They entered the small windowless room that housed the court documents, and Bobby flipped on a switch that brought the humming florescent overhead lights to life.

"I've certainly considered it. It's not like I'm doing a bang-up job at work or anything. What would I really be walking away from? But when I think about what our lives would be like with everything that's happened I feel we're better off as friends. I don't know if I could be with someone who asked me to give up everything I believe in. I don't think that's the right foundation for a relationship. All I want is Jules and I to be happy for each other, even if we can't be happy together. I'm not making any sense," Bobby stuttered, heading toward the computer and turning it on.

"It makes perfect sense to me. I completely understand why she doesn't want you to be a police officer, but I also understand why you feel like you have to be. It's amazing how one event can impact people so differently." Piper and Bobby hadn't ever talked about Stan's death, but he assumed Betty had shared it with her. If Piper was coming over for Wednesday dinners that meant Betty trusted her. Bobby was inclined to agree, but was taking a bit longer to form his full opinion.

"That's exactly it. Stan being murdered made me want to chase down criminals, and it made Jules want to protect everyone she loves and her own heart. When we were younger it didn't matter as much because doing either of those things was outside our control. Eventually, though, we grew up and had to decide if we were going to stay on our paths or make a new path together. I'm hoping there is some middle ground somewhere. I feel like we're finally on our way to finding it." Bobby pulled two chairs up to the computer and sat down. Piper joined him, her leg brushing his thigh as she sat. This man was solid muscle. She let her thoughts move from the melancholy of Bobby's heartache, to the idea of what he might look like under that uniform, then finally to the anxiety of what she was about to do. She wished now she had been firmer in her objections to his help, but she had to admit being here next to him had its perks, too.

"So," Bobby continued, "you tell me what you're looking for, and I'll use this program to drill down to the specific cases. The drill downs are almost endless. Just give me the criteria you need and I'll enter it. Then it will tell where in these filing cabinets we can find the public information linked to them. Also, by searching here in this field, you can pull up any news stories that may have been printed about it." Bobby sat with his fingertips over the keyboard waiting for Piper to direct him. She bit her lip and let her mind run through the possible repercussions of over-sharing here. As long as Bobby was under the impression that she was gathering the work for a friend then it seemed fairly safe. She decided that sitting quietly while he waited looked far more suspicious than having him dig up some old files in the name of research.

"I need to find case files from the last eighteen months where the sitting judge was Judge Lions. Then I need only the cases that were found in favor of the defendant. I'd like to drill down into cases that included special judicial rulings like the suppression of evidence for any reason, technicalities resulting in an acquittal, or petitions by either the defense or prosecution that were ruled in favor of the defense." Piper pulled her notebook onto her lap and waited as Bobby typed the information into the system.

"Okay, that gave us thirty-nine results. Now we just need to write down the reference numbers and then go dig them out." Bobby called the numbers off to Piper as she jotted them down.

It took them over an hour to gather all thirty-nine case files and, by the end of it, Piper's arms were tired and her eyes were strained. Every time they crossed paths Piper felt her body tingle and her face become warm.

"Why exactly do you need all this stuff anyway? Are you trying to site precedence in a case or something?" Bobby asked as he handed Piper another stack of documents.

"It's not for a case per se. It's more along the lines of a thesis, something for my friend Michael to publish eventually. He's a lawyer and you know how gigantic their egos are. Well apparently they like having their names in writing too. He's trying to show how strict adherence to the letter of the law in our society has prevented the spirit of the law from being enforced." Piper had spent the last twenty minutes getting that story straight in her head.

"I know all about that. Catching a guy with a box of illegal guns and getting your ass kicked means nothing unless you Mirandize him. If that isn't bullshit I don't know what is." Bobby sat down at the computer again and grimaced. "Let's not get into that though, what other information do you need about these cases?"

"Well I'll need a list of the defendants and the charges against them." Piper rolled her chair back over to his side. She quickly realized another absolute difference between Bobby and Michael—the way they smelled. Michael wore expensive cologne that always made Piper imagine him dressed in a sweater vest, holding a polo mallet and posing for a clothing store ad. Bobby, on the other hand, just smelled clean, like soap and maybe some shaving cream.

"Here's the list, alphabetized." He scanned it as Piper read over his shoulder. She noticed a trend immediately.

"That's odd. Of all these cases, fourteen of them have the same last name—Donavan. And here, five of them have the last name Cheval. That doesn't seem normal, does it?" If Bobby hadn't been with her, she'd be running those names through every search engine she could find, frantically looking for more information on them.

"It's not that odd, really. Donavans are a pretty notorious family in this part of the state. It doesn't surprise me they've had a lot of cases. Duke Cheval is a known associate of theirs. There aren't too many really bad guys in this area luckily, but they are certainly on the short list. I would have expected to see their names on here." Bobby passed the list over to Piper.

"What makes them so bad?" asked Piper as she rolled her chair over to the piles of folders on the table. She tried to look as though she were only half listening to what Bobby was saying, when in reality she was hanging on every word.

"Christian Donavan, Jr. is said to have followed pretty closely in his father's footsteps. Christian Sr. was a notorious gambler who ran an enormous bookie business. When things were going his way he was living the high life, but when times got tough he started to invest in some shady deals. He was around in Stan's heyday. I remember hearing stories of how Christian Sr. was the number one source for illegal guns at the time. The homicide rate had almost doubled in the underprivileged sections of the state where he had been running prostitution rings and gun sales. A lot of people actually looked at him pretty favorably since he had an unwritten code about not selling the guns in Edenville. Who says there's no honor among thieves?" Bobby rolled his chair over to sit next to Piper, hoping he'd be able to help her sort through the documents in front of her.

"I love the irony in that name. Christian, it's so fitting. So all these Donavans on here are related to him?" Piper passed the list back to Bobby and continued to pretend to be otherwise occupied.

"It looks like it. Christian, Jr. is the brains of the operation as far as rumor has it. He picked up pretty much where his dad left off. These two cases here are his cousin Tommy's. I know of his brother, Sean. He has three cases on this list. He's not so bright. He's known for being a bigmouth skirt-chaser, and that's not conducive to a successful life of crime. If I were going to take these guys down, I'd start with him. Not that it matters—I'll be working traffic for the next ten years." Bobby took his hands and rubbed at his temples as though the thought of directing traffic gave him an instant headache.

"I'm sure you'll be back taking down huge crime rings before you know it. One mistake doesn't ruin your entire career." She put her hand on his shoulder and was instantly impressed by how muscular it was. There didn't seem to be an ounce of fat on him anywhere.

"I think I'll be asking to stay on traffic actually. The mistake I made had nothing to do with forgetting to read the Miranda rights. It was being overconfident enough to think I could manage that type of investigation and take down those guys my rookie year. I was trying to prove something, to Jules or myself or maybe to Stan. I don't want to be just an average cop, because if I am then I gave up someone I loved in order to do a mediocre job. I guess I was trying to overcome that. Realistically, I had no business getting involved. I could have blown more than an opportunity, I could have gotten myself and Rylie killed. Those two weeks of suspension were some of the darkest of my life."

Piper's hand lingered on his shoulder, and he felt it burning through his shirt. He wanted to believe that it was all the time they had been spending together lately that made the thought of her touching him intoxicating, and hoped it wasn't the fact that all he could picture was that lace bra of hers. He didn't want to be that kind of guy.

"I wish I had known you then, because I would have told you I was proud of you. It took someone with an enormous amount of courage to do what you did. You should have no regrets. I wouldn't have let you stay in that dark place for too long." She saw a look of gratitude fill Bobby's face as she spoke.

With a swift movement toward her, Bobby leaned in and pressed his lips against hers. It wasn't a kiss full of passion and hunger. It was a kiss that two old friends might share. To Piper, even though it was brief, it felt powerful.

"I'm sorry," Bobby whispered. "No one else has said that to me since this whole thing started, and I needed to hear it more than I thought. I didn't mean to ambush you like that." For the second time today Bobby couldn't look at Piper directly.

"That's all right, I completely understand. It was nothing." Piper smiled and waved her hands, indicating it was no big deal, though inside, her mind was reeling. She thought the only thing worse than the awkwardness of a kiss would be a lingering silence to follow it, so she kept speaking. "You found a box of guns and three pretty terrible guys and none of it mattered because you didn't follow every single step in the process. The justice system is completely flawed and set you up to fail. Those guys should be in jail right now, and you should be a hero."

Bobby followed Piper's lead and kept the chatter going. "The system is there for a reason. I'm supposed to execute it exactly how it's been laid out so that everyone gets treated fairly. I made a mistake. It's taken me a little while to own up to that, but I know now that, ultimately, I might have had the right motivations, but those guys deserve the same opportunities you or I would have." Bobby tried to nonchalantly lean back in his chair to create some distance between them. Kissing Piper felt right in the moment, but sliding the piles of folders off the table and slowly peeling off her clothes didn't seem as appropriate.

"You've got to be kidding me." Piper was completely annoyed now and it was obvious all over her face. "I'd imagine you know where all those guns go. They're involved in robberies, homicides, and drive-by shootings every day. Those guns kill children. The drugs they push ruin people's lives. If I had my way, those guys would have been begging to go to jail when I was done with them. Look at this case." Piper pulled open a folder she had been browsing earlier. "Duke Cheval was arrested for holding the lease to an apartment where seven women were being kept as sex slaves. The notes in the prosecutor's file say that the women were too afraid to testify against him and, therefore, he was found not guilty. He claimed that the people were squatters, and he had no knowledge they were using his apartment as a brothel. There were pictures of Duke entering and leaving the building on at least two occasions, but Judge Lions suppressed the evidence due to a mishandling in the storage process. Apparently the pictures were coded incorrectly by the person cataloging them and they were filed with another case. By the time they were found the judge felt there was too much opportunity for them to have been tampered with. The youngest victim was sixteen years old and had restraint marks on her ankles and wrists, as well as cigarette burns all over her body. Can you honestly tell me that you think he had no idea what was going on in that place? Are you telling me that he doesn't deserve a fate worse than prison?" Piper didn't need the extra space Bobby had given her by leaning back in his chair in order to keep them from kissing again. His ridiculous idealism about the justice system was enough of a deterrent.

"So what exactly is your solution, vigilantism? We all go get our pitchforks and torches and hand out punishment as we see fit? How can someone with any interest in criminal justice have that opinion?" Bobby loved a good debate as much as anyone but he was desperately hoping that Piper would break into a laugh any minute and admit she was joking.

"Why do you think I'm not in school anymore? The entire thing is a joke, and I don't want to be a part of it. Maybe retribution outside the system is exactly what they need." Piper closed the file in front of her with a huff, exasperated by Bobby's stubbornness. They both sat for a minute in silence, their faces twisted in frustration at the other's view. Just as Bobby began to defend his point further, a voice broke in.

"I am so sorry guys. I swear they can't do anything up there without me. Bobby, were you able to help Piper?" Bobby stood, and Jules, knowing him well, recognized the annoyance on his face.

"I think she needs more help than I can give." Immediately regretting the dig he tried to change the subject quickly. "I completely forgot, Jules, I came here to ask you what kind of cake you want for tonight. I'm going to pick it up on my way."

"I think I'd like a strawberry cake with white frosting," Jules said as she looked back and forth between Piper and Bobby, trying to make sense of the tension in the room.

Bobby nodded and headed for the door. "I'll see you guys tonight then." He leaned in and kissed Jules on the cheek as he hurried away.

"What was that about?" Jules asked with her hands on her hips looking suspiciously at Piper. "Did I walk in on you two about to make out or about to fistfight?"

"We were definitely not about to make out. We were having a fiery debate about my feelings that legal mechanisms for criminal punishment are either nonexistent or insufficient, and maybe a little justice outside the law is occasionally in order. He, however, feels that the rules are there for a reason and the law is completely black and white." Piper started to stack the files up and found herself doing it with a little more annoyance than she intended.

"In other words you want to go kick some ass and he wants to let the law do its job. That sounds a lot like Bobby. He plays by the rules, almost to a fault. That's how my dad was, and he feels like anything else would be doing a disservice to his memory. He might be a little sensitive today. The cake he's going to get is for my dad's birthday. Every year my dad used to let me pick whatever cake I wanted and every year I picked something different. We've tried to keep that tradition alive. We'll have it after dinner tonight." Jules swallowed hard as she smiled through the pain she still carried with her about losing her father. It didn't matter how many years went by, how many cakes she picked, it always felt like she had just lost him.

Piper stopped forcefully stacking folders and turned herself toward Jules. She felt like a bratty little child now and wanted to slink away and die of embarrassment. "I feel like such an idiot now. I didn't know. I get so caught up in my own convictions sometimes that I lose sight of the fact that people have reasons for believing what they do. I don't want to intrude on your celebration tonight or upset Bobby any more than I have. I should skip dinner this time."

"I want you to come," Jules whispered, with a disarming smile. "My father would have liked you. He always appreciated a good discussion of opposing views. Plus, I know Bobby wants you there. When you know someone as long as I've known Bobby you can read 'em like a book. I've actually been fixing to tell you that if something should happen between you and Bobby, I'd be all right with it. I'm always going to love him, but I don't ever see us being together again. I want him to be happy, and if that comes from being with you then I'm all for it," Jules said, flashing her magnificent smile at Piper. It was hard to even listen to Jules speak sometimes without getting caught up in how stunning she was.

"You don't have to worry about that at all, Jules. Bobby is a really nice guy, and getting to know him better has been great, but nothing is going to happen between us. I know it's kind of a cliché, but I have an enormous amount of baggage. I'm hardly in a position to be anyone's friend right now let alone anything more than that. I don't have any room in my life for it." Piper hoped this brief moment of honesty on her part wouldn't lead to a barrage of questions from Jules.

"Oh darling, Bobby is the kind of guy you make room for. He'll open your car door, drive twenty minutes to kill a spider you've trapped under a jar, and he'll forgive you before you even realize you're sorry. That boy has been by my side for every hard moment of my life. Whatever woman makes room for Bobby will be eternally blessed," Jules said with a knowing look on her face. Letting Bobby's love slip through her fingers was a regret she'd have to live with, but if she could stop someone else from making the same mistake maybe she'd find some peace with it.

CHAPTER 8

Piper kept thinking to herself, this isn't at all like the movies. She was an average person with no notable skills trying to do something most people wouldn't be delusional enough to attempt. It had been two weeks since digging through court records had helped her make the connection between the Donavan family and the judge, yet she still found herself buried in more research. She couldn't decide if she was stalling or being thorough.

Two more trips to the town hall had proven helpful. She was able to read an abundance of articles that had been printed about the Donavan family along with personal notes by various attorneys. This gave her insight into people's perceptions of them. None of the material offered cold hard facts, but there was something to be said for rumors; they almost always held some truth. Two prosecutors had actually made notes in the margins of their pads that made vague references to judicial bias.

Piper was also very grateful for the job with the cable company. Not only did the staggered shifts give her ample time to piece the puzzle together, but the company's data base was a gold mine of information. It was amazing what you could learn about someone from television and Internet choices. She compiled a spreadsheet of addresses for each member of the Donavan family she could find. Something Bobby had said kept running through her head. *If I was going to take them down, I'd start with Sean.* And everything Piper found was pointing in that same direction.

Sean didn't seem to be employed as he spent most of his time during the day utilizing the gaming system and chat function that ran through the cable company. At night he rented an ungodly number of porn movies. His overall Internet and television usage was astronomical. He seemed to be a deadbeat, just as Bobby had described him.

All of this was helpful information, but Piper still had no idea how to use it. She knew that the quickest and most effective way to remove the judge was to turn his allies against him. She was now fairly certain that the Donavans were the cohorts in question, but what was her next move?

She did have a slight advantage over the average person. Her childhood provided an inside track to the unwritten code of criminals. Most people would incorrectly assume that a family of crime would be far too indebted to a judge who consistently acted in their interest. But Piper knew there were at least three things the judge could do to undermine his relationship with the Donavans.

First, you never mess with an associate's children or sleep with his wife. Even if they are divorced, she is still off limits. Second, you don't double dip, meaning if you are currently taking bribes from the Donavans you don't go getting greedy and start looking to expand your dealings with other groups. And third, you are perfectly allowed to sleep with women of any age. You can frequent strip clubs, pay for sex, and even rough the girls up if that's your thing. Regardless of how young they are, in the eyes of these men, you are not a pedophile. But if you make the same habit with young men and boys, then you are a monster and considered the lowest of low on the criminal food chain. If the judge were to cross any of those lines it would be a fast track to dissolving their alliance.

So Piper would follow Bobby's unwitting advice and start with Sean. She wasn't sure where he would lead her, but she felt if anyone was going to further her plan it would be him.

Now all she needed to do was set the trap. Finding a way into his house wouldn't be all that difficult. Sean certainly couldn't live long without his cable and Internet, so disrupting those would result in an urgent call for a technician in that area. The hard part would be what she would do once she was there. No one really opens up much to some stranger from the cable company. She would need this encounter to be a bridge to a more intimate rendezvous between them. She decided that she would need Sean to ask her out on a date. Judging by his inability to put down the remote control, this might not be an easy task. Somehow she would have to come across as someone worth leaving the house for.

That meant more research. She studied the video games he played in great detail and watched many of the movies he ordered through pay-per-view, but she stopped short of diving into the ones that fell under the adult subscription. She hoped that sharing his interest in *Smoking Hot Moms* wouldn't be necessary to win him over.

Before she knew it, Piper was standing outside the door of Sean Donavan's third-floor apartment choking back the urge to vomit. She blamed the feeling on the repulsive smell of marijuana and garbage that seemed to fill the hallway, but realistically, her nerves had begun to catch up with her.

She knocked hesitantly and clutched her toolbag tightly with her sweaty hand. She heard a muffled grumbling noise and then the shuffling of feet coming toward her. The door swung open and a disheveled man who had clearly just woken up stood before her. His eyes were puffy and red, which Piper assumed was from doing drugs of some sort. His hair, which was somewhere between blond and brown, was matted in some areas and then looked as though it was attempting to escape from his head in other areas.

He wore baggy gray sweatpants and a green buttoned-down shirt that was wide open, exposing his chest and stomach. Piper noticed he was fit and had a thick, raised scar running from his chest down to his belly button. Even with the repulsive lack of grooming he had a gorgeous face. The structure of his lips and cheeks were rigid and incredibly masculine. He reminded Piper of a young James Dean, weathered but smolderingly handsome.

"They send a freaking skirt to fix my cable? What the hell is this world coming to?" Sean asked as he squinted to look Piper over. The bright lights of the hallway were too much for his cloudy and watery eyes. Piper was beginning to wonder what kind of backward town Edenville must be. Its occupants had such a hard time wrapping their mind around a woman being able to run some wires and drill some holes. She wasn't sure if they thought work at the cable company was so complicated or that girls weren't capable of manual labor. "At least you're hot. Let's get this over with already. I've got shit, like work, to do on my computer."

Piper wanted to interject that chatting with other unmotivated strangers while blowing things up in the latest video game didn't count as work. Instead, she smiled and followed Sean into his apartment. Not surprisingly, it was a mess. The apartment itself was quite nice, with a brick fireplace and granite countertops in the kitchen, but it was overrun with beer bottles, ashtrays, and piles of clothes.

"Sorry you're having trouble with your cable. I'm sure I can get it fixed so you can get back to work," Piper spoke in a coy, quiet voice and smiled warmly at Sean. She made her way to the first television in the room. She knew full well that the problem with his cable didn't lie in the house. She had disconnected his service from outside.

Sean plopped down on the couch, and she could feel his eyes on her. Piper had on a lace tank top beneath her uniform and had left most of the buttons on her shirt undone. In a very degrading move she had searched through her old clothes to find a pair of thong underwear that she hiked up above the line of her khaki pants. It was all incredibly demeaning to her, but she had known guys like Sean her whole life. She knew what he'd be thinking as she bent down to get access behind the television.

"Oh wow," Piper sang, feigning surprise. "You have the Demons from the Depths Five? I've been on the waiting list to get a copy of that for weeks. You're so lucky." Piper felt her face warm a little as she tried to sound like an envious fellow gamer.

"It's not luck. You have to be someone in this town to get access to shit like that so early. You play?" She assumed that was some kind of gamer slang and that he was asking her if she liked video games.

"A little," she answered. "I can hold my own. But I guess it doesn't matter, since I'm not *someone in this town* I won't get a chance to play it for a while," Piper used her fingers to make air quotes and show a sassy side.

"If you ever get my shit fixed here, then maybe I'll let you lose to me for a while." Sean had clearly spotted the lacey clues Piper had left for him to find all over her body. She could feel his interest in her growing. He had a devilish smile creeping across his face.

"I'll have it fixed in just a few minutes, but I have other jobs to get to so I can't stay, even though I'd really like to hang for a while." Piper wasn't sure if people still said things like hang, and she could feel her nerves raging. She winked at him and gave her best attempt at a naughty crooked grin.

"I think if you stayed we'd find other things to play." Sean rose from the couch and Piper felt her heart skip a beat. She wanted to be flirty and mysterious, but she knew she might claw his eyes out if he actually tried to touch her right now.

"I don't play anything without dinner, or at least drinks." Piper slowly started putting her tools back in her bag and stood.

"You might be worth a drink or two. How about you meet me at Lorenzo's Bar on Thursday night at nine?" Sean moved closer to her and she could feel her skin begin to crawl. She sidestepped him as he approached and headed for the door.

"That sounds great. I'll see you there. Your cable should be all set in about ten minutes. I'll just show myself out," she spoke fast and moved even faster toward the door. Mission accomplished, she thought, no need to stick around and give Sean a chance to get any ideas.

As Piper reconnected Sean's cable from the box outside his place, she could feel her heart pounding against her chest. Every time she took one step further down this path she felt herself falling slightly more out of control.

CHAPTER 9

"Are you ready to go?" Bobby asked Piper as they sat on Betty's porch swing watching the night unfold before them. Lightning bugs were beginning to sparkle across the open field of the front yard, and the crickets were chirping loudly. Piper looked forward to Wednesday nights week after week. They were brief moments in time filled with calmness and tranquility mixed with laughter. For the last two weeks Bobby had given her a ride there. Betty had insisted that it didn't make sense for two people coming from the same direction to drive in different cars. Whether she was playing matchmaker or mother hen, it didn't seem up for debate.

"I'm never ready to leave here," Piper answered, with a little pout. "Don't you wish you could stay forever? This creaky old swing, the sounds of the night and all these stars? I'm not sure there is anywhere on earth more peaceful than this." Bobby watched the wonder dance on Piper's face and realized how different her life must have been from his growing up. He appreciated a little front porch sitting as much as the next southerner, but Piper seemed completely in love with the concept of quietly watching the world around her, as if she had never really done it before. Until his parents moved back up north two years ago, Bobby had lived at home, just next door, with them. Most of his nights ended exactly this way. Now, since moving into downtown Edenville, Wednesday night was the only way he could enjoy the outdoors this way. But if he had to, he'd sit on a pile of rotting trash at the landfill to be next to Piper.

"Come on," he said, standing and pulling her up by her outstretched hands. "It'll be next Wednesday night before you know it. I'll be honking the horn outside your house and we'll be on our way back here." Bobby poked his head back through the screen door and called a goodbye to Betty who was drying the dishes and humming a song.

"Bye kids, drive safe." Betty walked out on the porch as they got into Bobby's big red truck and waved at them as she always did. Piper loved that about Betty. She loved that she stood on the threshold of her house and waved all of them off every time they left.

There was something so comforting about knowing no matter how many times you looked back she'd still be there. She'd stand with her dishrag draped over her shoulder waving her hand and smiling until you were out of sight. Piper felt like she had waited her whole life for gestures like that.

Being a passenger in Bobby's truck was oddly exciting. It was an antique but so comfortable and well-kept that you'd never know how old it really was. It was nice not to have to navigate the dark country roads, and to simply sit back and watch the world go by. They usually talked about how work was going for both of them, how much of an idiot Scott was that night, and occasionally about Betty and Stan. Piper had learned their love story was one you might see in a movie. Bobby painted them as the perfect parents and fiercely loyal to each other. He had mentioned on more than one occasion that he would never settle for a relationship that was less than what Betty and Stan had.

"So I've been meaning to ask you something," Bobby started

timidly, and Piper could tell he was feeling a little awkward about his question. "Did Jules give you the same speech about how we have her blessing if anything should happen between us?" Bobby looked straight ahead, focusing on the road.

"She did. It was strange and uncomfortable but very sweet. Don't worry though, I told her nothing was going to happen." Piper was desperate to move on from this conversation. She hated any deep discussion that didn't come with an exit strategy, unless she considered diving out of a moving truck an acceptable form of ending a chat. She knew everything she had been doing over the past weeks was playing with fire. She couldn't go around blending herself into this peculiar but delightful group without them wanting more from her. And she couldn't go around swinging on a porch swing week after week with a gorgeous cop and not think he'd expect something to come of it.

"Well that's not completely true. We kissed." Bobby felt a small pang of disappointment at Piper's reaction. He had hoped this conversation might be a jumping off point for something more.

"That wasn't really a kiss. It was a thank you between friends. It didn't mean anything. It was how you would kiss your grandmother for goodness sake."

"I guess the next time I kiss you I better not leave any doubt about my intentions then," he smiled unapologetically at her.

"There isn't going to be a next time. I'm not sure how to put this so bear with me while I think of the right way to say it." She bit her lip and searched out her window, hoping maybe the right words would be painted on the passing trees.

When Piper remained silent for several moments, Bobby spoke up. "You're very beautiful when you're speechless. Let me see if I can help you. Are you dating that lawyer guy you're doing all that research for? Because that won't stop me from pursuing you. I'm not above stealing another guy's girl," Bobby said with a forced seriousness that broke into a smile.

"No, Michael and I are barely even friends. We're more like

acquaintances. That isn't it at all." She looked down at her lap still searching for the right words to say. She fiddled nervously with her hands until Bobby reached over to hold one.

He intertwined his fingers with hers, and she was taken aback by how warm and large his hand felt. Her hands were always cold regardless of the outside temperature. It seemed to be ages since she had felt the warmth of another person in this intimate way. She let the comfort and connection of his hand take over for a moment before realizing what she had to do. She pulled her hand away and began to speak.

"I'm not even a whole person, Bobby. I'm no Betty to your Stan. There are some girls out there who are worth the fight and the hard work, but you're going to have to trust me when I tell you that I'm not one of them." She had her hands back in her lap now and stared down at them. It had only been a minute and she already missed the feeling of his hand enveloping hers.

"I'm a pretty insightful guy, Piper. By now I've realized that you don't talk about your past. If you haven't noticed, I've stopped asking. I can see that you've got some history that maybe you're still dealing with. That doesn't make you some damaged girl unworthy of a relationship." Bobby pulled the truck up to the front of Piper's house. The thought of the conversation ending was relieving to Piper and disappointing to Bobby. She pushed open her car door instead of waiting for Bobby to come around and do it for her as he usually did, another gesture she had always imagined but never expected. Before she could hit the first step of her apartment she heard Bobby following behind.

"Bobby, I know you have this whole hero complex thing, and you probably see me as this great cause you can work on. I don't need that right now. I need a friend, and you, Jules, and Betty have been wonderful. That's all I have room for at the moment." She fumbled for her front door key as she climbed the stairs, not looking over her shoulder to see his reaction or if he was following her. He certainly was.

They were both at the top of the stairs now, her keys in hand and her forehead pressed against the door in frustration. He turned her around to face him and pulled her chin up so he could look into her eyes.

"I'm going to kiss you right now unless you explicitly tell me not to." He paused, and Piper was frantically searching for the words to tell him to stop, but none came.

Bobby leaned in and kissed her, hesitating slightly as if he were afraid to scare her off. After a moment of passively fighting it, Piper parted her lips, inviting him to kiss her passionately. Bobby's warm hand was resting softly on her cheek. His tongue danced lightly across her lips. He used his free hand to pull her body up against his and she felt herself shake with passion. It didn't matter how many times she had touched him over the last few weeks she was always surprised by the tightness of his muscles and the width of his shoulders.

Time seemed to cease, until the sound of a honking car somewhere in the distance freed them both from the trance. As their lips moved away from each other's, their foreheads came together, and Bobby looked into Piper's eyes, searching for a reaction.

Her face read only stunned. She was surprised at how magical the moment felt, how she had made it all the way into her twenties without ever feeling anything like that before. She was even more surprised that she had let it happen. Bobby kissed her cheek, tucked her frazzled brown hair behind her ear and leaned in to whisper to her, "That was no Grandma kiss." He took the keys from her hand, unlocked her door, and swung it open. Piper, who was still reeling from the kiss, felt his hand on the small of her back as he nudged her in. For a moment she thought he'd be joining her and the kiss would be only a gateway to a night of passion. But in true gentlemanly fashion, he nodded and winked as he turned back toward the street, pulling the door closed between them.

It took another long minute before she could will herself to move toward the window to watch his taillights as he pulled away. She had kissed and been kissed by men in the past, but none had ever felt so breathtaking. She could still taste the mint of his gum on her lips and smell his fresh, soapy skin. She knew now that she felt something for Bobby that she had never experienced before, and it meant one of two things. Either she'd have to let him in or push him away. Both options seemed suffocating.

CHAPTER 10

Piper opened her eyes wide as she brushed mascara across her lashes. It had been so long since she had gone through the entire process of getting herself made-up. She had to dig deep into her closet to find something edgy enough to wear on a date with Sean. This method of preparation even required a trip to the store for additional makeup supplies and perfume, two things she had almost completely stopped buying years ago. As the picture of her primped self started to come together in the mirror, Piper began feeling warm with excitement. The thought of a date with Sean was repulsive, but the act of getting ready for an evening that didn't include sweatpants or flip-flops was a little enticing.

The problem was, as hard as she tried to force the memory of her kiss with Bobby out of her head, it continued to creep its way back in again and again. She spread her ruby red gloss across her lips and all she could think about was how nice it would have been for this date to be with Bobby tonight. How he would come to her door with flowers and be floored by how beautiful she looked. She wouldn't need to wear this black cocktail dress, just something simple. She would feel his eyes on the curve of her hips and his hand on the small of her back as he walked her to his truck and opened the door. They'd have a romantic picnic under the stars somewhere so quiet it teetered on spooky, because Bobby knew her well enough to know that was what would make her happiest, not drinks in some overcrowded noisy bar.

When she was finally done getting ready, Piper stood in front of her full-length mirror and reviewed her handiwork. Her thick hair, which she usually let air dry, was silky and full of volume thanks to forty-five minutes of blow drying with a giant round brush. Her dress was cut low, and it hugged tight to her waist. Piper's modesty would never allow her to admit it, but she did have the figure for perfectly showcasing a snug fitting dress.

As she walked the ten blocks to the restaurant in heels, she realized this would be daunting to most people in Edenville. People hardly walked anywhere in this town if they didn't have to. For Piper, however, her whole life had been spent walking the streets of Brooklyn. Her parents never owned a car, and Piper avoided public transportation as often as possible. As a result, she frequently found herself walking miles to her destination. She thought it very funny that she had a car and a driver's license now. It had all been included in her relocation. The fact that she never took a driving class, passed the necessary test, or had even been behind the wheel, didn't seem to matter to anyone. Those types of details fall through the cracks when you're handed a prefabricated new life. She had taught herself to drive in the parking lot of a closed supermarket. It took three weeks before she was willing to venture out onto the streets, but, even now, she walked whenever possible.

Walking in Edenville was so different than walking in Brooklyn. In Edenville, there were no herds of people moving like cattle. You didn't have to jump to avoid oily puddles loaded with floating cigarette butts. There were no homeless people to step over and passively ignore. Edenville had charm, but Brooklyn had character, and Piper knew there was a big distinction. You could search all of Edenville and still probably not be able to find a group of people to represent every race, creed, and religion whereas in Brooklyn you could find it all walking down the street. No matter what time of night, you could get any type of food you wanted in Brooklyn. A Viennese deli, a food truck, an upscale restaurant—they were all just steps away from each other. For Piper, Brooklyn was full of toxic memories, but they were the only ones she had.

The contrast between New York and Edenville was most glaring in some of the simplest scenarios. Piper would watch a school bus stop every hundred feet in Edenville to gather up children of all ages. Back in Brooklyn once you reached middle school, there were no school buses to transport you. Students ventured out onto the subway, walked, or hopped three or four different bus routes to bravely make their way to school, unaccompanied and trying hard to appear unafraid.

The tallest building in Edenville was the bank, standing three stories high. In Manhattan, where Piper would escape to as often as possible, she'd get vertigo just by staring up at the enormous structures that towered over the busy streets. As a child, Piper's favorite thing to do was ride the elevators up the highest buildings and stare out the large glass windows at the skyline of New York. There was no shortage of differences between the two places she had lived, but Edenville had one thing New York didn't—Bobby. She let herself smile slightly at the thought of him, and replayed in her mind for the hundredth time, the kiss they had shared.

Pulling the door to the restaurant open Piper pushed out the thoughts of her past and Bobby. She took a seat at the bar and started to refocus on what her goal was tonight. She was going to attempt to determine through which avenue it would be best to annihilate the judge's relationship with the Donavans. Would it be Christian's wife? Would it be his family? She might not get everything she needed from Sean tonight, but even the most general conversation could open up a new door for her to explore.

It was now a full thirty minutes past the time Sean was supposed to arrive and Piper was getting annoyed as she sat looking quite pathetic at the bar. Finally, after telling herself she'd give him five more minutes, the door swung open and in walked Sean. He was wearing dark denim jeans that were a few sizes too big and hung low around his waist, not so low that he could be an extra in a rap video, but low enough to look ridiculous as far as Piper was concerned.

He had on the same green button-up shirt she had seen him in just days before, but now, thankfully, it was buttoned. His hair was combed back and greased in true mafia fashion. She hated that he was good-looking; that she had even the slightest attraction to him infuriated her. The muddled chatter around the bar subsided for a moment as patrons watched Sean approach. When he sidled up next to Piper, conversations quickly resumed, though Piper could now feel a dozen pair of eyes on her.

Sean leaned in toward her and kissed her cheek, lingering for a moment to smell her hair. He pulled out his stool and sat down beside her, looking her over from top to bottom. "Damn girl, you clean up nice." As a true New Yorker herself, Piper was annoyed by Sean's attempts to sound like anyone other than the Southern-born kid he was. He tried hard to hide his drawl and speak like one of the Italian tough guys you'd see outside of the bakeries in Brooklyn. He did a terrible job at it, and every word grated on her nerves.

He flagged the bartender down, which wasn't hard as he seemed eager to serve in a moment's notice. "Hey Chuck," he said as the two shook hands across the bar. Piper could read an air of anxiety on the bartender's face.

"Hey Sean, how's things going?" Chuck asked, stumbling slightly on his words. "What can I get you two to drink tonight?

On the house, of course." He stood wringing his towel in his hands nervously.

"I'll have the usual, and she'll have a seven and ginger," Sean said, not even looking at the bartender. His eyes were locked on Piper's body, and he grinned like a child who had found an extra toy in his happy meal. Piper ignored the fact that he hadn't actually asked her what she'd like to drink. That didn't really matter, because if she'd had her choice it would have been a root beer. She hated the taste of alcohol and usually struggled to pick a drink for herself.

"Great guess. That's one of my favorite drinks," Piper giggled, batting her mascara-laden eyelashes.

"So since I guessed right, does that mean I get a prize? Maybe we should drink these fast and get out of here." Sean put his cold, clammy hand on her thigh just under the hem line of her dress. It was incredible to her how two hands could feel so different. The night before, Bobby's hands were warm and comforting, and tonight Sean's hands felt intrusive and dirty.

"Maybe I gave you the wrong impression over at your house," Piper explained, trying to slow the night down a bit. "I think you're a cool guy, and I'm glad we're out having drinks, but I don't even really know you. Let's at least talk a bit before we take this any further."

Sean rolled his eyes and grabbed for his beer the bartender had just put down in front of him. "I knew you weren't going to be as easy as I hoped." He rolled his eyes and took a swig of his beer with his free hand, the other still planted on her leg. "Fine, what do you want to know about me? Bring on the stupid chitchat."

"I guess my questions changed the minute you walked in here tonight, because originally I did want to ask you some dreary questions about your favorite movies, but not anymore." Piper leaned in and looked into his eyes, talking barely above a whisper in an effort to seem more seductive. "Now what I really want to know is why the whole bar got quiet when you walked in, why everyone seems a little nervous you're here, and why you drink for free in one of the only decent bars in this town. I could give a shit what your favorite movie is now; all I want to know is who the hell I'm sitting with here." She knew what this would do to a man like Sean. She knew making him feel important and bolstering his ego would put him in the mood to talk.

"You're a very observant girl, aren't you? I'm guessing you're not from Edenville because you'd already know plenty about me. If you were smart you'd've asked around before coming out tonight." His finger danced in a circled on the top of her thigh and under her dress as he flashed a devilish grin.

"And what would I have heard, exactly? I don't tend to listen to rumors much. I like to get my information right from the source." She slowly reached across and fixed the corner of his collar that was sticking up slightly. She did this partially because she thought it would be a sexy gesture and partially because it was annoying the hell out of her.

"I come from a very important family in this town. We have a lot of history, here. My dad was a businessman until he died five years ago. My older brother and I, we've picked up where he left off. Don't bother asking me what kind of business, you don't want to know." He threw his beer back, took another mouthful, and it reminded Piper she hadn't even sipped her drink yet. She reached for it, pulled some up through the tiny straw and used all of her willpower not to wince.

"Very mysterious, I like that. So if you're such an important businessman, what were you doing home in the middle of the day waiting to play video games?" She placed her drink back on the bar and tried to ignore the vibrating of her phone in her bag. The noise was loud enough to distract them and it was the third time it had gone off.

"I handle the family side of the business. Up until school started I watched my nephew every day. Now I have him every afternoon. My brother is very protective, and he doesn't trust him with anyone but family. It sounds like a lame gig, but it pays well, that's for sure." Somehow Sean had already managed to finish his beer and before even thinking of waving down the bartender another had appeared before him.

"That sounds like a nice setup. How old is he? Doesn't he have a mom who can watch him?" Piper didn't want the questions to come too fast and sound like she was gathering information.

"Chris is eight. His mom didn't exactly like the lifestyle that came along with the family business, so she took off a few years ago. She's a real bitch." Piper assumed Chris was short for Christian III. What a lucky kid, part of such a wonderful legacy.

"That is really cute. I think guys who get along well with kids are so hot." She reached into her bag trying to get a glimpse of who was calling her while grabbing her lip gloss. No luck, she couldn't see the caller ID without being more conspicuous, but luckily it had stopped vibrating. She smeared the lip gloss across her lips and puckered them together.

"So is that enough to get you to finish that drink and get out of here?" His hand moved another inch up her leg as he leaned in toward her ear whispering, "My car is right out front."

"How do I know you're telling the truth? You prove it to me." Her phone began vibrating again, and she could see Sean becoming irritated, either with the phone or her protests about leaving. "A good uncle would have picture of his nephew in his wallet."

He huffed and finally released her leg, leaned over and pulled his wallet from his back pocket. He flipped it open and there was a school picture of a little boy. He was perched in front of a fake autumn scene wearing the uniform of a private school. Piper leaned in to get a good look at the crest on his shirt and cooed over how adorable he was.

She slid off her stool and whispered in his ear, "Let me go find out who is calling me and run to the ladies' room. Then I'll be right back, and we'll talk about getting out of here."

"I'm done talking," he hissed back, half angrily half playfully as he grabbed a handful of her ass on her way by.

She looked over her shoulder at him and winked, "We'll see." As she rounded the corner of the restaurant and was out of sight she wrestled her stupid oversized bag for her phone. It rang again and the screen read *Michael.*

"Hello?" she said in an exasperated tone. There was no answer, she heard the phone click and disconnect.

"What the hell are you doing?" Michael's voice called from behind her, sending her jumping. "Are you seriously on a date with Sean Donavan, or am I having some sort of stroke?"

"Michael, you scared the hell out of me. What are you doing here, and why are you calling me every five seconds?" She knew the answer to the latter question, but faking ignorance seemed like her only card to play.

"Look at you," he said, pointing to her dress and hair. "I barely recognized you. I tried for fifteen minutes to convince myself it wasn't you sitting at the bar with that complete degenerate. So tell me, do you have the nastiest taste in men or the faultiest judgment on earth? Because you are either out on a date with him or poking your nose where it doesn't belong, either of which would be a terrible choice." Michael's face turned from hard-lined disappointment to genuine concern. "What have you gotten yourself into, Piper? When I told you to go check out those court records I had hoped you would either be too dumb to figure it out, or too smart to do anything more with them."

"Seriously?" Piper couldn't believe what she was hearing. "So you knew all along what I would find? You had the answer and wouldn't give it to me? More importantly, you're too much a coward to do anything about it yourself. I'm writing a paper Michael, stop being so dramatic." Piper tried to storm past him but he used his body to block her. He put his hands on her shoulders, not with force but enough for her to stay put.

"What I believe and what I know are two different things. In this case I believe there may be more than meets the eye when it comes to a judge and a crime family. I'm certain you are in absolutely no position to go trying to find out on your own. I have tried two cases against Sean, and both were sexual assaults. He is a dangerous guy and as tough and smart as you are, you can't outrun wickedness, it will catch up to you. Please, make an excuse to leave and meet me at my office. We'll talk this out." Michael brought himself down to her level and looked her in the eye. "Please."

"Fine." Piper had gotten all she could out of Sean without actually having to sleep with him which she never intended to do anyway. Michael's incessant phone calls had actually acted as a decent exit strategy, but she wouldn't give him the satisfaction of meeting him after. "I don't need the lecture though, so I'll skip the little meeting at your office. Thanks anyway." She shook his hands off her shoulders and stormed past him.

As Piper approached the bar she worked fast to concoct a decent story. "The pipes in my place burst," she huffed, sounding flustered and put out. "I've got to get back there and deal with the damage. My landlord is having a meltdown. I'll have to take a rain check on tonight." She had prepared herself for some pouting, whining, and overall childish behavior on his part and was surprised at how calm he was.

"Oh, that sucks. Why don't you just finish your drink, that's what we came here for, right?" He pointed to her bar stool and smiled crookedly at her. "The pipes won't be any less broken in ten minutes."

She didn't have time to dispute, her story was not thought out well enough to ad lib reasons she must leave right this second. When nothing came to her, she acquiesced and sat back down. She knew Michael's eyes would have been on her. She knew he must be steaming mad, but she thought finishing her drink was a small price to pay for exiting this horrible date unscathed and with a little more information than she had when she arrived.

The drink only tasted worse the longer it sat, and Piper decided to drink it quickly and make short work of it. With five or six large swigs that she tried to work in between more idle conversation, the drink was finished. Why she was worried about being rude was beyond her, but she thought she should wait at least another five minutes or so before taking off.

It was in the middle of a discussion about video games that Piper realized something was amiss. She had been half-listening to Sean speak and half-organizing the thoughts of her plan in her head as she processed the information he had given her and considered ways to use it. Then she was doing neither; her thoughts seemed to be sloshing around in her head like a boat at sea. She felt dizzy and confused, her vision failing her slightly.

When she grimaced and brought her hand to her forehead to try to steady the spinning room she heard Sean's voice, now seeming far away. "You don't look so good. We better get you out of here." He lifted her arm, the one closest to him, and swung it up over his neck. In an instant she realized what was happening. He had put something in her drink and now was trying to take her out of the bar.

Even though her limbs were heavy and she couldn't find her voice, she used her free arm to swat at Sean's beer bottle and knocked it to the floor where it smashed loudly. All she needed to do was draw some attention to herself and then someone, hopefully Michael, would intervene.

"Hey." She heard Michael's voice swimming around in her head. She could barely keep her eyes open now and her legs were shaking, hardly able to support her weight. She didn't want to keep holding on to Sean, but if he were to let go she knew she would fall to the floor.

"What the hell do you think you're doing?" Michael stood

between Sean and the door. "Did you drug her? You honestly think you're walking out of here with some girl who can't even see straight. That doesn't sound like a good idea with a record like yours." Michael was ready to fight, either with his professional skills or his fists, it didn't matter. There was no way Piper was leaving with Sean while he was standing there.

"I don't have a record. I've never been convicted of anything. You're the lawyer, you should know that. Just because you can't win a case doesn't mean you have to go around making shit up. She had a few too many drinks, I'm taking her home." Michael was a full five inches taller than Sean and significantly stronger. As long as Sean didn't have a weapon on him, or was stupid enough to show it in a busy restaurant, then Michael felt confident. Sean tried to push past him and in one fell swoop Michael pulled Piper to his side and shoved Sean in the other direction.

Chuck the bartender, still meek in his approach, came out from behind the bar and talked quietly to Sean. "Sean, buddy, if you catch another case your brother is going to kill you, especially if you draw any more attention to this place. Just get out of here and I'll cover for you." He ushered Sean toward the door.

"Wait," Michael shouted, having a last minute epiphany. "What the hell did you give her and how much?" He knew this information would be vital to figuring out what to do next with the lifeless girl pressed to his side.

"Right, like I'm going to tell a lawyer. That tease wasn't worth it anyway." Sean pushed open the door and proceeded to flash his middle finger back at Michael. If there had been a safe place to lay Piper down he would have followed Sean into the parking lot and beat him senseless.

The bartender waved back at Michael signaling that he would try to find out and to stay right where he was. Michael looked down at Piper who was now limp and seemed as though she were sleeping. He watched her chest rise and fall and was relieved to see she was still breathing. A few moments later Chuck reemerged from the doors and tossed a pill bottle over to Michael.

"There's an ambulance on the way, but you've got to meet them at the corner," Chuck said, motioning toward the street. "Sean said he only put one in her drink, and all she'll need to do is sleep it off." Chuck was shaking his head as he crossed back behind the bar and went right back to work. "I can't have this shit here," he mumbled.

Michael adjusted his grip on Piper's upper half and scooped her up from behind her legs, cradling her in his arms. He had stood next to Piper, leaned in close to her over some documents a few times, but it wasn't until this very moment he realized how tiny she was. He pushed his way through the entrance and was stunned by the lack of offers to help. People didn't want anything to do with this and certainly would have let Sean walk right out with Piper regardless of what state she was in.

Outside the restaurant, Michael sat down on a bench under a flickering street lamp, his arms starting to ache from holding Piper for so long. He was still supporting her under the legs, and her face was now pressed against his neck. He took comfort in the repetition of her breath and was whispering encouraging words in her ear.

The ambulance pulled up one block over from the restaurant, and Michael was relieved to recognize the EMT. It was an old acquaintance of his, Johnny Thompson. He saw him occasionally testifying in court and they still had some friends in common. They had partied together in Michael's early days in Edenville. The move to a small town where he hadn't known anyone had seemed like such a good idea until the loneliness had started to set in. Johnny had been a dependable drinking buddy for a while.

"Hey Mikey, what's going on?" Johnny asked, as he and his partner, a young stout woman, hustled over toward them.

"Hey Johnny, it's been a crazy night." There was a good chance that Johnny Thompson no longer preferred to be called Johnny.

He was probably just John now, much like Michael had converted from Mikey years ago. But the relationships you form in your youth, as casual as they might be, always seem to transport you back in time.

Michael relayed the story to Johnny and handed over the bottle of pills. They loaded Piper into the ambulance and took her vitals.

"So what's the plan here, Mikey? If I bring her into the hospital this turns into a police report, and it won't be something we can forget about tomorrow. Her vitals are stable. There's been no impact to her blood pressure or blood oxygen levels. Most likely she needs to sleep this off, so if you want to leave the cops out of this..." Johnny's voice trailed off as a police car pulled up to the scene. "Never mind, looks like this will be a police matter after all." Johnny walked over to the police car and Michael watched a young, dark-haired cop exit his car. He could tell by his military posture and unsmiling face that this cop wasn't one of the good ol' boys.

Great, Michael thought, at least one of the older cops would be willing to let this go to avoid the paperwork. But an eager young rookie would be a thorough bastard tonight. Michael was confident whatever Piper was doing here tonight, she wouldn't want it to be the start of a long-drawn-out court case. She'd want it to go away.

"Hey Bobby," Johnny said, pulling his rubber glove off and extending a hand out to greet the officer. Michael felt slightly relieved that at least they knew each other.

"Did this get called in? I didn't hear anything about it over the radio. I was passing by and thought maybe you could use a hand. What's going on?" Bobby approached the open doors of the ambulance and glanced inside. Immediately recognizing Piper, his heart popped in his chest, and he felt panic briefly overtake him. "Piper?" he quaked, pulling himself into the back of the ambulance to be by her side. "What the hell happened, is she all right?"

"You know her?" Michael asked, feeling like this night was one of the strangest of his life. Living in Edenville you grew accustomed to knowing someone almost everywhere you went, but Piper wasn't from here, and from what Michael knew she was somewhat of a loner. She never talked about having friends or family in the area. Now suddenly she was associating with cops and criminals.

"She's my friend," Bobby said, hesitating a little on the words. Piper certainly had become a friend over the past months, but after the kiss they shared last night Bobby had been wondering if they were becoming more. He reached for her hand and pulled it up to his chest and over his heart.

"She was out tonight with Sean Donavan. Apparently the date wasn't moving fast enough for him and he put something in her drink. I saw him trying to get her out of the bar, clearly not of her own volition, and I stepped in. This being one of the Donavan-owned establishments we didn't get much support from the staff, which is why we are sitting here, a block away from the place, and no one else seems to be worried about how she's doing." Michael found himself still itching to fight, his nerves still on edge, and the thought of all those complacent people enjoying their meals was making him crazy.

"Is she going to be okay? Are you taking her to the hospital?" Bobby had urgency in his voice that spoke volumes about his feelings for Piper.

"We were talking that over," Johnny cut in. "Her vitals are stable. We know what kind of pill he gave her. It was rohypnol, or ruffies. She isn't showing any signs of an allergic reaction, most likely she needs to sleep it off as long as someone can stay and watch her. We've got to get back to the station, so I don't want to rush you but we need to make a decision."

"I don't think she'd want this to turn into a big thing," Michael said, forgetting for a minute that he hadn't really introduced himself as more than a stranger in the right place at the right time. "Dealing with the Donavans, especially in court, is no easy process. There is a restaurant full of people ready to cover for Sean. Unfortunately I've been through this process with him before. They'll drag her through the mud in any kind of case we try to make. Piper got lucky tonight; maybe we should just cut our losses and move on. I think that's what she would want."

"You know Piper?" Bobby asked with a skeptical glare. He let his mind run through the scenarios of how this man might somehow be involved.

"I'm sorry, I haven't introduced myself." Michael leaned into the ambulance and shook Bobby's free hand. "I'm Michael Cooper. I'm a lawyer and a friend of Piper. I was out tonight having drinks with some people from work and saw her up at the bar."

"I'm Bobby Wright," he answered, skeptical of this entire situation. "So you're *the* Michael? You're the one Piper has been doing all this research for? I find it odd that one day she's digging up cases on these guys for you and the next she's risking her life at the bar with them. It sounds like maybe you were looking for a little more information and decided to use her as bait?" Bobby put Piper's hand back down gently and exited the ambulance to get a better view of Michael. Bobby was excellent at reading body language, facial cues, and tone of voice. If he was going to get an accurate read on this guy he'd need to get closer.

"She isn't doing any research on my behalf," Michael barked defensively. "She's writing some paper for school, and I've been giving her pointers. I have no idea what she was thinking being out with Sean tonight, but you can be damn sure I didn't put her up to it. If you guys are such good friends why didn't you know where she was?" Michael was dumbfounded at the attack. All he had tried to do up until this point was steer Piper away from danger. He certainly wasn't putting her in harm's way.

"She dropped out of school months ago. She isn't writing any paper. What the hell is going on?" Bobby replied, looking back over his shoulder at Piper.

"Guys," Johnny said. "I'm sorry but I need to either get her to the hospital or not. Can someone keep an eye on her tonight?"

"Bobby, I don't have all the answers, but I think you should get her home. Getting any deeper into this isn't going to help her." Michael wasn't naive enough to think his knowledge of Piper or their friendship was that deep. He did, however, know the Donavans and the lengths they would go, to avoid prosecution.

Bobby climbed back into the ambulance and lifted Piper, holding her close to his body. Michael shook hands with Johnny, nodded a thank you to his partner and opened the rear door of Bobby's cruiser.

Once Bobby had placed Piper in the back of his car and positioned her in a way he thought she'd be safe, he turned back to Michael. The ambulance had driven off and now it was only the two men standing uneasily on the quiet corner.

"Thanks for keeping her safe tonight. I'm glad you were there. I don't want to think about what might have happened if Sean left with her." Bobby's mind was churning with questions and worry. He wasn't completely sure what he thought of Michael yet, but, at a minimum, he seemed to have stepped in when Piper needed him.

"Cindy Martin," Michael whispered, shaking his head. "I know you don't want to think about what might have happened, and tomorrow neither will she, but you both should. She's mixed up in something, Bobby, and tonight could have ended much differently. Sean has been charged twice with some pretty serious crimes, one of which was drug facilitated sexual assault. The details of that crime will be seared into my mind forever. Cindy Martin, the girl he drugged and assaulted had three broken ribs, a fractured cheek bone, and was covered in scrapes and bruises. He rolled her out of his moving car and left her on the side of the road in the middle of December. She was on the verge of hypothermia when she was discovered by a woman driving home that night. Yet, there was a parade of people willing to corroborate his alibi. Once they had destroyed Cindy's credibility on the stand because she had a history of recreational drug use in her past, the case started to fall apart." Michael was speaking mostly through his teeth with an angry hiss. He was motioning his hands animatedly as if he were giving an impassioned closing argument.

"I almost didn't come out tonight. I was tired and had more work to do, and if it weren't for my buddies convincing me I needed a break, I'd be at home trying to find a way to prosecute a crime while Sean was out committing another one. Tomorrow when she wakes up and doesn't want to tell you what the hell she was doing here tonight, when she tells you she's fine and that she had it all under control, you tell her about Cindy Martin. You tell her about the beautiful twenty-two-year-old girl who can't eat out at a restaurant anymore without having a panic attack, has three locks on her door, and hasn't been on a date in a year and a half. Here's my card," Michael said, pulling a business card out from his pocket. "If you're really her friend you'll get her to tell you what she was doing with Sean tonight, and you'll convince her to stop before it's too late. Give me a call in the morning to let me know she's all right."

Bobby tucked the card into the breast pocket of his uniform shirt. "I hear you," he said, shaking Michael's hand. "I'll see what I can find out tomorrow. Hopefully a scare like this will be enough to get her out of whatever stuff she's mixed up in."

Michael nodded a goodbye. As he turned back toward his car he spoke over his shoulder. "I don't know what it is about this girl that makes me give a damn. It's impossible to cut my losses and mind my business. The easiest thing in the world for me to do would be to get in my car and forget this night ever happened, forget about Piper all together. She shoots down every date I ask her on, she plays me like a fool, and I know almost nothing about her. She's like fireworks, captivating and gorgeous, you can't help but watch and be amazed, but you better keep your distance or you'll get burned."

CHAPTER 11

Piper refused to open her eyes. She had woken up a few moments earlier and realized something terrible had happened. She thought if she could only keep her eyes closed and attempt to piece the previous night's events together she could make sense of it all. She knew once she let herself come fully awake, she may not like what she faced. She remembered talking to Michael in the back of the bar, she remembered finishing her awful drink and making idle conversation with Sean, and she remembered rapidly losing control of her faculties. Had Michael come over and intervened, and now she was safely sleeping in his bed? Had Sean been able to slip her out of the restaurant unnoticed and now she was who-knows-where and in further danger? As fear began to overcome her she took mental stock of what she could with her other senses, still unwilling to open her eyes.

She was dressed, still in the uncomfortable black cocktail dress, though her shoes were off. These sheets felt like her own, the flannel set she had just put on the previous day. Her body was sore and her head ached, but she didn't feel violated or injured in anyway. All these things brought her anxiety level to a manageable place, and she dared to let the light pour in as she cracked her eyes open.

There was her dresser, her nightstand, and her curtains. She was in her own room, in her own bed, seemingly safe. But who had brought her here? Michael didn't know where she lived; perhaps he had looked at her driver's license and used her key to put her to bed?

"Piper?" a man's voice called from behind her. She was still cloudy and her reflexes sluggish, but she was fairly certain it was Bobby. She rolled over toward him and groaned. She didn't think of the repercussions or the questions he may have for her, all she could think was how glad she was that he was there.

"You were given a dose of Royhpnol last night, it's a powerful sedative that causes a person to blackout and usually have memory loss and some fatigue the following day." Bobby had pulled the chair from Piper's desk over to the side of her bed. He had spent the night perched there, as she slept.

"The date rape drug?" Piper whispered. Her voice was hoarse and her throat dry. She closed her eyes again. It was hard to focus on anything and the light was making her head pound.

Bobby reached for her hand and laced his fingers in between hers. "Nothing happened. Your friend Michael got you out of there before Sean could do anything. I was driving by when I saw the ambulance and stopped to see if they needed help."

As wonderful as Bobby's hand felt in hers, as sweet as his voice was, thick with concern—all those words brought reality back into focus. Bobby met Michael, he knew she was out with Sean, and there was an ambulance involved, probably a police report. Bobby was too insightful, too good of a friend to not pry into this situation. However happy she had been to wake up and see him sitting vigil by her, she knew everything was about to change the moment he wanted to know more.

"Piper, I'm going to ask you some questions, but first there is something I want to say. We haven't known each other very long, but I care about you. The kiss we shared, the time we've been spending together, for me it isn't some flirty game I'm trying to play. I can see myself with you. I can see this working between us. I think it's important that you know that so when I'm asking you these questions you understand my motivation. Does that make sense to you?" Bobby had ample time that night to think about how he would approach this precarious conversation. He waited for Piper to nod that she understood and then he pulled her hand, still linked with his own, up to his lips and kissed it gently.

"When you first started coming around Betty's house I wanted to know more about you, but you weren't very forthcoming with information. No one else seemed to notice, but I kept leaving every Wednesday night with more questions about you than answers. Jules and Betty mean the world to me, and I was concerned that you had some ulterior motive. I called in a few favors and did a background check on you. The preliminary one came back as though you didn't exist prior to two years ago. I thought maybe it was a glitch in the system so I pushed for more information. I went up as high as I could and even indebted myself to some guys with pretty high clearance, and still there was nothing. It really freaked me out at first, but the more I got to know you, the more I started to care about you, and the less I let it bother me. I convinced myself that you had your reasons for not sharing your past with me and that when you were ready, I'd be here to listen. I decided that you were not a threat to Jules and Betty and that I would give you time to open up to me. I committed myself to trusting you even though it wasn't in my nature." Bobby could feel Piper's grip on his hand loosening, and he knew it was her recoiling from his harsh honesty, but she didn't speak, so he continued.

"That was, until last night when I found out you've been untruthful about why you're so interested in the Donavans' criminal history. I couldn't understand, and still can't really, why you'd be out with Sean. I don't know why just weeks after you and I are rummaging through their court cases, discussing how unworthy they are of the benefits of our justice system, you're sitting across from one of them having drinks. So what I'm asking is: who are you? Who were you two years ago? And what were you doing last night? If you can tell me that, I promise you I'll help you in any way I can. You need to trust me." With that last sentence, Piper pulled her hand away from his, and he felt a piece of his heart go with it.

"Sure I'll trust you, let me run a background check on you first." She pulled herself up to a sitting position knowing she looked too weak crumpled under her blankets to be taken seriously. "I think you're being a little dramatic, and I'm guessing so was Michael. The two of you together probably blew this whole thing out of proportion. I'm sorry that I'm not turning out to be who you hoped I was, but I'm not going to sit here and be accused of having questionable motives. I think you should go." Piper pointed at the door, and she wondered how her mouth and her mind could betray her heart so deeply. Would there ever be a time in her life that they pulled in the same direction?

"I don't want to go, Piper. I'm not looking for an easy out." Bobby stood and raised his voice slightly. He felt this conversation, this woman, getting away from him and it wasn't how he wanted it.

"What do you want?" She threw her arms up in exasperation and immediately regretted the sudden movement. She had momentarily forgotten how much her body was hurting and how fast her head was spinning. She didn't want him to leave, but she wanted him to take back everything he had just said.

"What do I want? I want to take off this uniform and crawl into bed with you. I want to spend the entire day under these covers. I'd tell you how terrified I was when I saw you lying in the back of that ambulance. I'd tell you how I've never been so full of rage or had such a desire to track a man down and kill him for what he had done, what he could have done to you." Bobby's hands clenched into fists as he thought of Sean. "I want you to feel like you can tell me everything about yourself, the hard stuff, the scary stuff. I want you to talk until you lose your voice, and I want to hold you until I can't figure out where I end and you begin. I want today to be the first day of something incredible for us. There is nothing that you can tell me that would scare me away, nothing that could change how I feel about you."

He was practically yelling now, his face red with frustration. He realized how worked up he had become, and he softened his voice. "I want to stay here and find out who you are."

Piper forced the tears forming at the corners of her eyes to stay right where they were. She swallowed back the lump in her throat and dug her fingernails into the palm of her hand to help redirect the pain away from her heart. She let the thought flash through her mind for a moment. What if she did tell Bobby who she was and what she had planned? Would he do as he said and stay?

"I don't think there is anything more real to you than your convictions, Bobby, and I can assure you there isn't anything more important to me than mine. The problem is that ours happen to sit at opposite sides of the moral spectrum. I won't ask you to stand by me when I know it would mean you'd have to set aside things that make you who you are. I'm also not naïve enough to believe you're even capable of that. Who I was two years ago isn't something I'll share with you. What I was doing last night isn't something you'll approve of. So the only thing I can do, because I do care about you, is not lie. I'm asking you to go, so that I don't have to." Piper knew it would be more convincing, more final if she could be staring into Bobby's eyes as she spoke, but she couldn't bring herself to do it. She thought if she raised her eyes and looked at him, she'd see his heart being pulled from his chest, and she couldn't stand to think of him hurting.

He didn't dissect her words about morals and convictions or try to argue his way to the truth. He grabbed his things from her desk and quietly made his way to the door of her bedroom. He dropped his head, and rubbed at his eyes, clearly feeling like he was out of options. "When I go, you need to understand that's it for us. I won't stand by and watch you put yourself in danger. If I walk out this door right now, you're on your own. That goes for Betty and Jules, too." He was facing away from her as he spoke.

"You really think they'll just stop talking to me because you tell them to?" Piper, for the first time in this conversation, felt a righteous indignation about Bobby's decree and ultimatum.

"No, I won't tell them they can't talk to you. I'm hoping that the person I started to care about is as principled as I thought. If you're putting yourself in a compromising position I hope you won't be selfish enough to subject anyone else to it. Especially people who have suffered enough already. If you truly can't let anyone in, at least you can minimize the collateral damage. I might not know who you were, but I'd like to think I was starting to know who you are." He didn't wait for her response, he didn't look back to see if his words had impacted her. There was nothing left to do but leave.

When she heard the thud of his truck door slam and the rumbling of his engine starting up she knew she was in the clear. She let a few warm tears roll down her cheeks, thinking they'd be enough to release the pressure of emotion that had built up inside her. Instead they were the beginning of a flood. She lay back down and pulled the blankets up over her face and sobbed. She cried at the thought of losing Jules and Betty's friendship. She cried for what could have happened last night, where she could be waking up this morning if it weren't for Michael. And she cried at the thought of living the rest of her life without ever being kissed by Bobby again.

As she lay in bed aching mentally and physically she realized stories like these, the ones filled with revenge and vigilantism, all had one thing hers did not. A capable, trained person with a litany of abilities. She was not an assassin skilled in martial arts and able to physically protect herself. She wasn't a robotic, cold-hearted black widow void of all emotion. She didn't carry a gun. She didn't even have mace for that matter. She was like someone who'd never played football joining the NFL and playing without pads. Yet, even all that wasn't enough to stop her. She might be the underdog here, but it wasn't impossible, and that's all she needed to know to keep driving forward. There was a chance that this journey was a self-inflicted masochistic punishment for the failures of her past. Happiness seemed at her fingertips, but she wasn't ready to indulge in it, and there were miles to go before she'd feel worthy of it.

Her eyes were puffy and burning from the salt of her tears. She had managed to stop blubbering and wailing long enough to reach for her phone. She squinted and queued up a familiar number. It rang three times and finally an answer.

"Michael," she mumbled, trying to mask the devastation in her voice. She may not have been able to give Bobby what he needed to keep him around, but Michael needed much less from her, and she wasn't ready to go back to being completely alone in this world.

CHAPTER 12

Seventy-one days. That's how long it had been since Piper had spoken to Bobby. She had seen him and Betty, twice through the window of the diner, but she stealthily avoided being seen by them. She had almost called him a handful of times, but managed to fight off the moments of weakness with the reminder of what that phone call would entail.

Once, in the middle of another sleepless night, she came to the depressing realization that she might love Bobby. It was baffling to her how she could meet someone and be so annoyed by him and then just as quickly become so caught up in him. The first couple of Wednesday nights since arguing with Bobby were like torture for Piper. She'd spend hours looking out her window up at the stars and cursing the noise that came from the street and the stores below. Nothing would ever be as tranquil and serene as her time spent with Bobby swinging on Betty's porch, watching the night unfold before them.

She occasionally saw Scott at work. Whatever story Bobby had told them about Piper's absence had been enough to have him walking the other way when he saw her coming. Her emotions ran the gamut. There were days she was saddened by the barrenness of her life. Other days she was angry that she didn't mean enough to any of these people for them to track her down and find out how she was. Did she mean that little to them? Had she misread their friendship?

Michael had been a steady presence in her life since the night after her date with Sean. She had asked him for coffee and told him that she was sorry for putting him in that position. She had genuinely thanked him for his help that night and even let a few tears fall when relaying her gratitude. She admitted she had been stupid, overzealous, and caught up in the idea of what she thought was wrong with the justice system. She told Michael she wasn't putting this all behind her quite yet but she wouldn't put herself back in a position like that ever again. She knew that was probably a lie, but it was one he needed to hear in order to forgive her.

They shared long nights together talking only about topics that pertained to Michael, never what was going on with Piper. They discussed his dysfunctional family, his cases, and his future. He picked her brain and loved to bounce new ideas off her. It was nice to see the spark slowly come back into her eyes after her brush with danger.

Many nights he felt himself on the verge of kissing her, staring at her lips as she spoke. She had told him time and again there would never be anything more than a friendship between them. Yet, somehow he kept finding himself caught up in the idea of running his tongue along her neck and making love to her on his desk. It was an internal conflict he fought hard to keep at bay.

He had spoken with Bobby the morning after Piper's date with Sean. Bobby had told him he wasn't able to get through to her. It was a large part of Michael's job to read between the lines and it was clear that Bobby cared deeply for Piper. But Bobby explained he had other people in his life to worry about, and Piper was too much of a liability to them right now. He asked

Michael to keep an eye on her, and to do his best to keep her safe just as he had that night with Sean.

At first Michael wasn't sure how he felt about being someone's keeper. He was a successful, handsome, and wealthy man with his pick of woman and an abundant social network. Babysitting wasn't in his job description, and he assumed it would put a cramp in his social life. However, the more time he spent with Piper the more he realized how alone she was in this world. She had told him that first day over coffee she needed him to refrain from asking her questions about her family or her past. She wanted to spend time with Michael but it couldn't be an interrogation, she wasn't a puzzle needing to be pieced together. "Let's go back to being funny, laid-back people who have a good time together," she begged, and, begrudgingly, he agreed. However, even through casual conversation, he found Piper to be more damaged and lonely than anyone he had ever met before. So why commit to keeping watch over her. Frankly, he was lonely too.

When he felt himself wanting to scoop her up into his arms and make love to her until she felt whole, he reminded himself that even though he wanted her he didn't love her. And even if Bobby couldn't be around her right now, Bobby did love her. If Piper was going to be happy someday it wouldn't be because of a passionate night in a dark office. He wasn't going to be the guy sleeping with her when Bobby returned on his white horse.

"So have you thought about what you're going to get your mom for her birthday?" asked Piper as she curled a ring of hair around her finger and read a file Michael had given her. She loved being in his office. She loved being in his presence. He had done exactly what she needed, been there for her without needing to be everything to her.

"I think I'm going to send her one of those fruit things that look like flowers. I'm pretty sure she likes fruit and flowers. So what do you think of that opening argument?" he gestured to the file in her hands.

"It's all right. It seems a little weak though. Have you thought about talking more about the children? You said there are seven women on the jury, four with kids. I would talk more about the impact the crime had on the kids. Their mother was beat up by their father right in front of them while he was in a meth-induced rage. Sure she was sleeping with another man, that might bias a few people on the jury, but she wasn't sleeping with the man in front of her kids. The defendant is the only one who crossed that line. That's not something they can get over. How are their grades? How are they sleeping? Have they had any therapy? I would tell the whole story from the perspective of the youngest... what was he, nine? My opening statement would read like a journal entry from that little boy on the scariest day of his life. That'll make an impact for sure." She closed the folder and slid it across the desk to Michael.

"What a horrible misuse of talent, Miss Anderson. That is simply genius, and I fully intend to steal the idea from you and pass it off as my own. You should really consider going back to school. Maybe even law school down the road." Michael knew he was on thin ice. Bringing up school with her was something they had put on the taboo list early on. But he was tired of her skills being wasted, though he was certainly benefiting from them.

"Nope, I'm perfectly happy being your muse here and tinkering around at the cable company. Besides, I'd probably end up taking your job someday if I did that." She stood up and took his school conversation as a great cue to leave. Things between them had been working so well, and some of it simply came down to a well-timed exit on her part. "Give me a call once you have that drafted if you want to talk it through." She pulled her bag over her shoulder and saw herself out.

Michael swiveled his chair so he could look out his window and watch her get into her car and drive off. He thought it was finally time to do something he had been thinking about for weeks. He picked up his phone and dialed.

"Hey Bobby, it's Michael Cooper, do you think we could get together sometime this week? I have a few things I'd like to chat about." Going behind Piper's back wasn't ideal but she hadn't left him with much choice.

Piper had planned on being at Michael's office for at least another hour before he had brought up school. It was only six o'clock on Wednesday night which meant she'd have too much time to sit alone and think of Bobby if she went home now. She normally would have had dinner with Michael, or they would have had takeout delivered to the office. The only upside of knowing that everyone would be at Betty's house was it meant no one she knew would be at the diner. At least she could get a bite to eat and even sit in the seat she knew Bobby had sat in earlier that day.

As she pushed her mashed potatoes around on her plate she realized how quiet the diner was this time of night. She was ready to pay her bill and slink back to her lonely apartment when the booming voice of a man broke the silence as he pushed his way through the front door. It was Judge Lions, and his face was flustered and dotted with beads of sweat.

"You better believe I'm pissed," he thundered as he hastily settled himself down into his booth. "I can't talk about this right now, but I want to get it resolved as soon as possible. Meet me at nine tomorrow morning at the mill." He punched a button on his cell phone and slammed it down on the table. He pulled a handkerchief from his breast pocket and wiped the sweat off his brow. Something had flustered the normally even-keeled judge, and Piper was determined to find out what.

Over the last few weeks, she had been able to identify which school young Chris Donavan attended by researching the crest she had seen on the picture Sean had shown her. She had finally settled on Chris being the linchpin, that, if pulled, would collapse the relationship between the judge and the Donavans. Her best bet was to combine two cardinal sins, "don't mess with the kids and don't have an unhealthy interest in young boys."

Determining how that would play out had slowed Piper down a bit. She was certain that she never actually wanted Chris to be in any danger, it would only need to look as though the judge was targeting him. She had begun spending time watching Chris's comings and goings. He was a simple boy who didn't seem as though he had been tainted yet by the power of his family. He played fairly on the playground and took time to stop and watch the bugs crawling across the sidewalk on his way home from school. He was always accompanied by someone. It was either his father or another man who Piper didn't recognize.

She thought that she may, at some point, have to lay eyes on Sean again if he was ever appointed to walking-home-from-school duty, and she had decided it didn't matter. She intended to seek retribution at some point, but she could be patient. She wouldn't let her personal vendetta overshadow her main objective.

The judge's presence at the diner tonight and his cryptic conversation had Piper's senses tingling with excitement. She didn't know what had upset him or who was on the other end of the line, but she was pretty certain she knew which mill he was talking about. Back when she was tailing him more closely he had pulled into the old complex of mills that had once housed a textile company years ago. She wasn't able to follow him into the long empty parking lot, but from the street she had seen him pull up to a loading dock and climb the stairs to a side door.

She had become savvier at using the database at the cable company to find the information she was looking for. Both Christian and the judge had a GPS system on their cell phones that was tied to their data plans. The information ran through a sister company of ComCable. She had access to their information and could track their past locations as well as anytime they had been in close proximity to each other. After seeing the judge enter the old mill she had cross-referenced their two phones to see if Christian had ever been in that area at the same time. With this information she was able to determine that the mill was a preferred meeting place for the judge and Christian.

She paid her bill and hustled out the diner while the judge was chatting with the waitress. Piper slipped out the door and quickly crossed the street. If she was going to be ready to do surveillance on that meeting tomorrow she'd need all night to prepare.

CHAPTER 13

God bless search engines, she thought to herself. Over the last few weeks the Internet had provided her with ample sites that sold interesting spy gear. She had invested in a small hearing enhancement system that would help amplify any conversations she was trying to overhear. She decided she needed some form of protection so a stun gun had been her weapon of choice since she assumed her background, or lack thereof, may keep her from being able to secure a gun permit. She had two micro cameras that she still couldn't figure out how to work. Hollywood had certainly made all this espionage stuff look much easier than it was.

She pulled a dark pair of jeans, a black sweatshirt, and a baseball hat from her closet. The key to all of this would be to continue to maintain anonymity. The advantage of not being a professional was she didn't have to pretend to be a nobody in their world because she genuinely was.

Piper knew it was important to sleep. She had triple-checked her alarm clock to ensure it was set for four a.m., but she still couldn't manage to quiet her mind long enough for sleep to come. She watched the minutes tick by and thought of the different things tomorrow's meeting could be about, or who it could be with. She was hoping it would be Christian Donavan. She was dying to see the dynamics between the two men. It was important for her to know if they had a reluctant or tenuous business relationship or if they were as close as family. Knowing this would help her determine how irrefutable her intended evidence against the judge would need to be in order to sever their ties.

Arriving under the cover of early morning darkness to set up her hearing enhancement equipment was important. She wanted to be settled in hours before their arrival and have an opportunity to find a sufficient hiding spot. The mill was at least a thirty minute walk from her house, but she didn't want to have the hindrance of finding a covert place to park her car. It was a cool morning, and she wasn't looking forward to the long trek, but her adrenaline had her body moving without much thought at all.

As she finally approached the mill she waited until there was no sign of a car coming down the quiet street. She looked around for any sign of life, and when she felt sure the whole world was still asleep she made her move through the parking lot and toward the stairs. Her heart jumped in her chest as she reached the door and pulled at the knob.

Why had she not assumed that the door would be locked? Of course an old abandoned mill wouldn't simply be left wide open for anyone to come and go as they please. She berated herself for such an oversight. She remembered the lock-picking set she nearly bought the week before and realized it wouldn't have done her any good. She'd probably be as hopeless at that skill as she had been at working the micro cameras.

She climbed back down the stairs and started looking for an alternative entrance. There were multiple windows she could shimmy through but they were out of her reach. She could touch the bottom of the sills with her fingertips but her embarrassing lack of upper body strength would keep her from being able to pull herself up. She searched around for something to stand on. She found a rusty barrel around the back of the mill that seemed like it would do. She climbed onto it awkwardly, steadied herself, and peered in. She'd need to break this window. She pulled her sweatshirt over her head and wrapped it around her arm like she had seen this in a movie. She cocked her arm back and punched at the glass. It made a thud and she squeaked at the pain vibrating its way up her arm. Perhaps there was some movie magic involved in the window breaking she had seen. She unwrapped her hand and put the sweatshirt over her elbow instead. She was losing the advantage of her early start and felt panic set in. With all her might she slammed her elbow into the glass, and it shattered. She broke away the remaining shards and while pulling at a few stubborn pieces she felt the window tilt out toward her. It had been unlocked the entire time. She cursed herself for not simply trying to open it first. These were the moments she was glad she didn't have a partner.

Piper lowered herself through the window and into the large open space of the mill. She pulled a flashlight from her pocket and put her sweatshirt back on. Using her foot she swept the glass from the unnecessarily broken window under a nearby shelf. The floor was loaded with dust and she realized too much moving would leave foot prints and possibly draw attention to her presence if someone was astute enough to notice. She could see a large area of the floor with most of the dust already disturbed. It was under one of the only hanging lights that still had a bulb in it and she deduced this was probably where the judge held his surreptitious business meetings. With that in mind she began searching for the right spot to settle in and wait.

A few steps to her left were some stacked crates pushed catty-cornered against the wall. There was enough space for her if she curled up the right way. The small spaces between the crates would give her a possible line of sight and at least a place to point her microphone for the hearing enhancer.

Time seemed to be moving at warp speed as she set up her equipment and wedged herself behind the crates, trying multiple positions in an attempt to give herself the best chance to have a view of the meeting. She knew full well this was all a gamble. Maybe the meeting would be held at the complete opposite end of the mill. Maybe they'd sit outside in a car and never even come in. She knew she needed a lot of stars to align in order for this to work, but she was willing to have some faith. Something out there kept sending her signs to will her forward. She knew she wasn't very skilled and maybe she made some rookie mistakes, but so far when it counted she'd been successful.

She had done one final run-through of everything and decided she wouldn't emerge from her hiding spot again until either the meeting had taken place or it had gotten late enough that she was sure it wasn't going to happen.

Her watch read seven-forty-five and she knew this last stretch of waiting would be the hardest. She refused to let her mind fall into thoughts of Bobby or what would happen if she was caught here. She decided, instead, to think only of old songs she loved and her favorite books. She would fill this time with quiet reflection on things she enjoyed rather than regret and fear.

Not sleeping the night before was proving to be more detrimental to her mission than she had anticipated. The dark, quiet mill was lulling her into an overdue sleep. Time and again she felt her head slipping downward and repeatedly she jolted back up.

When the sound of a key in the door came into Piper's ear through the headphones of her hearing device she instantly felt the exhaustion fall away. She had never been more awake in her life. She realized she would need to move her head backward in order to get a better view and see who had come in, but she was frozen with fear. She heard the large, metal door slam shut and the amplified noise shocked her ears.

Her fear hadn't just limited her ability to move, she also found herself unable to breathe, blink, or swallow. It took a full minute for her to realize if she didn't do these things she might pass out.

The door once again squeaked open and slammed shut, and Piper heard a conversation start up and two hands slap together for a handshake.

"Sorry to take you away from a busy day in court, but you know I wouldn't have done so if it weren't critical. The good news is, I think the situation is pretty well contained at the moment." The voice sounded like that of an older man, not Christian's, which Piper had heard on two occasions when watching him walk his son home from school.

"I certainly hope so. If not what the hell am I paying you for? Tell me everything." The judge seemed as aggravated as he had the previous night on the phone. Piper was relieved to know her equipment was working properly. She'd be able to hear the conversation clearly as long as they kept talking at this volume.

"There's this rookie cop who's got a little too much free time on his hands and apparently some lofty goals for his first year. Remember the kid who dug up that stuff on Manton and tried to take him down? Well he damn near would have done it if you and I hadn't intervened. It's not like we give a damn about Manton, but he was set to have a meeting with our guy that day for some guns. If we hadn't gotten Manton's guys off, they would have flipped on Christian. That was a complete nightmare, but I thought we put the kid through the ringer enough to knock him down a few pegs. I guess he's back at it and interested in your extracurricular activities. He came to me yesterday with a couple of photos of you leaving the motel. He said he hadn't dug into it enough to give any details yet, but he thought he spotted two of Christian's guys out front and that you might be involved in something worth checking out. I told him to hit the brakes and let me look into it a bit, that those kinds of accusations against someone like you were nothing to mess around with. Now I've got to figure out what to do." The man's voice was quiet as he broke the bad news.

"Are you sure he hasn't been flashing the pictures around anywhere else? Why would he bring them to you? We can't be that lucky." The judge's tone changed from frustration to alarm.

"I know the kid. You're going to be pissed to hear this, but he was Grafton's neighbor. He practically idolized the guy. Grafton's the reason he became a cop in the first place. He thinks I'm one of the old timer good guys like Grafton was. He thinks he can trust me," the man said and Piper could hear his growing irritation with the situation.

"So let's take care of him the same way we did Grafton, and let's do it quickly before he realizes you're not quite as good a guy as he thinks," the judge retorted sarcastically.

"Things are different now. We can't go around taking guys out anymore, Randy. Luring a cop into a building, shooting him, and pinning it on some mystery criminal won't fly anymore. There's too much technology, too many people with damn camera phones everywhere. Not to mention, Internal Investigations isn't on our side. We don't have as many of the guys as we used to in there. They've all retired. We've got to be smart about this." The man's voice was forceful as he tried to deter the judge from making a rash decision.

"Come on, Red. Buy him off, everyone has a price. If he's such a determined kid I'm sure we can find a place for him in our organization," the judge snapped, clearly underestimating the situation.

"You don't get it," the other man roared, pounding his fist against a desk or a wall that Piper couldn't see. "He's like Grafton reincarnated, it's actually scary sometimes. I can tell you right now a payoff wouldn't have worked on Stan and it won't work on this kid either."

"So what exactly are you proposing? I'm hearing a lot of objections and not too many solutions. You know this kid, what's it going to take to get him off this?" The Judge was now pacing the room and Piper could hear his voice growing louder as he came closer to her, then fading as he headed back in the other direction.

"I've been wracking my brain and the only thing I can come up with is we hit him where it hurts. He's got a thing for Grafton's daughter I think, and I know he's real close with Grafton's old lady too. Maybe we let him know if he doesn't drop this then they're not safe." The man cleared his throat frequently as he spoke and Piper tried to make a mental note of this habit. If she couldn't turn and get a good look at him, then she'd need to try to piece together his identity any way possible.

"If we can't kill him, and we can't buy him off then let's scare the hell out of him and see if that works," the judge said arrogantly.

"I'm going to try one more time to get him off this whole kick first. Maybe I can get through to him. I really don't want to start messing with anyone's damn family, especially a dead cop's wife and kid. I'm getting too old for this shit." The man's voice trailed off as he turned in the other direction away from where Piper was hiding.

"Well if you find yourself getting cold feet about this then I'll have Christian take care of it for me. He's got no problem doing what needs to be done. Maybe that's why he's stepping on your toes so much lately. Maybe it's time you retire." The judge knew this was a hot button and he enjoyed exploiting it.

"Christian might have the stomach for all this, but he'll never be able to give you what I do as a cop on the force. We haven't found one decent officer to recruit, and I'm one of your last guys left on the inside. You might want to drop the retirement bullshit. If anyone should be bowing out of this game, it's you. You're getting sloppy. We wouldn't be in this position right now if you could keep away from teenage girls." The tension in the room was palpable. Piper could sense it even from behind the crates.

"You take care of this kid before I decide your pussy diplomatic approach is a sign of weakness. Get your hands on those pictures, and put this to bed. Now get the hell out of here. I'm supposed to be in court in fifteen minutes." As the first man, the one the judge called Red, left he mumbled something under his breath that Piper couldn't make out.

A few minutes later the door pulled open and slammed shut again. Piper heard the key turning in the door again. She sat motionless. The amount of information buzzing in her mind was almost too much to process. The meeting wasn't between the judge and Christian, it was much bigger than that. The meeting was between the judge and a corrupt police officer, and more than that the rookie cop causing trouble was Bobby. As all the pieces came together, her head spun with the reality of it all. The person they were talking about murdering ten years ago was Betty's husband.

CHAPTER 14

"Bobby, I know I'm the last person in the world you want to talk to right now, but I need you to come to my house. It's important." Piper skipped the niceties; she needed to get to Bobby before that cop did.

"Piper, I think we were both pretty clear that day. If you didn't want my help I wasn't going to let you put people I care about in danger." Bobby's voice was quiet and she heard the noise of the diner crowd in the background.

"I'm not the one putting Jules and Betty in danger, you are. I know you're across the street at the diner eating that same old breakfast. Pay your bill and get over here." Piper hung up the phone and tossed it onto the kitchen counter. It was so nice to hear Bobby's voice again even though the circumstances were tense.

Fifteen minutes passed before she heard a knock on her door. She looked through the peephole and saw Bobby standing there, looking annoyed and impatient. She knew that nothing about this conversation was going to be easy, but what choice did she have?

She opened the door and waved Bobby in, then headed for the

living room without speaking. She hadn't had time to change her clothes, put on any makeup or even tidy up her house. This wasn't how she had wanted her reunion with Bobby to go. When she dreamed about it at night it always involved him having some kind of injury leading to memory loss that allowed them to start fresh and move on from all the friction that had grown between them.

"I've only got a half hour. I have to get to work. So in the interest of time, let's cut through all the bullshit and figure out if this conversation is going to go anywhere." Bobby only took two steps inside the house and folded his arms across his chest in childish resistance.

"Fine, I won't mince words. Have you been digging around for information on Judge Lions since the last time we spoke?" Piper didn't care if he didn't want to come in. She wasn't going to stand in the entryway and have this conversation. If he wanted to know more he'd have to at least stand in the living room with her.

"I don't really see how that's any of your business. I don't know anything about you, remember? For all I know you're in on whatever scheme he's running and you're pumping me for information. If you can't prove to me that you're worthy of my trust then nothing you say is going to mean anything. Even if you pull that crap about Jules and Betty being in danger, I'll chalk it up to one of your lies." Bobby had indeed followed her to the living room but stopped in the doorway. His stubbornness was so frustrating. She had hoped enough time had passed to soften him. Instead it seemed to have made him more scornful toward her.

"So even though Betty and Jules are in danger, and I have important information about that, you don't want to hear it unless I'm willing to dredge up everything I really am. I have to prove to you that I'm not some drifter con artist who changes her identity to uphold her charade?" The question was full of sarcasm and petulance. The idea of having to bare herself to him, to dig up parts of her past that she had intentionally buried to keep herself sane and safe, made her so angry. She was only trying to help him. Why couldn't he accept that and let her keep her secrets hidden where they belonged?

"Yes, that's it exactly," he replied curtly. He wanted to know that she was capable of telling the truth, of letting him in. If she could do that, then he'd be willing to hear her out.

"You have no idea what you're asking of me, and you're completely minimizing the impact it will have, but I don't care because Betty and Jules are in danger, and that's all that matters. If you're juvenile enough to think knowing the *real me* makes a difference then I'll appease you, even if it crushes me to talk about it. But if I'm doing this it's not going to be while you have one hand on the door ready to leave. If you want my story, you're going to get all of it, and you're going to sit here with me and listen. Also, this never leaves this room. What I tell you about me is my story to tell, not yours." Piper sat down on the couch and Bobby came and joined her. He had a look on his face like he had won something, something he wasn't really sure he wanted anymore.

"I'm not trying to minimize this, I'm sorry. I don't want you to have to dredge up everything about your past just for my entertainment. I want to believe that I can trust you, but you need to show me I'm not making a mistake by doing so. I swear, I won't tell anyone what you tell me here today." Bobby wanted to hold her hand, to brush the loose strands of hair out of her face. She looked so tired, so alone. He wanted to hold her and forget all of this, but it was too late now. He needed her to come through for him.

"Promise me that you'll take what I say about the judge seriously and that you'll heed my advice. If you guarantee me that then I'll tell you everything you want to know about me. But remember, Bobby, this is a bell you can't unring. Once you know where I come from and what I've done chances are everything between us will change." She swallowed hard and could barely believe she was about to share the dysfunctional narrative of her upbringing with Bobby. He nodded in agreement, and she took in a deep breath and tried to start from the beginning.

"My name, my real name, is Isabella Lawson. I haven't said that name out loud in two years. Can you imagine what it's like to not be able to say your own name, like it's a curse word? My father was Roberto Lee Lawson, my mother, Carolina Murphy. They never married. I was what you would call an accident, but that would be a nice way of saying it. I found out as I grew up I was a *mistake,* a pregnancy that went undetected too long to be erased by an abortion. My parents were neglectful, sadistic drug addicts who spent their entire lives dabbling in one crime or another. My mother would sell her body in order to bankroll her next fix. My father would find out, and after partaking in half of her score, would violently beat her. I was in school only frequently enough to pass my classes and fly under the radar. Half the kids there should have been taken from their parents. The system wasn't equipped to deal with every bruised child who looked a little hungry. I spent days locked in my room as my parents binged on drugs and threw rowdy parties. I went without eating, without having a bathroom to use. My childhood was one horrific moment after another. The ironic thing is, that's not even why I'm here. That's not why I changed my name. It isn't even the darkest part of my life, and I can already feel you looking at me differently." Piper stared straight ahead as she spoke. Bobby wanted to put his arm around her and pull her up against him but he hesitated.

"When I was twenty years old, and on the verge of getting the hell out of that place, my mother got arrested again for prostitution. Living in the projects was miserably oppressive at times, but I saw plenty of people succeed. My parents just weren't those people. They were swallowed up by it. After that last arrest my mom was locked up for ninety days. She came out completely sober, and you know the old cliché—she had *found God.* She told me we were leaving, to pack up whatever I could before my father got home because we were getting out of there. The clergyman in the prison had found us a shelter sixty miles away and had arranged a ride for us. She told me she was tired of protecting my father. At the time I had no idea what she meant. It seemed like my father was doing just fine taking care of himself. It was the two of us that needed protection. I was so happy to be leaving that place, and my mother was like a new person. She got a job at the mall next to the shelter. A few months later we transitioned from the shelter to a place of our own," Piper gulped back the lump in her throat.

"That was the closest to normalcy and contentment I had ever experienced. We didn't have to worry about my father's beatings or ripped-off drug dealers coming to our house on a vendetta. I thought I finally had a chance at a real life. We lived that way for twenty-one months and twelve days." Piper wanted to look over and see what type of expression Bobby had on his face. Was he horrified? Sad? Maybe he didn't believe her at all. Either way she couldn't bring herself to turn toward him. She carried on with her story.

"Then my mother came home one night from work high out of her mind. She had fallen off the wagon. I had suspected it for a while, but I couldn't bring myself to believe it. She told me she had made a mistake, that in a moment of weakness she had called my father and told him where we were. She said he was furious and that we'd need to leave as soon as possible before he came to get us. I couldn't believe after all this time, after all the hard work, my mother would be so stupid and selfish. We packed our duffle bags and gathered up every dollar we had in the apartment, pulling even the loose change from the couch cushions. It didn't matter though, we weren't fast enough. There was a loud thumping on our door, and I heard my father's voice booming in the hallway. I thought we'd get the beating of a lifetime and have no choice but to return back home with him. Unfortunately, it was worse than that."

There were warm tears rolling down Piper's cheeks now. She could feel them forging itchy paths on her face, but she didn't wipe them away. If Bobby was going to insist on hearing this then he could deal with the consequences of what it did to her.

"My mother finally opened the door and without a word my father cocked his fist back and punched her across the face. She fell backward onto the floor and was disorientated. I pressed myself up against the living room wall, feeling like a helpless child again. I thought about grabbing a knife from the kitchen or the baseball bat from under my mother's bed, but my father was too strong and too fast for me to take such a chance. I had resolved to endure the thrashing and beg for mercy as my mother was doing on the floor. But my father changed the game, he pulled a large metal spike from his jacket, and my mom shrieked in a way I had never heard before. She begged him not to do it, she begged him to let her live. I didn't know it then, but my mother knew exactly what my father was about to do. He struck her again in the face with his fist and then pinned her down by sitting on her stomach, his back to her face so that he could hold down her legs. He raised the spike over his head and plunged it into her thigh. He yanked it back out and blood, an ungodly amount of blood, poured out of her. I did nothing. I didn't scream or run over to her or try to stop him." Piper choked back her quivering voice.

"I stood, still pressed against the wall, praying he would forget I was there. When my mother stopped moving and the blood had stopped spurting from her wound, my father pulled out a switchblade that was clipped to his belt. I couldn't see what he was doing from where I stood, but whatever it was took precision. When he stood up, I begged him to let me go. I promised that I wouldn't tell anyone. He didn't blink, he didn't speak. He walked slowly up to me, hit me in the face, and shoved me to the ground.

He was about to pin me down when we both heard the sound of sirens approaching. I thought, he'd stop and run. But he didn't. The sirens had distracted him but not stopped him. I decided in that moment, that I didn't want to die that way. I didn't want to be someone who didn't fight back. As he tried to pin me down the sirens grew closer, and he finally just raised his arm up, spike in hand, and plunged it into my leg as I tried to twist away from him. I was pulling at his hair and clawing at his back. Finally, he spun around, grabbed my hair, and slammed my head into the floor, knocking me out." Piper might have been furious at Bobby for forcing her to tell this story, but there was something cathartic in saying the words out loud, about admitting what had happened to her.

"There is a lot more to this story, Bobby, but I know you need to get to work and it's important that I tell you the information I have."

"I don't need to go to work. I have the afternoon shift today. I was being a jerk. I've got time and I want to listen. I'm sorry this is so painful for you, but I promise none of this changes how I feel about you," Bobby said, wiping a tear from Piper's warm red cheek. It felt so good to touch her again.

"That's easy to say, Bobby, but there are things I still can't forgive myself for. Don't assume you'll be able to look past it," she said, pulling away from him slightly. "I don't want to stay here anymore. Can we please get in your truck and go for a ride? I don't want to talk about it here." Piper stood up and ran her fingers through her hair pulling the loose pieces away from her face and tying them back into a messy bun. She knew her lack of sleep, lack of makeup, and overall ragged appearance should have kept her from leaving the apartment, but all she wanted was to be riding in the passenger seat of Bobby's truck watching the world zip by. Most people would assume that the memory of nearly being killed and watching your mother take her last breath, would be the hardest thing to reminisce about, but really it's what happened next that Piper struggled with the most.

Bobby and Piper climbed into his truck, and he started to drive with no real direction in mind. Piper waited until they were out of town and heading down a long stretch of open road before she started to speak again.

"The police came and stopped my bleeding just in time. My father had fled, and, because I wasn't conscious, they had no leads to start hunting him down. When I woke up in the hospital there was a woman sitting next to me." Piper conjured up the memory of that haunting and familiar face she had awoken to. She remembered she had short jet-black hair and the darkest eyes she'd ever seen. Her skin was a rich dark espresso.

"I remember thinking how beautiful and strong she looked. She was dressed in a perfectly tailored gray suit, and she smelled like peppermint. I thought for a minute that maybe I was dead and she was some kind of spirit. But I realized quickly I was alive and that life was about to get much harder for me. The woman told me her name was Special Agent Lydia Carlson of the FBI. She was sorry to inform me that my mother had not survived the brutal attack in our apartment but that, miraculously, I had. She told me she knew I was tired, and this was not an ideal time to have to rehash the horrific details, but time was of the essence.

"I wanted to speak but my mouth and throat were so dry, and Special Agent Carlson kept talking and talking, hardly allowing an opportunity for me to speak even if I could. Finally she asked me a question that made no sense to me. She inquired if I had ever heard of the Railway Killer. I hadn't, so I shook my head no. She continued on, telling me that over the last nineteen years the Railway Killer had murdered twenty-two women with the same MO each time. Agent Carlson had been part of the task force assigned to catch him for over ten of those years. They had been waiting for a break in the case, and now they finally had one, she said.

"I couldn't understand what she was talking about, what this had to do with my mother and me. As she continued to speak the fog lifted and everything became painfully clear. She told me the Railway Killer targeted young women. He utilized brute force and the element of surprise. He would pin them down and drive a railroad spike into their femoral artery, severing it, causing massive blood loss and eventual death. Then he would carve a number into their leg that corresponded to how many women he had killed before them. 'Your mother had the number twenty-two carved into her leg, and you have the number twenty-three. You are the only surviving victim of a man I have spent a decade hunting. Anything you can tell me will help bring him to justice,' Agent Carlson said.

"You would think I would have sat up in bed and cried out that not only did I have details that would help the case, but I knew the name of the man they were searching for." This was the hardest part for Piper, reliving this dark moment of her past was like slicing open an old wound. But she had gone too far to stop now.

"That's what any rational person would have done in that situation, but instead I lay there, silent. After nearly an hour had passed and she had made her case in every way possible, she left and told me she'd be back the following day and we could talk then. She did come back, every day for five weeks, and I never spoke a word to her. She would tell me how they could keep me safe, how they had reported in the news that I was dead in order to protect me from any more harm. She'd fluctuate between empathy and frustration, but nothing would make me speak. I didn't want to be the daughter of a serial killer, or the victim of one. I wanted to rewind my life to when things had started to feel right, to when my mom was alive and sober. I knew the moment I told Agent Carlson that my father was the Railway Killer, I could never take it back."

Piper sobbed with her hands covering her face and her head

pressed against the passenger window. She had never admitted her horrible mistake to anyone, let alone someone whose opinion she valued so much. Even if Bobby could overlook the dysfunction of her roots, she found it hard to believe he could move past her not coming clean to Agent Carlson. She assumed he would see it the way she did, as a selfish attempt at self-preservation.

"Piper, you were in shock. You had gone through a horrible event, had nearly been killed, and had watched your mother die. Any officer knows that victims need time. Even when you're anxious to solve a case, you can't do it at the expense of the victim." Bobby reached across the truck and tried to calm Piper by rubbing her shoulder. It killed him to see her fall apart like this.

"You don't understand. I wasn't traumatized over the death of my mother. I was sorry she was dead, but she was equally as sadistic and violent toward me as my father had been. She wasn't my advocate or my protector. Even when we moved on and tried to piece our lives together, we barely spoke. We mostly just coexisted. I think, to her, I was a reminder of a past she wanted to forget. To me she was an enemy I couldn't forgive. She called my father that day, she did drugs, and she told him where we were. I believe my mother covered up his crimes for years. I don't think anyone deserves to die that way, but that wasn't what was keeping me quiet. I didn't want to deal with the spectacle that would come from telling the truth. I didn't want my parents stealing any more life from me than they already had, and in that self-absorbed decision I was a part of something that I will carry around with me for the rest of my life.

After my recovery, when on the verge of being released from the hospital, Agent Carlson came storming into my hospital room and threw a handful of pictures onto my bed. They were crime scene photos, and I remember turning away at the sight of a dead girl sprawled out in a puddle of blood. Agent Carlson put her face close to my ear and hissed, 'Delanie Morrison, a twenty-one-year-old waitress, was murdered last night on her way home from work.' She pointed to a picture of the girl's thigh, which had the number twenty-four carved into it. 'Every number after twenty-three is more blood on your hands,' she told me." Piper's eyes were spilling over with guilt and tears.

"She was right, I could have prevented that murder and because I didn't, it made me just as guilty as my father. That idea destroyed me." Remembering the day she had found out about Delanie was harder for Piper than the day she had almost died. She had never felt more alone, more immoral and guilty in her entire life. She felt the air in her lungs turning to gravel. She wanted to pull open the door of the truck and jump out. She begged Bobby to pull over.

When the truck came to a stop in a small clearing on the side of a quiet stretch of road, Piper pushed the door open and jumped out, gasping for air. Bobby ran around the truck to try to calm her in any way he could. What she did next took him completely by surprise.

Piper unbuttoned her jeans and pulled them down slightly on one side, exposing her upper thigh. Bobby's heart broke at the sight of a large, circular raised scar from the number twenty-three carved in her leg. He had asked for the truth and assumed it would be murky and tainted in some way. But he never imagined anything like this.

"I could have stopped him, but instead I kept my mouth shut. After I saw those pictures of Delanie I told Agent Carlson everything. I promised to testify against my father and do anything I could to make sure he was brought to justice. It didn't matter though, nothing would bring back Delaine, give her parents back their child." Piper was frantic and her words were hardly coherent.

Bobby came to her slowly. He took her hand from the top of her jeans brought it to his mouth and kissed it. He touched the raised skin of her scar and stared into her eyes. "That was not your fault. What Carlson did was a technique to get you to give her what she needed. They literally train you on this stuff, on getting victims to talk. Your father was the murderer. The blood is on his hands, not yours. The important thing is that you told her everything you knew and they were able to catch him. You did the right thing, and it's understandable that it took you a little time to process it all."

"You don't get it! I'm here in North Carolina because they haven't caught him. I waited too long, and he had time to run. Someone leaked to the press there was a break in the case and they were pursuing a person of interest due to an eyewitness ready to testify. He is one of the most wanted men in America and no one can seem to find him. I was put in witness protection until he's apprehended, and I can be called to testify against him. *He's still out there.*"

Piper wrapped her arms around Bobby's waist and rested her head on his chest. Carrying this burden alone for the last two years had been suffocating. Knowing she could say this all aloud and someone would still be there to hold her was liberating, even if the rehashing of her mistake was painful.

"Piper, I'm so sorry that you had to go through all that, and you've spent all this time blaming yourself. You're not alone in this. I'm still here, and I'm not going anywhere. I'm sorry I doubted you, but I'm glad you told me. Living with that burden by yourself is too much. I'm here to listen to whatever you want to tell me." Bobby squeezed her tighter and then crouched to lower himself to her eye level. She was still breathing erratically through her tears, and as much as he wanted to kiss her, he didn't think this was appropriate. Piper needed his support, and he didn't want any of it to be clouded by passion.

Piper let herself melt into him for a moment before she spoke. "I need you to hear what I have to say about Judge Lions. It's important, and I'm not sure I can talk much more about my past right now." Piper wiped at her cheeks and drew a deep, composing breath.

"All right, if you're sure you're up to talking about it then go ahead. But can we get back in the truck? It's getting cold out here and I don't want you getting sick." Bobby walked over and opened her door. As she walked by him to hop in, he grabbed her elbow and spun her gently back around toward him, hugging her one more time before the seats in his truck would force space between them.

Piper wasn't sure exactly how to start this difficult conversation, but she dove in. "I saw something in the alley behind my house one day. I was feeling so lost, school hadn't panned out, and this seemed like a sign. Judge Lions was assaulting a young girl. I overheard enough of what he was saying to learn he was paying her to have sex with him. At first I didn't know what to do or who to tell. I felt like the whole system had failed me, and everything I had learned in school led me to believe there was no way a man like Judge Lions would be held accountable for his actions. I started to concoct a plan to take down the judge without having to go through the normal channels I knew wouldn't work. I saw that girl bleeding in the alley, and all I could think was that I wasn't going to let someone else get hurt or killed when there might be something I could do about it. I've spent the last couple of months slowly gathering information. Well, that search led me to a mill this morning where I was listening in on a meeting between the judge and who I thought would be Christian Donavan." Piper hadn't fully recovered from telling her own story. She felt like there was no way she had the emotional energy to tell Bobby what she knew about Stan's death, but she had no choice.

Bobby cut in, shocked by the thought of her solo surveillance. "Wait, what do you mean you were listening in on a meeting? Like you were hiding in this mill while the judge and Christian Donavan were there? Please tell me sometime in your life you've had some training or experience to prepare you for this. Maybe that's part of the story you haven't shared with me yet?"

"No," Piper continued. "And I know that sounds crazy. I've mostly been taking it all really slow, thinking through my next move. The meeting this morning was a little impromptu, and I had to make a decision whether or not to go. I'm glad I did though. The person meeting with the judge wasn't Christian, he was a cop. I need to know, Bobby, if and why you've been digging into Judge Lions's business, because this cop was on to you."

"I have been," Bobby answered shocked at her knowledge of his recent activities. "I started a few weeks ago. I thought if you were involved in something this is how I would find out, and if you were in trouble, this is how I'd protect you. I thought if I could figure out what was going on I'd be able to get ahead of this, ahead of you." He wanted her to know that even though they hadn't been speaking he was still thinking of her every moment they'd been apart the last couple of months.

"Well whoever you showed the pictures of the judge to is the cop who was at that meeting today. They were talking about how they were going to deal with the situation, deal with you. They decided that hitting you where it hurts would be their best bet to get you to back off. That meant making you realize Betty and Jules were in danger." Piper was half hoping that Bobby would say he hadn't shown the pictures to anyone. She was holding out hope that maybe the judge and the cop were talking about someone else, although her logic told her that was highly unlikely.

"That's not possible. I only showed the pictures to Rylie. There's no way he's on the take. He's one of the most respected guys on the force, and he was a good friend of Stan's. He wouldn't get involved with anything that put them in danger. Are you sure you heard all this right?" Bobby asked in disbelief.

The next piece of information would be more of a blow than finding out someone respected was not worthy of it, and Piper was not looking forward to delivering the news. "The judge called the man Red. I don't know if that means anything to you, but I can assure you, it was clear to me that this man knew you. It was also clear he knew Stan very well too."

"Yes, that's Rylie's nickname. I can't believe he'd be mixed up in all this. Maybe it's because he's so close to retirement. They're messing with pensions so much, maybe he needed the money." Bobby shook his head as he searched for any plausible reason why a cop like Rylie would go against the badge like this.

"Bobby, Rylie is going to come to you and try to convince you to back off this. It's going to be your last out before they take more drastic measures. You need to go along with that. Tell him you've been thinking about it, and you don't need another mark against you like Manton. Give him the pictures and tell him you trust him to do whatever he thinks is best with them. That's the only way to keep everyone safe." She was praying he'd agree and make this easy.

"I will, because there's no way I'm putting the girls at risk over this. He was there for Manton so he'll understand why I wouldn't want any more attention on me right now," Bobby said, trying to convince himself this was the right thing to do.

"There's more to the story here, Bobby. Rylie was there for the takedown on Manton because he was part of it. The Donavans were supposed to be there that day. Rylie set you up to protect them. He made sure Manton got off the hook so he wouldn't flip on them. I hate to say this and I haven't really thought of the right way yet, but there is something else I need to tell you. Something worse." Piper bit at her fingernail as she tried to find the right words. She was about to stomp on Bobby's chest, crushing him in a way he probably didn't believe possible. As much as she wanted him to know the truth, she wished she could protect him from it.

"Tell me," he said, reaching across and taking her hand, stopping her from ravaging her fingernails. "I don't see how it can get much worse."

"I need to know that you'll handle this right. This corruption is not limited to the judge and Rylie, it runs deep, and we have no idea who we can trust. So when I tell you this I need you to think through all the consequences of any action you take and realize at the end of the day you need to protect the people you care about first and foremost." Piper paused waiting for him to agree to her terms. He nodded his head impatiently. "The reason they want to target Jules and Betty rather than just take you out is because killing a police officer isn't as easy as it was ten years ago. Ten years ago the judge and Rylie had more people on the inside willing to help in the cover-up. There wasn't as much technology, times have changed. So ten years ago they were able to lure a police officer into an abandoned building and shoot him, passing it off as a random robbery gone wrong. They got away with it ten years ago when they killed Stan for digging around in their business and getting too close to the truth. Bobby, Rylie and Judge Lions killed Stan. I don't know which one of them pulled the trigger, but I know they orchestrated it and covered it up."

Piper was crying again though she wasn't sure why. She had never met Stan, but she felt like she had gotten to know him through his family, and the thought of him being betrayed by people he trusted sickened her.

Bobby tightened his hands over the steering wheel until his knuckles were white. Piper could see him grinding his teeth as he processed the new information.

He sat silently for several minutes. Piper kept wondering if she should say something, anything— but nothing she came up with sounded right in her head. She opened her mouth to speak, but Bobby had beaten her to it. "Betty was right all these years," he whispered. "I've been telling her over and over again that she was crazy, that if there were some kind of conspiracy it would have been uncovered by now. Everything I've ever believed about the sanctity of the shield and due process means nothing. If the system can't flush out the men who killed a cop —a great cop—in ten years, then what the hell are we all doing every day? I need to do something about this. They can't continue to live above the law." He punched his fist into the steering wheel and the horn blasted, sending Piper jumping in her seat.

"I have a plan," Piper said, hoping Bobby's resentment against Rylie would be enough to sway him. She needed him to ignore his normal instinct to obey the law and let her continue with her explanation without argument. "Originally I was only going to target the judge, but after I heard about Stan this morning I came up with a way to include Rylie and even Christian Donavan in all of it. I want you to know that I have this all under control. As long as you do your part with Rylie and convince him you're not interested in the judge anymore, then I'll take care of the rest. The less you know the better."

"Piper, do you have a gun or another way to protect yourself when you get caught doing surveillance on these guys? Have you ever even fired a weapon? You're intentions are great, Piper, but you aren't qualified to do any more of this on your own. Tell me what you're planning, and I can help." Bobby's brain had kicked into high gear as he processed all Piper was telling him. Maybe Stan's way of handling things was admirable, but it also got him killed. If Piper hadn't come to him this morning with this information he unknowingly would have put Betty and Jules in danger. He might not think Piper was qualified, but she was certainly doing everything right so far.

Piper continued, "Your instincts are going to tell you to shoot this plan down, so try to fight that. Remember your other options. You can drive your truck to Rylie's house right now and kill him in cold blood, spending the rest of your life in jail. Or you can take the information you do have, most of which is hearsay, and report it, crossing your fingers and hoping whoever you confide in doesn't have a hidden alliance of some sort. You'd spend the rest of your life looking over your shoulder and worrying that you've endangered people you love."

Piper thought a preemptive strike against Bobby's possible points of contention would be her best approach. "Knowing all that, my plan shouldn't sound so bad. I haven't worked out all the details yet but I'll give you the basic outline. The judge is a pedophile. He engages in sexual activity with underage girls. That doesn't matter to the men he's aligned with. If the judge was more inclined to engage in this type of behavior with underage boys, this may change some minds. But I'm not willing to take a chance on *maybe* swaying someone against an association with the judge, so I plan to up the ante. Christian Donavan has a young son who attends Millersville West Academy. I intend to plant evidence that convinces Christian the judge is targeting his son as his next victim. There is no way Christian will continue any type of affiliation with the judge under those circumstances, leaving him vulnerable and with limited protection."

Bobby shook his head. His mouth was agape as he searched for the right words. Piper had hoped he was on the verge of calling her a genius, or that his next question would be about how he could help, but as he started to speak she knew she had further persuading to do. "You think he's going to simply discontinue his affiliation with the judge? Christian isn't an 'I'm taking my ball and going home' kind of guy. We'll be pulling the judge's bloated body out of the river within twenty-four hours of finding that evidence. Do you really think you're prepared to cope with what part you're going to play in that? I know it's not going to sit right with me, not to mention the legal implications if it comes back on us. And how does this tie in Rylie with Christian?"

Well, he didn't say *no* outright, so Piper felt like that was a start. She had been pretty sure what she was doing could very well result in the judge's death at the hands of Christian, but she didn't think that was a good starting point for attempting to win Bobby over.

"It's chess, Bobby. All I'm doing is setting up the pieces. They're the ones playing the game. If Christian wants to kill the judge, then that's on him, not me. As far as taking the other two down, think of how advantageous it will be to know a murder will be committed before it happens. Think of how easy it will be to gather crucial evidence when you know ahead of time both the victim and the murderer. Once Christian believes his son is in danger, I'm confident he'll seek some form of revenge. If we keep eyes and ears on him we'll be there to either catch him in the act or collect everything we need for an irrefutable slam-dunk case. I overheard in today's meeting there was bad blood between Christian and Rylie. We give Christian the opportunity to flip on Rylie. Christian is a smart guy. He'd be covering his bases and have some type of blackmail or evidence against Rylie in his back pocket in case he ever needs it." This was the first time Piper had talked out loud about anything regarding the judge. It was exhilarating, yet still strange, to think how far she had come all on her own.

"You'd be comfortable with giving a plea deal to a guy like Christian?" Bobby had to admit Piper had some solid ideas and, implemented correctly, there was a chance all of it could work. Whether or not they could live with themselves when all this was over was a different story.

"A plea deal for killing a man I already want dead? Yes, I think I can live with that," Piper said, immediately regretting the admission, knowing it made her sound cold. "As much as I think Christian probably deserves to spend the rest of his life in jail, he didn't conspire to kill Stan. Christian would have barely been out of high school back then. I thought I was doing this because I wanted a man like the judge to be held accountable for his crimes against that young girl. I thought it was shameful to live above the law and that his abuse of power needed to end. Now, it's also about what they did to Stan, what they took from Jules and Betty all because of money and influence. Christian is good collateral damage, but I want to see the judge and Rylie pay for what they've done."

Piper knew this wasn't how Bobby would want to handle any of this. Vengeance wasn't as appealing to him as straightforward legal justice, but she took his allowing her the opportunity to speak as a good sign.

Bobby looked hesitant. "There has to be a way we can do this without risking the judge's life. I want him held accountable, but I'm not sure how I'll sleep at night if I know we put into motion actions that led to his death. I need time to think about it. For now, I'll do my part with Rylie today and let him know I'm not moving forward with the pursuit of the judge."

Bobby tapped his fingers on the steering wheel and bit his lip. This was a position he thought he'd never find himself in. When faced with moral dilemmas there always seemed to be a clear right and wrong, but Piper was making him think maybe there had to be more options than that. Maybe rules are important, but when they stop working you have to create your own in order to stay one step ahead of dangerous people.

CHAPTER 15

"Where the hell is he?" Bobby grumbled to himself as he drove his squad car up and down the streets of Edenville. It was nearly dark and Bobby felt the last fifteen minutes of his shift melting away. It seemed as though Rylie was being incredibly elusive today, which was frustrating the hell out of Bobby. He didn't want to be transparent and call Rylie. He needed their conversation to seem unprompted, and chasing Rylie down ran the risk of seeming desperate. He crisscrossed side streets of Rylie's normal routes and continued to curse under his breath. Finally, he suspended his search and decided to check in on Jules on his way home. He was sure to see Rylie tomorrow as Friday mornings always included a little gathering of the first shift for coffee at the precinct.

He pulled his squad car up to the front of town hall. He only planned to make a quick stop and no one tended to complain about a cop's car out front. Every Thursday was Jules's day to work the late shift. The only part of the building that was left open this late was the records department so that officers and court personnel could gather what they needed. It tended to be pretty quiet, and Jules always appreciated company on these long days.

Bobby pushed open the large revolving door and, after seeing that Jules wasn't in her office, headed down the hall to the records room. He felt a flash of heat flow through his body as he remembered this was the first place he had kissed Piper, the first time he had realized how much he cared for her.

"Hey Jules, just stopping in to say hello," Bobby called as he peeked his head into the large room lined with filing cabinets and storage boxes. There was no one there, no sign of Jules. This room and her office were the only two places she'd normally be once the front desk was closed for the day. She'd never leave the front door unlocked and not be around to meet anyone coming in for the records room. Bobby felt his chest tighten at the thought of Piper's warning about Rylie. Maybe he should have tried harder to track him down and convince him that he wasn't interested in pursuing the judge any longer. Perhaps Rylie had already acted on his plan to hit Bobby where it hurt.

The silence in the old, drafty building was broken by a loud deep voice coming from the front desk. Bobby darted in that direction not sure what he might find.

There, at her usual post for the daytime hours, stood Jules with an enormous grin on her face. "Oh Bobby, I was wondering if you were going to stop by tonight. You know Officer Rylie." Standing across from Jules with the cap of his uniform tucked dutifully under his arm was the redheaded backstabber who had killed Stan. Bobby worked quickly to assess the situation and determine if Jules was under any type of distress. She seemed to be oblivious to any danger.

"Why aren't you in your office or the records room? It's late. Isn't the front desk usually closed this time of night?" asked Bobby, pulling the small swinging half-door that led to the large desk Jules was standing behind. He wanted to be closer to her than Rylie was and being next to her behind the high oak counter was the best he could do right now.

"Office Rylie came in looking for a burning permit, and I said I would help him out. I know you guys work odd shifts, and it's not always easy to get in here during the day." Jules turned toward the filing cabinet and thumbed through the folders, searching for the necessary paperwork.

"A burning permit?" Bobby raised an eyebrow skeptically at Rylie.

"Hey there, kid. Yeah I've got some stuff I need to get rid of, and I figured the best way to do it would be to burn it. Sometimes you need to reduce things down to ashes in order to be done with them. You know how it goes." Rylie winked at Bobby and flashed him a crooked grin.

"Yeah, I know how it goes. Hey listen, Jules, can you finish up the paperwork? I've got to talk to Officer Rylie out front. Work stuff." Bobby crossed back through the swinging half-door and waved for Rylie to follow him out.

"No problem. Officer Rylie, it was good seeing you. I'll put this in the mail tomorrow and you'll have it in time for the weekend," Jules said, waving to them.

As the two men pushed out the front door Bobby reached into his coat and pulled out an envelope containing all the pictures he had taken of the judge.

"Rylie, I've been doing a lot of thinking and I'm really not in a position to do anything with these pictures. I'm practically the laughing stock of the department right now, and I don't think I'll survive another mess. I'm in over my head, and I'm not really sure what to do. It's none of my business if a judge wants to screw around on his wife. Here are all the pictures I took. I want to put this behind me. Can you help me out?" Bobby handed the envelope over to Rylie who struggled to mask his delight. He had a "this is easier than I thought it would be" look on his face.

"I hear you, kid. I was going to warn you if you want a

career in this town this isn't the way to go about it. I've got some guys I can trust, and I'll pass these pictures along to them. They'll look into it, and if there is anything, and I mean *anything*, going on here they'll handle it. You don't need to be a superhero. Keep your head down and do your job. Messing around with stuff like this will get you or someone you love hurt. A pretty girl like that in there, it would be shame to see anything happen to her." Rylie tucked the envelope into his jacket pocket and put his cap back on his head. Rain started to sprinkle down and a rumble of thunder sounded in the distance. "I'm out of here, kid, before this storm starts. It's supposed to be a bad one. You made the right call though. See you in the morning at the precinct."

It took an enormous amount of self-control for Bobby to not get in his car and run the man down. He was a slimy, arrogant, corrupt bastard who didn't deserve to wear that uniform. He stood outside for a few minutes after Rylie pulled away and tried to calm himself down.

Even with the extra time outside Bobby couldn't help but storm down the hallway boiling with rage as he made his way back to Jules. "I've told you so many times it's not safe to be here by yourself with the door unlocked. You need to change your schedule so that you're not a sitting duck in this big building. Someone could come in here, murder you, and no one would even hear you scream. This is the last time I'm going to warn you about it. You're smarter than this, Jules." Bobby's face was red and his voice was a booming echo in the large empty building.

Jules had initially jumped at the sound of Bobby's voice but her fear turned quickly to annoyance. They'd had this argument many times before, but it was the first time Bobby had been so resolute about it. She rolled her eyes and returned back to her work as she spoke, "The only people who come in here at night are cops and lawyers. You're acting like we live in a crime-ridden metropolis and I'm some kind of target." Jules tucked the paperwork into a file and came out from behind the counter. She brushed past Bobby dismissively and headed for her office.

"Well maybe you should take your mom's advice and stop trusting everyone wearing a uniform. All I'm saying is there has to be a better way to run this late shift on Thursdays." Bobby was marching right behind Jules not letting her brush the situation off so easily.

"You're the one always talking Ma out of that asinine conspiracy theory crap. You're not my keeper, Bobby. I hear what you're saying but I think you're being a little over-protective. It's sweet and all, but it's getting old." Before Bobby could retort, his phone rang and Piper's name lit up his screen. Jules spun around and grabbed his wrist to see who was calling. "Wait, you still get to talk to Piper, but we have to give her space? I really like her, and I don't understand why we haven't seen or heard from her in two months. I already told you that if there is something going on between you guys I'm fine with it. You don't need to keep her from me because you think it's going to hurt my feelings or something twisted like that."

"That's not it Jules, give me a second." Bobby shook Jules's hand from his wrist and walked back out the front doors. He felt a nervous shiver run up his spine as he stood in the misting rain. "Hello?"

"Bobby, I've got some bad news. I was at the diner, and the judge was there. I guess his wife is traveling or something so he's eating there all week. I heard him take a call, and it didn't go well. He said he didn't care if the situation sounded under control- it was too risky for them to sit back and do nothing. He told the person on the other end of the phone that he thought they should stick with the plan. I'm guessing it was Rylie he was talking to, and he didn't like what he was hearing. The judge said if he wasn't interested in the job then Christian would be. They talked for a bit more, and it sounded like the judge might have been coming around to Rylie's side on the whole thing, but all he said was they would talk more about it later. I don't know if Jules and Betty are safe at this point, it's all going to come down to how convincing Rylie can be. Until we know more, you have to be hyper-vigilant." Piper was short of breath from the sprint she made back to her apartment after hearing the judge's phone conversation.

"I'm with Jules now. Betty would have gotten home an hour and a half ago. I'm not sure exactly how we should handle this. Neither of them will be willing to blindly trust any warning I give them right now. Jules is already pushing back. I think we should talk to them tonight. We don't have to tell them everything but we should let them know they may be in danger. Can you get to Betty's house in about an hour? I'll stay with Jules while she locks up and we'll head over there, too." Bobby felt another chill run down his spine. He wasn't sure if it was from the cold rain or the thought of an impending threat on the dearest people in his life.

Piper hesitated on the other end of the phone, not sure how to ask a question weighing heavily on her. "What did you tell them about me? About why I wasn't around? The way Scott was avoiding me at work I figured it had to be something pretty substantial. I want to know what I'm walking into." Piper went from being winded to feeling sheepish. Somehow the thought of Jules or Betty thinking negatively about her was more intimidating than anything she was doing with the judge.

"I told them you were going through some stuff, and that you needed some space. I said that you'd come around when you were ready and as hard as it was to stay out of it, we needed to. The reason Scott was avoiding you is because he and Jules separated last month. They filed for an annulment." Now that Bobby had learned more about Piper he found himself looking for little moments of vulnerability. Moments like this reminded him she wasn't quite as damaged as she liked to think she was. She cared so much about the girls and about what they might think of her.

"Thank you. I know you were only watching out for them and that you weren't intentionally trying to hurt me by keeping me away. They are lucky to have you. I'll get over there soon. We'll figure this all out." Piper waited for Bobby to say goodbye and then hung up the phone from her end. She wasn't sure sharing anything with Jules and Betty would be in their best interest, but Bobby knew them better than anyone. If he thought it was the only way to keep them safe then it was the right thing to do.

CHAPTER 16

Pulling into Betty's long dirt driveway felt incredibly right to Piper, even if her stomach was fluttering from nerves. She had missed this place. If she had to sum up the feeling of Betty's home in one word it would be *unconditional*. That seemed like the perfect way to describe the love Betty showered on everyone, and the friendship around her table.

Bobby's truck was already in the driveway, and the light on the porch was shining brightly, cutting into the dark night. Piper tapped on the screen door, no longer feeling that her old blank check about "come right in, no need to knock" still applied. Betty came barreling around the corner with her arms stretched wide.

"Child you better not be knocking on that door. You come right in, I don't care how long it's been between your visits—this house is always open to you." Betty beamed animatedly, scurrying across her kitchen toward the screen door where Piper stood. "I've been as nervous as a long-tailed cat in a room full of rocking chairs about you. The only reason I knew you were still alive was because I had some spies at the diner. They served you dinner a few nights and reported back to me that you seemed all right." Piper pulled the door open and let Betty fold her arms around her in a warm embrace. Piper had survived a lifetime without being embraced by a mother, and until this moment she hadn't realized what she had been missing. She had never been held so tightly and so gently all at once. In subtle ways, through small gestures, it felt like Betty was handing Piper little pieces of love. Like she was giving her something to keep and string together. Maybe one day it would be a road map to a place where Piper could feel whole.

There was a chance the hug went on too long- Piper wasn't sure when she was supposed to let go. She knew she never wanted to. She took in a deep breath, and realized Betty smelled like she had imagined every mother should. It was a combination of a flowery perfume and some kind of sweet pastry.

"Thank you, Betty. I'm sorry I haven't been around. It's been a bumpy couple of months, but I'm happy to be turning a corner. I can't tell you how much it means to me that you are welcoming me back like this." Piper spoke into Betty's shoulder and she could feel warm tears gathering at the corners of her eyes. She had expected to be excited to see Betty but her tender welcome had moved Piper deeply.

"Sweetheart," Betty said, pulling away and maternally stroking Piper's hair, "we don't just want you here, we need you here."

"Come on in and sit down, Piper," Bobby called from the doorway of the sitting room. Piper had hoped she and Bobby would have had a chance to calibrate their talking points before sitting with Betty and Jules, but she decided to follow his lead.

"You're really starting to spook me with all this, Bobby. You're being very odd about this big important meeting, even though I was already in my housecoat and curlers. You're lucky you gave me a few minutes' notice so I could get myself decent," Betty said, as she and Piper took a seat on the couch.

"I know. I'm sorry to have to spring this on you. I've gone back and forth with myself about whether or not sharing this is the right thing to do. My gut tells me the more you know the more of a liability it is for you, but at the end of the day you are two capable, strong women who deserve the most information possible. I'm not even really sure where to start." Bobby looked over at Piper for some assistance. She didn't know exactly what or how much he was planning on sharing, so a starting point would be up to him.

Before Piper could even nod some encouragement in Bobby's direction Jules chimed in, "Bobby, spit it out. If I thought what you were doing at the town hall was irritating I should have prepared myself for how annoying all this talking in code would be. You have our attention; just say what you need to say. Oh my word, did you get Piper pregnant? Well that happened faster than a knife fight in a phone booth." Jules's expression changed quickly from exasperation to glee. She covered her mouth with her hands and shrieked with joy.

"No!" shouted Piper and Bobby in unison. Bobby felt his face redden at the thought of getting Piper pregnant. He certainly wasn't in the market to be a dad, but the idea of sex with Piper was something he had a hard time not thinking about. From the moment he had walked in to Jules's office and caught a glimpse of Piper without her shirt, he found it hard not to undress her with his eyes. He pictured them at her place, at his, and sprawled out on blankets in the bed of his pickup parked down by the lake. Even now, with more than enough distraction and stress, he was picturing himself peeling away layers of Piper's clothes.

"This is about work," Bobby continued, refocusing himself. "I know that neither of you are very keen on the job I've chosen, but you both know it's important to me. You also know at times it can be complicated. I'm currently working on something, and it's come to my attention that I may be a target for some less than reputable people. In turn, that puts anyone I care about at risk as well. That's why I was jumping down your throat today at work, Jules. I need you both to bear with me over the next couple weeks while I work on eliminating the threat. In the meantime you have to stay very alert and be aware of your surroundings constantly. We need to come up with a plan to ensure you're safe. I've started thinking of some simple schedule changes that will help, but I thought we could all brainstorm together on what would work best." Jules stood up before Bobby could finish speaking.

"How dare you," she said, glaring at him with fire in her eyes. "You know what we went through with Daddy. You saw what it did to us. This is exactly why I didn't want you to become a cop. It wasn't me throwing some temper tantrum about not getting what I wanted. It was about not ever wanting to go through all that pain again. I can't believe you're sitting here asking us to uproot parts of our lives for the choices you've made at work. That's so selfish of you." Jules's voice was climbing and becoming shakier with every word.

"Sit down young lady," Betty thundered in a stern voice Piper hadn't heard from her before. As quickly as Jules had stood up, the sound of her mother's voice had her seated again. "That's what people do, they ask their loved ones to make sacrifices to support what they believe. We don't have to understand it, but we sure as hell have the responsibility to be there for him when he needs us. I don't like the risk that comes with Bobby's job either, but there isn't a single day that goes by I am not filled to the brim with pride." She turned her stare from Jules over to Bobby. "If you're telling us to be on guard for a couple weeks then that's what we'll do. One of the hardest things I've ever been through with Stan was being in the dark. It would have been much easier for you to keep this to yourself and hope nothing happened. In my humble opinion, doing it by himself is what got my Stan killed. You tell us what to do, and we'll do it. You have our support like you've always supported us."

"Thanks, Betty," Bobby said, hanging his head. "I'm so sorry Jules. I never wanted to put you in any danger, but the only thing worse than that would be leaving you in the dark about it. I promise it will be over soon and we'll all be better for it." Bobby needed Jules's forgiveness to make all this work. More than that, he needed her support, not because Betty was telling her to, but because she believed in him.

Jules lowered her voice but it was still filled with anger. "Screw you. I'll do whatever you want for the next couple weeks, but after that you either quit your job or you quit this friendship. As far as I'm concerned if you really cared about us, you'd never put us in this position. No case should ever be important enough to take these kinds of risks." Jules's cheeks were flush with anger and she could feel blood rushing around her body.

Betty shook her head in disappointment at her daughter's reaction. "Don't waste your breath, Bobby. Trying to get her to understand is like trying to nail jelly to a tree. I swear she's as thickheaded as her daddy and as stubborn as her mama. You don't stand a chance."

"I get it," Bobby murmured looking defeated. "Let's discuss how to get through the next couple weeks. I get why you're upset, Jules. I don't blame you, and if it means we can't keep going this way then I'll understand that too." Bobby tried to focus on the issue at hand and ignore how much this was killing him. It became clear to Piper he didn't intend to share with them anything about the connection to Stan's death. Maybe she was out of line, maybe she was about to ruin everything, but she couldn't keep quiet any longer.

"Bobby," Piper cut in, "this is crazy. You need to tell them the truth." Piper gestured at Betty and Jules and stared hard into Bobby's eyes. She turned her attention back to the two now-bewildered women, each holding her breath. "You guys know Bobby is an intelligent, quick-thinking man with the best intentions and a fierce loyalty to you both. The question is, do you trust him?" Betty nodded her head with unwavering support.

"Yes," Jules said quietly, "I do think that he's loyal to us and would lay down his life to keep us safe. I only wish he wouldn't put himself in the position to have to do that. I wish he wouldn't make work more important than his life, or ours."

Piper locked eyes with Jules as she spoke. "Then you can rest easy, Jules, because this has nothing to do with work. Not one word of this leaves this room. I need you to give me your word on that." Piper pointed her finger directly at Betty and then at Jules as they both agreed. "I think the truth is the only thing that is going to get you to a place where you'll understand how serious this." She took a long breath, giving Bobby a chance to cut in. When he remained silent she took it as her sign to continue. "My interest in criminal justice led me down some unique paths here in Edenville, and along one of them I came across information about Stan's death." Piper paused, half expecting Bobby to shout at her.

"What?" Betty exclaimed, covering her heart with her hands. "What kind of information are you talking about?" Her voice was octaves higher than normal as she searched Bobby's face for answers.

"Bobby and I are looking into it. There isn't much we can share with you right now. It seems we've brought a little unwanted attention to both of you. It isn't some imminent threat, and it actually may already be behind us, but he thought you had the right to know there may be some risk to you. There will come a time when we can and will tell you everything. Right now Bobby needs your trust and support so he can continue chasing down this lead. We can't do anything if we think it will put you at further risk. Helping to minimize that by being vigilant and careful will help move us forward." Piper spoke in a steady, unemotional tone. She may have shed tears when she learned of Stan's betrayal, but in this moment she would need to be the strong person in the room.

Jules crumpled forward and covered her face with her hands as she sobbed. "I'm sorry," she said through her tears, "I didn't know it was about Daddy, I didn't know." Piper felt herself beginning to sweat. She could handle a lot of things but when people got emotional she immediately felt unprepared to help them. Luckily Bobby seemed more than equipped. He crossed the room and crouched in front of Jules, trying to convince her to stop crying.

Betty sat silently for a few minutes, stoic in expression and posture. Finally, she said in her no-nonsense, straightforward manner, "Bobby, you cannot trust anyone. There is no one on that force, young or old, who I would reach out to. I know someone there betrayed Stan, and I've carried that with me all these years. Don't go on this quest for me, or for Jules. I don't think there is a soul in this town who you could talk to who wouldn't double-cross you." Betty's bravado faltered as she practically whispered, "You'll end up like Stan." She stifled a small sob as she said her husband's name. "I know that I've been hoping for answers for years, but I don't want them at your expense. You believe there is good in everyone. You believe the system works the way it should, but it doesn't. If you're planning on turning over whatever you've found and betting on the fact that you can rely on one of the good guys, then please don't do it. Please let it go." Betty clasped her hands together as she begged Bobby.

Piper was quick to reassure her. "We already have that covered Betty. We have no intention of using the customary channels. You said that you trust Bobby, so you should know he's thought through every angle of this. We need to know you both will keep this to yourselves as it all unfolds. Know that as soon as we can share more with you, we will."

Piper leaned over on the couch and put her hand on Betty's shoulder. She couldn't imagine how overwhelming this would be for them to hear after such a long time.

"We won't say anything," Jules trembled, trying to gather herself. "You figure out who the hell killed my father, and make sure they pay for it. I don't care how, as long as you guys stay safe doing it."

Bobby turned back to Piper with grateful eyes. She had revealed enough to gain their buy-in but not so much that they might compromise their effort. It was exactly what he had hoped to do. He was glad Piper was there to pick up where he had faltered.

Bobby brushed Jules's wispy red hair away from her wet eyes and kissed her forehead before moving back to his chair. "I know you've been talking about staying here for a bit while Scott looks for a new place. I think you should start tonight. Having you both in one spot will be better. Betty, do you still have Stan's old pistol and hunting rifle?"

"You bet your ass I do. And I certainly haven't forgotten how to use them either." Betty folded her arms across her chest in defiance. "Part of me actually hopes someone comes around causing trouble, because I'd be as happy as a dead pig in the sunshine to shoot down the people who killed my husband."

Piper smirked as she tried to wrap her mind around that odd statement. Were dead pigs happiest when sitting in the sun, she wondered?

"Betty, I can't have you smacking a diner patron over the head with a frying pan because you think he's involved in this," Bobby said, raising an eyebrow at her. "I know it's frustrating that I'm not sharing more of the details with you, but I promise the people involved in Stan's death will pay for it." Bobby stood up and headed for the door of the sitting room. "Betty, why don't you take Jules upstairs and relax for a while? The best thing you can do is lay low, be alert, and try to keep your emotions in check."

Bobby nodded toward Piper, indicating she should follow him out. They headed for the porch, one of her favorite places to be with Bobby. Tonight, however, it felt different. "That didn't go like I planned," he said, rubbing at the stress that had gathered in his temples. He flopped down onto the swing, and Piper took her seat beside him. In spite of all of this, there was still something comforting about swinging with Bobby.

"I know. I was probably out of line back there. Maybe I over shared, but it felt like the right thing to do. Without her buy-in, Jules never would have taken the conversation seriously. I thought that was most important." Piper had hoped Bobby would agree. She knew she had taken a big risk.

"You're right, we were losing her, and she needs to understand how serious this is. I wanted to keep them clear of everything until the wheels were in motion, but I think you made the right choice. I'm glad you were here. We make a great team." He sent Piper a half-hearted smile, he wanted to be happy but what lay before them seemed too daunting. "I do, however, think that we need some more help. We can't possibly focus our efforts on your plan and protect Jules and Betty at the same time. We'd be stretched too thin, and both of those tasks are going to require an enormous amount of coordination and time. We need a third person." Bobby crossed his legs and lounged back on the swing. Being back in this peaceful moment with Piper wasn't enough to remove the stress of the things to come, but it certainly took the rough edges off it. He figured if he had to be knee-deep in a shitty situation at least he was there with a beautiful woman.

"I'm not sure that's a good idea. We have no clue who we can trust on the force, and the more people we involve the more likely we are to expose ourselves. The whole key to this is complete anonymity. I'm just a girl working for the cable company with no ties to any of these players. When all this goes down and people start digging, they won't even know I exist, let alone that I'd have a motive or means by which to play a part. That means I should be doing all the leg work, and you should be focused on Jules and Betty." Piper knew she was overestimating her abilities and oversimplifying the risk, but if she didn't believe she could do it, then who would?

"What about Michael? Is he someone you think we can trust?"

Bobby left the question hanging there between them. He didn't try to argue why he thought Michael could be trusted; he wanted to hear Piper's opinion.

"I trust Michael. He's a good friend and through his work I've come to believe he's a principled and reliable man. The problem is he thinks this type of thing is a disservice to the greater good. He's had ample opportunity to take on situations like this in his career, and I think he's turned a blind eye because he believes doing his job is his best bet for holding people accountable. I don't think he'd be interested even if we talked to him, but I don't doubt he could be trusted," Piper said, pulling her sweater closed as a small chill overtook her body. The nights had finally started to cool. That didn't matter though, because even if it were snowing, which it rarely did in North Carolina, she'd still stay out as long as she could, swinging with Bobby.

There was something sexy in the rhythm of his legs while rocking them both along. She rarely let her own feet hit the ground while they sat. She would kick off her shoes and curl her legs up close to her body. She liked that he did all the work, that he didn't mind keeping them both moving. It reminded her that Bobby was the kind of man who would gladly carry the heavier load when you needed him. You could fall—eyes closed, arms open—and know he'd be there every time to catch you. He'd keep the swing moving, he'd drive the truck, and he'd agree to help you carry out the most outrageous plan even though it went against his instincts. Piper recalled Jules's wise words from months earlier. Bobby was the kind of man you make room for in your life.

"Here," Bobby said, standing up and shaking himself out of his uniform jacket. "My adrenaline is pumping so much I don't need it." Piper leaned forward and Bobby wrapped his coat around her shoulders. The way the jacket completely enveloped her made her feel instantly warm and comfortable and seemed like the perfect metaphor for how this house and everyone in it was making her feel. She had no idea how this would play out, but she knew for certain when it was all over she wanted to be sitting right here with all of them.

Bobby smiled at the sight of Piper cuddled under his coat. He let his mind wander for a moment to the idea of her wearing only his coat, or maybe one of his shirts, waking up at his place. But he cleared his mind and throat as he continued on. "I think Michael would help if we asked him. I had a good read on him that night outside the bar, and I know you're not going to like this, but I've had a few conversations with him since. He actually called me on Wednesday. I was pulling in here for dinner, and he caught me off guard. I thought something may have happened to you. He wanted to let me know you seemed to be cooling off a little bit and you hadn't been on a date with a single Donavan since I had seen you last. He told me that if I really cared about you it was time to get over myself and call you. He warned me if I didn't make my move he couldn't continue to keep you from falling in love with him. He said it was a lot of work and he was getting tired of your constant advances." Bobby couldn't hold back his laugh as he recounted the conversation with Michael. "I think if we ask him, he'll help. I think it's the kind of guy he is. I also may have done a background check on him after I met him that first time." Bobby saw Piper's eyes narrow. "Don't give me that look. If you had access, you'd be running checks on everyone."

Bobby knew Piper didn't particularly like the idea of vetting everyone he met to ensure untainted reputations, but it was one of the very few perks of his job, and he found it necessary at times.

"He spent four years in the Marines. He was a sniper and had some time deployed. That's how he paid for law school, the G.I. Bill. He was honorably discharged and has a spotless record. His parents live back in Ohio, and his sister attends college at Ohio State. He doesn't have any extended family that he talks with regularly. It seems like all he does is work and go to the gym. We should reach out to him and give him a chance to meet Jules and Betty. I think we should have him over for dinner tomorrow night."

Piper laughed and rolled her eyes. "You mean you think he should have a chance to see Jules prior to asking him to play hero because he'll be blinded by her charm and beauty. He'll have no choice but to agree once he knows there is an actual damsel in distress. You are a wise but manipulative man, Bobby. I find your conniving side very attractive." Piper winked at him playfully and dug her elbow into his side.

"I only use my powers for good. I think this is the right move, but even if we get Michael on-board we still have a lot to work on. Our framework is solid, but there is going to be no shortage of details to be figured out. First, we need to make sure Jules and Betty are safe." Bobby put his arm around Piper and pulled her close to him. She felt so good under his arm, up against his body. He wanted her badly, but it wasn't blind lust pulsing between them. Piper already felt like a part of him, as vital as his lungs, as familiar as his own hands. It scared him to realize how deeply connected to her he felt. He rested his chin on the top of her head and spoke quietly, "This isn't at all what I pictured making up with you would be like. I hoped we'd be sitting here, and I hoped you'd be pressed up against me wearing my coat, but…" Bobby stopped and Piper worried that he was overwhelmed by what lay before them.

"But what?" she asked, afraid to hear the answer. She thought maybe Bobby was feeling that reuniting with her was more trouble than it was worth.

"I guess when I pictured this I didn't expect it to be so…" he paused again, and Piper tried to prepare herself for his words, mentally filling in the blank. Convoluted? Problematic? She held her breath bracing herself. Then finally he spoke. "Cold," he said, squeezing her tightly. "Shit it's freezing out here, give me back my coat." The two wrestled for a moment as Bobby pretended to struggle for his coat and instead tickled her relentlessly.

She quietly squealed and pleaded for him to stop, not wanting to disturb the others. When he finally let up, Piper was out of breath and her hair was tousled and unruly. Bobby effortlessly pulled her onto his lap as she tried to get her wild hair away from her face. He had never had to work so hard to not kiss someone before. "We're going to get through this, and when we do I intend to ask you some serious questions about us."

"Let's get through the next couple weeks alive, and then we'll see." Piper rested her head against Bobby's shoulder, letting her face come dangerously close to his neck. He felt her breath dancing on his skin and although his body was screaming to kiss her, his mind quieted the desires. There would be a moment, not long in the future, when becoming clouded and completely over-taken with passion would be the most important thing on his to-do list. Right now he knew it would have to wait.

CHAPTER 17

"Let me get this right," Jules said, standing in front of the mirror in Betty's upstairs bathroom and adjusting the curlers in her hair. To Piper, she looked a little like a space alien, but Jules assured her the time she spent putting the curlers in would amount to loads of extra volume in her hair, which was apparently a big deal. "I'm supposed to hit on this guy so he decides he wants to help our cause here. We're whoring me out?"

"No, don't think of it like that," Bobby said, as he sat on the edge of the tub, flashing his most charming smile. "I'm saying that it would help tremendously if you and Michael hit it off. If he decides to help, then you'll be spending a bit of time together, so making a good impression tonight would be to your advantage. I would hardly call that whoring you out. But out of curiosity, how far are you willing to go? You know, for the good of our cause. A little late night make-out session? Third base?" Piper leaned over from her seat on a small bench by the sink and smacked Bobby's arm.

"Very funny. Fine, I'll be nice, but I'm not making any promises. For goodness sake the ink on my annulment papers is barely dry." Jules applied her ruby red lipstick and pressed her silky lips together. Piper was still adjusting to the fact Jules and Bobby had the type of relationship that would have them all sitting around the bathroom, Jules fresh from the shower and wrapped only in a towel.

"Hurry up then. He'll be here any minute. We're going downstairs to make sure Betty doesn't scare him off before we have a chance to get him in the door," Bobby said, grabbing Piper's hand and pulling her off the bench and out of the bathroom. "So what did you say to Michael when you invited him over?" he asked Piper.

"I said that I was having dinner with some friends of mine, and I'd like it if he could come. I told him you'd be here, and that it would be nice if the two of you to got to know each other better. I also told him there was this incredibly beautiful redhead I wanted him to meet. I think he might be under the impression we're going to a restaurant, or out for drinks. It might be a bit of a shock to know we're having pot roast and then plan on hanging out on a porch. The good news, however, is there was a motion for an extension by the defense in the case he was working on. He's got at least two weeks with very little to do now. This case is a big one, so he's been focusing on it almost exclusively. He has all his legwork for the trial finished. He'll just be in a holding pattern until the defense is ready or the judge gets tired of their stalling. He's going to have some time on his hands."

Piper watched as Bobby hopped down the stairs and tapped the wooden beam above his head with his hand. It was something he seemed to do without any thought, a comforting habit formed out of hundreds of times up and down those stairs.

"That's good news as long as the idea of an 'at home country dinner' doesn't send him running for the hills. I hope we can pull this off. Without him I'm not sure how we move forward." Bobby headed for the porch as Michael's sleek black car pulled into the dirt driveway. "He's here," he called into the house, letting Jules know to hurry up.

As Michael stepped out of his car, Piper cringed at the sight of his tailored dress shirt and black slacks. His shoes, probably worth hundreds of dollars, were instantly covered with dust as he walked up the dry, overgrown walkway to the porch. Perhaps dinner out, in the environment to which Michael was more accustomed, would have been a better choice.

Jules came thudding with heavy feet down the stairs and pressed herself against the screen door speaking only loud enough for Piper and Bobby to hear.

"I changed my mind. Put me down for at least third base. How exactly did you fail to mention he could pass for a Swedish model and had buckets of money? Don't those seem like things I would have wanted to know? I can't wear this stupid sweater. I'm going to go change." Jules jumped back from the door and ran to her room for a more presentable outfit.

"Hey Michael," Piper said, waving guiltily at him. "Thanks for making the drive out. I know this is a little off the beaten path."

"That's no problem. It's beautiful out here," said Michael, stepping onto the porch and extending a hand to Bobby.

Just then, Betty burst from the screen door in her apron, a whisk still in one of her flour-covered hands. "Welcome to my home. I'm Betty, and you must be Michael. I'm so happy to have you over for dinner tonight." Piper winced. The plan they had arranged was already going off course. Piper and Bobby had hoped to meet Michael on the porch and apologetically ask him if he minded having dinner here at Betty's house. Then they would tell him briefly about Betty and Jules, and ease him into the introduction. Instead, Betty was in her normal position on the porch to greet any guest.

"It's a pleasure to meet you, Betty, and thank you for having me. Is that pot roast I smell?" Michael was one of the smoothest people Piper had ever met, able to morph himself into any crowd and act perfectly comfortable.

"You have a keen nose, my boy. Actually, by the looks of you, your nose probably isn't the only impressive thing you've got." Betty eyed Michael and shook her head approvingly. "It is pot roast with all the fixins and it's almost done. Why don't you come on in and you kids relax in the sitting room while I finish up." She shooed them all through the screen door, and Piper could feel sweat beginning to gather on the back of her neck.

As the three took a seat, Piper hoped someone would break the awkward silence that was beginning to choke her.

"Well, she's not a redhead and a bit older than I usually like my dates but she seems lovely. This should shape up to be an interesting night," Michael said, forcing Bobby to laugh, even though he knew it would anger Piper, who was obviously tense. "It might be a nice change actually. The girl I just broke it off with was a little intense. She didn't agree with my theory that when two people go for a long romantic walk together but only one of them knows about it, it's actually called stalking. I guess my point is, beggars can't be choosers. At least Betty doesn't seem the clingy type."

"No, Jules is upstairs still getting ready. That's her mom. Bobby grew up next door and they're all practically family. We were thinking of going out to dinner but decided a nice meal here would be better. If you're not comfortable though, I completely understand, and maybe the four of us can go for drinks somewhere instead." Piper could feel her face glowing with hot embarrassment. If Bobby didn't stop laughing he wouldn't have to worry about anyone else killing him because she'd do it right now.

"Are you nuts? Do you know how long it's been since I've had a home-cooked meal? I hate eating out, sitting at the bar with a bunch of morons from work. This is going to be perfect. I figure if Jules isn't my type, at least I know I've got Betty to fall back on." Michael shrugged his shoulders and grinned at the sight of Bobby once again losing his composure and infuriating Piper.

"Hi," squeaked Jules as she entered the sitting room. "I'm Jules, you must be Michael." She extended her hand and Michael stood up to take it. "We're sure glad you could join us tonight." Piper took note of the softer southern drawl Jules had seemed to switch on. The girl certainly knew how to be sexy, from her low-cut plum sweater to the soft flutter of her perfectly shadowed eyelids.

"I was just telling Piper and Bobby how happy I am to be here. It's been far too long since I've had a home-cooked meal around a real table with such beautiful women." Michael indicated for Jules to join him on the loveseat and waited, in true gentleman fashion, for her to sit first.

"So Michael, you're a lawyer. Are you a bleeding heart or an ambulance chaser?" Jules asked matter-of-factly, shocking everyone in the room. "What?" she asked, responding to the stunned looks she was receiving. "I see lawyers every day and to me, they all fall into one of those two categories. They're either out for money at any cost, or they're in it because they think they can change the world."

"I guess that's actually pretty right on," responded Michael. "I'd prefer to think I'm in the bleeding-heart category. I take some pro bono cases. Can I ask where you get this large sampling of lawyers?"

"I work at the town hall, and I set them all up in the records department. Mostly I point them in the right direction and then cleanup after them," she said, rolling her eyes at the thought of the inconsiderateness of most people she dealt with on a day-to-day basis.

"Oh, you're the town hall girl?" Michael asked slapping his knee and lighting up with recognition. "My clerks literally arm wrestle to see which of them will be going to the records department just so they can drool over you. I have to admit I can see why."

"They call me the town hall girl? That's pretty condescending don't you think?" Jules let her southern self-righteousness start to flare, and Piper cleared her throat in an effort to remind Jules of the purpose of this meeting.

"You've been called much worse," Bobby chimed in with a victorious smile. "Remember what they used to call you in middle school?"

"Shut your ugly mouth, Bobby Wright, or I'll tell Piper some of the most embarrassing things I know about you. Don't think I'm above it, you know I'm not." Jules pointed her finger at Bobby threateningly.

"Truce," Bobby shouted, not quite ready for Piper to hear about how he got stuck in a compromising position while trying to climb the Larson's chain-link fence, or how he burped accidently while playing spin the bottle with Stacy Parmer from down the road.

"It's ready," called Betty in her singsong voice as she carried a large tray of food past them and into the dining room.

As they all took their seats, Betty smiled with delight at the group gathered around her table. "Thank you, Jesus, for this wonderful company. Thank you for bringing Piper back to our table and for Michael joining us tonight."

"Amen to that," Bobby said, squeezing Piper's leg below the table. "Now pass the potatoes, I'm starving." By the look on Michael's face, if he wasn't completely won over by Jules's beauty then he might agree to help in order to get more of Betty's food.

The dinner was full of cordial conversation. Jules seemed to refocus her energy back on wooing Michael, and by all accounts, it seemed to be working. It was all going smoothly until, once again, Betty went off-script after dessert.

"Michael, I can't thank you enough for agreeing to be a part of all this. When I lost my husband, Stan, I thought I'd never be able to go on with my life. It devastated Jules and me beyond belief. These last ten years have been brimming over with regret and questions. When Piper and Bobby told me what they were going to do, it renewed my soul. I feel like Stan is sitting right here with us. I'd have to make you a thousand meals to ever come close to thanking you for your part in it." Betty folded her hands together and put them over her heart, looking sincerely around the table.

"It's my pleasure, Betty. I can't imagine what you've been through, and I'm so glad to hear that you're in the process of finding some peace," Michael said, smiling back at Betty and, much to Piper's amazement, not skipping a beat.

"Well I'm going to clear these dishes. Why don't y'all go sit on the porch and enjoy this beautiful night. Bobby, put some logs on the firepit out there so y'all don't freeze." Betty stood and filled her hands with dishes before disappearing into the next room.

"Jules, will you do me a favor and help your mom clear? I'm going to chat with Piper and Michael outside for a bit." Bobby spoke through his teeth and glared at Jules indicating she had better do what he asked.

"It does sound like we have a bit to chat about, now doesn't it?" Michael quipped, standing up with an awkward smile on his face.

The three moved onto the porch, all searching for an appropriate starting point for the conversation. Since Piper felt the most amount of responsibility for the three of them being there, she worked up the courage to speak first. "That wasn't exactly how we planned to ask you for your help. I'm sure you have a lot of questions, and I appreciate your not venting any frustration in front of Betty. She means well."

"I guess I'm wondering what all that was about. I think both Betty and Jules are lovely, and being here tonight was great. Right up until the speech about the endless gratitude, I thought things were going pretty well." Michael scratched at his head and looked perplexed.

Bobby thought he'd take a crack at an explanation. "I think you had a good idea of what Piper was doing when she was digging for information on Judge Lions and the Donavans. I know that when you and I spoke we decided that the best thing to do was try to talk her out of pushing it any further. Unfortunately, we didn't do a great job, and at some point information came to light that made all of this very personal for me, for everyone in this house actually. The judge is far more corrupt than we could have imagined, and Piper discovered that he and a cop currently on the force were responsible for Stan's death. Stan was like a father to me, and I watched his death destroy Betty and Jules. We have an opportunity to step in and seek some justice. The problem is, while Piper and I are out doing that, we have an enormous amount of liability here, and we need another person ensuring Jules and Betty are safe." Bobby had his back to Michael as he stuffed two more logs into the clay firepit that sat on the corner of the porch. It seemed easier than looking him in the eye and explaining their plan.

Michael looked back and forth between Piper and Bobby. He half expected them both to start laughing and reveal this all to be an after-dinner joke they had orchestrated for the newest guest at the table.

"Guys, I'm really hoping this is some kind of a prank you're playing on me. I'm hoping if you had evidence that the judge and a cop were involved in a murder, you wouldn't take it upon yourselves to seek retribution. You'd turn whatever you had over to the authorities and let the cards fall where they may." Michael was stern in his tone and now boring holes through Piper with his icy stare.

"They *are* the authorities, Michael," Piper said firmly. "We have no idea who we can trust anymore. Bobby almost got himself in too deep by going to a cop he thought was one of the most reputable and honorable guys he knew, and it turns out his hands are as dirty as they get. I trust you, and I know you wouldn't want anything to happen to these women. It's impossible to not adore them once you spend a little time in their company. I know with your case being continued you have some time on your hands. Couldn't you just spend it here? Maybe give them a ride to work every now and then, hang out in the records department while Jules is there?"

Michael was quiet as he stood up and leaned against the porch railing looking out into the night. He had to admit, Piper was right about one thing. Sitting around a table with kind, down-to-earth people had certainly felt nice. But so did minding your own damn business and protecting your job and your life.

"It's fine, Michael, if you don't want to get involved. I completely understand. This was a long shot, a lot to ask. Let's just call this a nice evening with great people and nothing more," Piper spoke quietly, afraid Michael might be on the verge of an emotional explosion. Luckily she didn't need to be loud out here where the whole world was placid. There were no car horns or bustling streets to contend with.

Michael couldn't believe what he was about to say, damn his chivalry. "I think you know me well enough to realize I'm not one to walk away from a lost cause, and, as far as I can tell, that's what the two of you are. I won't sit here and play babysitter while you go off trying to right some old wrongs and get yourselves killed. If you want my help, then I want the details. I want to know who the players are and what you plan to do. I have a skill set that can benefit you both greatly, but I'm not going to give my blind support. Either fill me in, or count me out."

He turned back toward the two and realized how far over their heads they were. If he did walk away now and something happened to any of them, he'd never forgive himself.

Piper and Bobby looked at each other and seemed to share a telepathic conversation about the pros and cons of fully informing Michael. There were certainly things he may be able to help with outside of what they originally considered, and if they were willing to trust him with Jules and Betty there shouldn't be anything holding them back.

"Fine," Piper said begrudgingly. "But Jules and Betty don't know the details yet. No one outside the three of us can know.

We're still at the beginning stages of planning, so don't jump down my throat if you don't like something you hear." She raised an eyebrow at Michael and continued without his even agreeing to her terms.

"The judge is—and has been—corrupt for some time. We know at least one police officer works closely with him to ensure the necessary outcomes on cases that provide them both with a large payoff. His name is Officer Rylie. I overheard a meeting between the two of them when they admitted to murdering Betty's husband, Stan. Also, they planned to threaten or harm Jules and Betty if they couldn't get Bobby to back off about some photos he had taken of the judge. You see, the judge has an affinity for underage prostitutes and uses his alliance with Christian Donavan to feed his addiction. The only reason the judge is so well protected and why going to the authorities isn't an option is because Christian and his people need the judge right where he is in order to continue their illegal ventures and avoid prosecution." She was leaving next to no room for him to interject as she spoke.

"Anyone bringing forth evidence on the judge or Rylie would be silenced in one way or another in order to keep the judge in his position. So my idea was to sever the ties between Christian and the judge, rendering him unprotected and vulnerable." Piper pulled a notebook from her purse, looking over her notes.

"How exactly do you plan to eliminate a mutually beneficial alliance that is held together by unlimited knowledge of the others' criminal exploits? Christian is not going to flip on the judge. In these circles, you're better off being anything besides a rat." Michael's demeanor was still blustery with doubt.

"Unfortunately, I have my share of knowledge about criminals and their inner workings. There is one thing worse than being a rat, and that's being a pedophile. You see, Christian has a young son who he fiercely protects. If evidence was brought to Christian's attention that suggested the judge has an unhealthy attraction to young boys, and then he's led to believe that his son is on the judge's radar, he would certainly take exception to that." Piper could feel her confidence grow as she spoke of this plan out loud for the second time.

Michael unfolded his arms from his chest and looked as though he had just taken a blow to the gut. "He'll kill him; Christian will kill the judge."

Bobby stood up and threw his hands in the air. "That's what I said. She seems perfectly fine with that and all the possible repercussions that could come from it. I, however, am racking my brain looking for some alternative solution. She thinks we set up the evidence and then track Christian until he makes his move to kill the judge. We let him and ensure there's enough evidence to charge Christian for the murder. We use our evidence as leverage to get him to turn on Rylie in exchange for a reduced sentence. This, in theory, eliminates all three men and serves as some kind of justice. I, for one, am not ready to have that blood on my hands. There has to be another way."

Michael shook his head, still in awe of what had been laid out in front of him. "You came up with this entire thing, Piper? I have to say, it's kind of genius and, frankly, very scary. I don't know your history, but it's got to be pretty twisted if you can work up a plan like that. It can't go down like that though. Planting evidence is one thing, but if it results in a murder we could all become accessories. There has to be a way we can accomplish the same thing and keep our hands cleaner. I need some time to think about it, but I'll admit you have the start of a plan here. I'll look at this from a legal perspective and try to limit all of our liability, but, first and foremost, no one can be murdered."

Piper had assumed this would be Michael's position on this point, but she was still holding firm. "Come up with something equally effective, and I'll go along with it, but if no one can offer any alternatives then the plan is going to move forward as is, and I'll understand if you guys don't want to be a part of it. I started this for my own reasons, and I'm prepared to follow through, even if that means I have to do it alone. Now, our next step is to come up with a schedule that has someone with Jules and Betty at all times. I've written down Bobby's and my schedule and where the biggest gaps are. Since you are going to have free time, take a look at it and let me know where you can help. Now, obviously, Bobby, you are armed. Michael, Betty has a handgun and a rifle here at the house. There is a chance we've completely minimized the threat because Bobby let Rylie know he doesn't have any interest in the judge anymore. We're just not sure the judge buys it, so we need to take precautions." Piper handed the notebook over to Michael, and he sighed as he looked at all the time he'd be spending watching after the women.

"How do you know I'm even capable of handling a weapon?" Michael furrowed his brow and started making note of what days and time he could be available.

"Colombo over here did a background check on you and saw you were in the Marines. Don't feel too violated or special, though, he does checks on everyone." Piper smirked up at Bobby who didn't seem to find his nickname all that funny.

"And how about you, do you have a weapon or any idea how to fire one? I get that you're the mastermind of all this, but you still need to protect yourself." Michael tossed the notebook back at Piper, and it bounced off her knees and hit the floor. She winced and rubbed the pain away. Michael rolled his eyes. "We can cross off high threshold for pain and cat-like reflexes from your list of talents."

"I'm going to take her out in the woods behind here tomorrow and give her a crash course. I have a small personal handgun I'm going to let her use," Bobby said, lowering his voice as he heard Betty and Jules approaching. "So we're good here, you're on board?"

"Reluctantly, yes. I'm in," Michael sighed. "But no one gets killed, and I get dibs on the redhead."

CHAPTER 18

In only three days Betty's sitting room had been converted to a war room. Michael had brought in a large whiteboard to map out their strategy. With many apologies to Betty he removed all the small porcelain clown figurines from the corner of the room in order to hang the board. In reality he could have worked around them, but they were by far the creepiest little things he had ever seen. He felt like their eyes were constantly on him. The couch and love seat had become makeshift beds for whoever was tasked with keeping Betty and Jules company for the evening.

Piper had done surprisingly well at target practice with Bobby out in the woods and she found herself feeling quite emboldened by the presence of the .22 magnum mini revolver in her purse. It had also been nice to feel Bobby pressed up against her back as he steadied her hands and showed her the correct stance for firing a weapon. She could have stayed like that all day, with his chin just above her ear, his arms wrapped around her, and his hands covering hers.

Because it had been decided that keeping the names of the judge and Rylie from Betty and Jules would be important, in order to prevent them from prematurely lashing out at the men, code names were created. The judge would be called Porky, for his uncanny resemblance to the cartoon character. Christian would be called Rico due to his constant violation of the Racketeering Influenced and Corrupt Organizations Act. Piper named Rylie "Eppolito." She realized it didn't exactly roll off the tongue, but it was fitting. Louis Eppolito was one of the most notoriously corrupt police officers in history. He had worked for the NYPD on paper, but in reality, took his orders from a prominent crime family. He was eventually convicted of racketeering, obstruction of justice, extortion and eight counts of murder and conspiracy. Piper liked that outcome and thought the name could be a good omen.

For some reason, Michael insisted they all needed aliases as well. Much to Bobby's disappointment, the name Colombo, which Piper had used to mock him, had stuck. Michael decided he'd like to be called Finch, for Atticus Finch. That character had been the reason he had become a lawyer in the first place. Betty was dubbed The Queen, which seemed to suit her. Michael decided Jules should be Princess since it seemed to infuriate her and flatter her all at once. He adored the way her eyes narrowed into a glare failing in her attempt to fight off a smile.

Piper shot down every nickname they had pitched so they had just begun calling her Captain. It was all a bit too hokey for Piper, and, frankly, hard to keep up with. She decided that placating Michael's desire to make this endeavor more like an espionage movie was a small price to pay for his help.

"So here are the pictures of Chris at school," Piper said, handing an envelope over to Bobby. "I also took a tour of the school and his classroom, telling them I had a younger sister who was considering attending. I managed to collect a lot of additional information, but I'm not sure how we can integrate it with the pictures. I know his favorite television show is something called The Idiot Squad, which sounds like good quality programming. His two best friends are Tristan and Corwin, which I didn't realize were even names. He listens to a band called The Stabbing Mothers and seems to enjoy trading these weird cards with monsters on them. So to sum up my findings, if the fate of humanity rests on the shoulders of this generation then we're all screwed."

"I love The Idiot Squad. You sound like an old lady, shaking her fists at the kids walking on her lawn," Bobby said, pulling the pictures out of the envelope and looking them over.

"You belong in The Idiot Squad," Piper said, throwing a nearby magazine in his direction, intentionally missing. "I still think it should be incorporated into the evidence we plant if possible. It makes it more authentic and personal. Maybe we can write some notes on the back of some of the pictures," Piper said, ripping out the page of her notebook and handing it over to Bobby, who flinched as though she was on the verge of slapping him.

"There's a chance that Rico would recognize Porky's handwriting. We'd need to be able to match it close enough to be convincing. I can get a sample from some court records and documents while I'm at town hall with Princess," Michael said making a note on the whiteboard.

"Do we really need to keep using these nicknames? I keep forgetting who is who," Piper said, scratching her head with the back of her pen.

"Well if we want to be able to walk down the street and have a conversation about it, or we truly want to keep Jules and Betty from knowing the players then yes, Captain, we do need the nicknames. I'm pretty sure if Betty knew that she was serving eggs to the man who killed her husband every morning she'd be plunging a butter knife into his temple tomorrow." Michael was right, but Piper had a feeling deep down there was an element to these codenames that was more about how cool they were than how necessary.

"All right Finch," Piper said, throwing her arms up in surrender. "I can forge Porky's handwriting on the back of the pictures. I made a decent profit writing excuse notes in high school for anyone willing to pay. Get me a sample, and I'll get this packet all ready to plant in Porky's house."

"Have we figured out how and when that's going to go down yet?" asked Bobby, sitting up in his seat ready to get down to business.

"The judge is a big fan of boxing. There is a boxing thing on Saturday. I'm thinking if I cut the cable Friday afternoon they'll be anxious to have it fixed in time and call in for an urgent repair." Piper assumed her forethought regarding the timing would earn her some accolades, but she was finding this was a cynical group of relentless clowns who were always looking for the next punch line. Jules was very similar, and when the four of them were together it was a parade of one-liners and zings.

"A boxing thing?" Bobby exclaimed incredulously with one eyebrow raised. "Saturday is one of the biggest boxing matches of the *decade*. Oliver Johnson and London Travis are two of the greatest fighters we've seen in years, and this is the first time they meet in the ring. I swear if you weren't pretty you'd be tough to like."

"Shut up Bobby. I don't think two guys beating each other senseless and suffering lifelong repercussions should be considered a sport. The fact that you enjoy it is very telling. You're such a caveman." Piper rolled her eyes and decided to turn her back to Bobby and speak only to Michael. "I'm going to bring this envelope in the house and plant it somewhere it wouldn't be stumbled upon accidently before Christian is made aware of it. I'm thinking we need to get the wife out of the house for a bit, and I have an idea I know neither of you will like. I'm very aware of why we want to keep Jules at a distance from this. However, I think this is the only viable option. The judge and his wife head a non-profit organization called Legal Buddies. It's a program that pairs children who have been exposed to the system—either through their own crimes or their parents'—with a mentor. They learn to have a positive appreciation for the legal system rather than distrust."

Michael cut in, unable to contain his clever snipe. "Sounds like a program that would have benefited you, my contemptuous little vigilante."

Piper tossed her head back in exasperation. "I honestly have no idea what to do with you two. You're both so hilarious I'm not sure how we'll get through all this before your comedy careers take off. As I was saying, the program is a non-profit that would have filed all its paperwork down at town hall. We can get Jules to contact the wife and say they're expecting an audit and some paperwork is missing that has to be corrected immediately. If not, the status of the charity would be at risk. Hopefully she'll find it urgent enough, and my presence innocent enough, to consider leaving me there to work. I know this exposes us slightly with Jules, but I can't think of another way." The joking nature of the room seemed to subside as both Michael and Bobby began to consider the details Piper had laid out.

"It certainly makes sense," said Michael. "I think if Jules was able to create a sense of urgency and you were to tell Mrs. Porky that you weren't able to come back for the rest of the repair until Monday she'd most likely leave you there. You'll need to be personable right out of the gate; she'll have to like you."

"Believe it or not, I'm very capable of being likable." Piper turned back toward Bobby. "What do you think? I know you don't want them involved, but I can't think of any other way."

"I think you're right. This would give you much needed time in the house alone and not raise suspicion down the road. If Michael or I were to try to create a diversion, it would likely blow back on us. I want to be the one to talk to Jules about it though." Bobby's mischievous grin had faded and the seriousness of all they were trying to do had seemed to suck the air out of the room.

"I understand," Piper said, as she tried to fight off the very foreign feeling of jealousy that had begun to creep its way in over the last few days of watching Bobby and Jules. Their connection was deeper than any Piper had witnessed in her life. They had endless stories of their past and would tell them, barely coherent, through breathless laughter. Piper tried to remind herself of the budding romance between Michael and Jules.

It was clear that Michael had caught Jules's eye and that she was vying for his attention, finding reasons to be next to him. It was also clear that Michael was reciprocating the feeling. Piper had seen them engaged in a late night kissing session out on the porch just yesterday. They seemed to be getting along quite well.

Given the choice, which he frequently was, Bobby always tried to find ways to be with Piper. But for them there had been no stolen kisses or holding of hands, as both had agreed that it would draw focus away from their mission. It wasn't easy for Piper to keep her hands and her lips to herself. When there was time to think about something other than the judge, her mind would drift to that night on her doorstep before everything got so convoluted, and the only thing that seemed to matter was Bobby kissing her goodnight.

She frequently caught Bobby looking her way, smiling, presumably lost in the same memory. The knowledge of these things should have been enough to calm Piper's anxiety and jealousy. Still, there were times she thought infringing on the bond that Jules and Bobby shared was a futile task.

Piper continued letting the business at hand trump her feelings. "Along with the pictures I'll also be planting some micro cameras to ensure that we can keep tabs on the evidence and who is aware of it and when. I'll use this burn phone to contact Christian." She saw the look of frustration on Michael's face as he huffed with annoyance. "Sorry, I mean Rico," Piper corrected. "Then once we know he's in possession of the photos we'll tail him until he makes his move. I'm guessing it'll be pretty quick, since there will most likely be an enormous amount of emotion involved in all this. I doubt he'll be doing anything but seeking some revenge."

"You're oversimplifying this a bit. How exactly do you plan to tell him about the photos? Don't you think he's going to have some questions? It's not going to be quite as easy as making a quick phone call," Bobby chimed in. He was concerned that on paper, they were heading in the right direction, but in reality things wouldn't go as smoothly.

"I've got that conversation under control. I'm prepared for it. What we're not prepared for is what happens when these two men are face to face. I know you're both against any bloodshed here, but I haven't heard any other solutions. We can't let that piece of the puzzle put the brakes on everything else. We move forward on Friday." Piper heard loud footsteps move above her and then down the stairs toward them. She had learned to tell the difference between Betty's slow and quiet steps and Jules's quick and heavy gait. For a small person the girl could certainly stomp around the house.

Like every night before this, she was bored and frustrated to be cut out of the details like a child. She came sulking into the sitting room and planted herself down next to Michael.

"Are you guys finished yet? I'm tired of being grounded," Jules said, folding her arms obstinately across her chest.

Michael wrapped his arm around her and pulled her into his side. "Yes, we're done for tonight. Sorry you have to wait around so much. I know this isn't easy on you. We're in the homestretch now. There won't be many more nights like this."

It was so odd to see Michael comforting Jules. Piper had grown so accustomed to his silly side that she hadn't realized how good he was at being serious, at being someone's rock. He was a good man in a storm, and this was certainly turning out to be turbulent weather. They had only come together a few days ago, yet they seemed to balance each other perfectly. Jules was a bit dramatic and emotional while Michael was steady and logical. Certainly, under different circumstances, they'd never grow so close so quickly, but something about this ordeal seemed to make it right to seek comfort in each other.

Jules had spent hours telling Michael about her father and what his death had done to her as well as how grateful she was for Michael's role in all of this. It had made Michael's resolve and commitment to see the endeavor through even stronger.

Piper turned toward Bobby, expecting to find him watching begrudgingly as his childhood companion sought solace in the arms of another man. Instead, his eyes were fixed on Piper, and his look was one of deep longing. He knew he didn't need the distraction, he didn't need to be clouded by his emotions for her, but it didn't mean he wasn't finding it near impossible not to hold her.

CHAPTER 19

Piper took in a deep breath as she rang the doorbell outside the judge's house. She could feel sweat gathering all over her body, and she reminded herself that everything hinged on the proper execution of the task at hand. There were so many moving parts, so many things that had to fall into place. She didn't pray often and didn't even believe that God would be supportive of what she was about to do, but she sent up a small silent prayer all the same.

The door pulled open and Mrs. Lions stood there smiling warmly. Piper was slightly shocked by her beauty. She assumed perhaps the exotic features she had seen from a distance would look more weathered up close and her age would show. It was quite the opposite. The judge's wife was stunningly pretty. Her hair was silky black, and perfectly styled. She wore a tracksuit made of luscious pink suede that hugged her fit body. Her jewelry was simple and elegant, but her most attractive accessory seemed to be her confidence.

The smell of cinnamon poured from the house and filled Piper with a sense of temporary calm as the woman began to speak. "I'm so glad you were able to come out so quickly," she gestured for Piper to come in. The house was so warm, not in temperature, but in its welcoming feel. Flickering candles filled the house with the scent of fall. There was a plate of baked goods laid out on the kitchen counter next to a small plate, cloth napkin, and an empty glass. "Please have a seat and enjoy a little refreshment first. I know how hard you work all day, you deserve a little break." She waved Piper over to the bar stool in the kitchen.

"Ma'am that is so kind of you. Unfortunately my schedule today is really full, and I have some appointments I've already had to push back. I should get right to work. I want to make sure we get you up and running before the end of the day. If not, you'll probably have to wait until Monday, and I don't want that to happen." Piper kept running the word personable through her mind. Michael had been successful in slightly psyching her out about her likability.

"I completely understand. My husband will just die if I don't have this all sorted out tonight. There is a boxing match this weekend, and we are expecting company. I can't stand it, such unnecessary violence, but you know how it is, we do anything for our husbands." She smiled big enough to show her perfect white teeth and, again, Piper couldn't understand how anyone could turn outside his marriage to such a beautiful woman.

Right on cue, the chimes of Mrs. Lion's phone began to ring. "The television is right through those doors. I'll take this call and be right back with you." She brought the phone to her ear and gave a cheerful greeting. Piper wanted to listen in on the call to ensure it was going as planned but knew she should set up her tools and look thoroughly busy by the time the judge's wife rejoined her.

"Oh, you've already started?" she said as she came fluttering into the room where Piper had laid out numerous tools and rolls of unnecessary cable. "I've got to run out for a few minutes and take care of some paperwork down at town hall, is it possible you can come back later on today?"

"I'm sorry, we've got so many people anxious to get their cable working before the boxing match that we're a little flooded. I think I have the problem figured out here. I'll need about an hour to get it all squared away. I guess if I hurry I could be out of here in forty-five minutes." Piper knew if Jules had done her job then she had created an urgency Mrs. Lions would not be able to ignore. If Jules had told the story properly then she would have relayed how an auditor was making his way through their files and it was imperative she arrive quickly to correct some missing paperwork.

"I really must go get this paperwork fixed. I know I'm not supposed to, but can I leave you here for just a few minutes? I won't be long at all." Mrs. Lions was already pulling on her coat and searching for her keys.

"It is against the rules, but as long as you won't be too long I won't tell anyone. I might need to access other televisions in the house; can you point them out quickly before you go?" Piper could feel the corners of her mouth tugging into a smile and she fought the urge to prematurely celebrate.

"Sure, there is another television here in the kitchen that folds down from under the cabinet, and one in the spare bedroom at the top of the stairs. Around the corner here in my husband's office, but you can't go in there. All the other rooms are fine but that room is off limits, I'm barely allowed in there," she laughed awkwardly. "My husband is a judge and has a lot of privileged information. If that television isn't working he'll have one of his guys come by and look at it another time." Mrs. Lions already had her hand on the door as she threw her purse over her shoulder.

"I understand. I'll probably still be working on this one by the time you get back. Drive safely." Piper flashed the southern charm smile she had been practicing and waved warmly.

"Bless your heart. I'll pack up some scones for you to take with you when I return." She pulled the door closed behind her, and Piper waited until the car pulled away before fishing her phone out of her pocket and dialing Bobby's number.

"She's on her way to town hall now. It sounds like Jules did great. I'm going to be heading into his office and looking for the right spot for the cameras and the pictures." Piper could feel her heart thumping against her ribs as she pulled everything she needed from her toolbag and moved toward his office.

Bobby sounded all together different to Piper as he began to speak. She assumed this was the serious tone he used at work. "Great job. Michael is at town hall now and he'll give us a heads-up when she's leaving. I'm on duty, so I'll take a couple of swings by the judge's house and make sure everything still looks clear for you. How are you doing?" Even with the firmer tone, Bobby's voice was the comforting beacon of a lighthouse that kept Piper from losing herself in the intensity of the moment.

"I'm fine. I want to get this done and get out of here," she stuttered nervously, hearing her words catch.

"Piper, stop for a second and breathe. I know this is overwhelming but you have this under control. Take it one step at a time. I'll stay on the phone with you," Bobby said, with a calm he must have learned in some hostage negotiation class.

Piper drew a long calming breath as she stepped through the threshold of the judge's home office. The massive furniture was made of rich, dark wood. The walls were a textured espresso color. There was a wall of shelves covered in books and another wall covered in pictures of the judge with various celebrities and noteworthy people.

"What do you see?" Bobby asked, breaking Piper's momentary frozen state while she assessed the room. He may have wanted her to be calm, but that didn't include being slow. They were still up against the clock.

"There are a few filing cabinets, a huge bookshelf that's the size of the whole wall, and his desk." She pulled the handles of the filing cabinet and they were locked. She ran her hands over the tops of the books that were within reach looking for any gaps or hiding places.

"Take a good look around. If you were going to hide something in there, something you didn't want to be found, where would you put it?" Bobby felt helpless, like his part in all of this was small and it wasn't fair to Piper to be in there alone.

Piper closed her eyes and imagined she lived here. She imagined this was her office and she was the judge, trying to live a double life. She opened her eyes and scanned the room until her gaze was pulled upward. "There's a gap between the top of the bookshelf and the ceiling. I think I could pull a chair over to it and get the pictures up there. I'm going to put the phone down for a minute. Don't hang up." She may have been alone in the house, but Bobby was her lifeline and she needed him to keep talking to her.

"I'm not going anywhere," he said reassuringly. He turned onto the judge's street and drove by the house wishing he could pull over and help Piper.

She wheeled the desk chair over and lifted herself up so she could see the top of the bookshelf. There was a good six inches from ceiling to shelf and it ran the length of the room. It would be a great spot to plant the pictures. The judge wouldn't be likely to accidently find them before Christian could.

As she tried to position herself better on the bulky office chair she felt the top of the bookshelf give way slightly under the weight of her arm. She noticed a piece of it didn't match the rest and seemed to be loose. She pulled her keys from her pocket and used one to pry up the wood. It came loose and exposed a small cubby filled with notes and photographs. Piper reached her hand in to pull some out.

She covered her mouth in shock as the reality of what she had found began to solidify in her brain. There were pictures of various boys in compromising positions at the hands of the judge. The boys seemed to range in age from ten to early teens and all had the same empty-eyed look of fear and pain in their eyes. The papers Piper was trying to gather up were all written on the letterhead of the charity, Legal Buddies. They seemed to be files of the young boys and in the margins were handwritten notes in the judge's familiar scrawl. Piper could hear Bobby's faint voice from her phone on the desk and knew if she didn't come down and let him know she was all right he'd be busting down the door any minute. She took a handful of the pictures and paperwork down with her as she dismounted the chair.

"Bobby, I found something. I don't know if it changes things," she stammered. "I don't know what to do here, I don't know what I'm supposed to do." Piper's voice was high and Bobby could tell she was beginning to panic.

"What is it? What did you find?" He didn't want to fluster her further but they needed to be finishing up soon, and the alarm in her voice was scaring the hell out of him.

"I was going to put the pictures on top of the bookshelf and there was this piece of the shelf that seemed like it was loose. I pulled it up and I found all these pictures." Piper looked down at her hands and felt tears filling her eyes. "Bobby these boys, these poor little boys." She let the tears fall as she flipped the photographs over, unable to look at the tormented faces of the judge's victims.

"There are all these papers here, too, from Legal Buddies. It's like profiles on all these little kids, and the judge has notes written all over them about how to get them to keep quiet. Here's one that says he'll rule to reduce the sentence of this little boy's father if he complies and doesn't tell anyone about their secrets. This man is a monster." She felt her hands shaking and her knees starting to buckle. She wanted to grab the pictures and run from the house directly to the police department and scream until someone would help her.

"Piper, I need you to listen to me. Put everything back where you found it and slip the photos of Chris in there with them. Set up the cameras then pack up your tools. We keep with the plan exactly how it is." Bobby kept his voice steady but rigid. There was no room for emotion right now, not with so much on the line and so little time. "Do you hear me? I just got a text from Michael that the judge's wife is leaving now."

"I hear you," Piper whispered. "I'm okay, I'm putting everything back." Piper flipped one photograph over and stared at it for a long moment. There was no place on this earth for someone so evil, and she'd never believed that more than this moment.

Piper mounted the micro cameras pointing to the bookshelf, replaced everything, and backed slowly out of the office, trying to confirm that it looked exactly as it had before she entered. She dried all the tears from her eyes and tried to cool the redness in her cheeks with the back of her hands. She hurried back to her toolbag and began collecting all her things. As she zipped it up she heard the car pull into the driveway and readied herself to cheerfully greet Mrs. Lions.

"Are you all done?" she chirped, as she entered the house with a wide grin, surprised to see Piper all packed up and looking ready to leave.

"I am," Piper responded unreservedly, returning a warm smile. "Your cable will be all set in about ten minutes. I need to work on the box outside for a minute and then you'll be good to go." Piper wondered what the judge's wife really knew about her husband's crimes, reminding her of her own mother's willingness to harbor a monster.

"Let me pack some scones for you, dear. You sound like you have a long day ahead of you. We're so grateful you were able to fit us in, it's the least we can do." The judge's wife tucked four scones into a beautifully decorated paper bag.

"You are so kind. I wish all my customers were as wonderful as you. I'm not sure I'll have time to stop for lunch today, so these will be a nice treat." Piper hardly recognized her own voice.

Perhaps Michael was right and being nice was indeed in stark contrast to her normal personality.

Piper waved goodbye as she shut the door behind her, toolbag and scones in hand. As she made her way to the van she saw Bobby's squad car approaching. She knew he wouldn't stop. They couldn't chat here, but as he passed, their eyes met, bringing a sense of relief that filled her entire body. There was something magic about that man, even a glance from him could calm her when it seemed like nothing could.

Unfortunately, as his car drove out of sight the magic wore off. Piper backed out the driveway and, after driving a safe distance from the judge's house, pulled the van over. She swung her door open and vomited onto a pile of freshly fallen leaves. The vileness of the world and the lack of protection for children were too much for her stomach to handle. As she pulled herself back into the van she felt the tears begin again, and she ached for this day to be over, to be safe at Betty's house.

CHAPTER 20

"Are you going to tell us what this is all about?" Michael asked in a demanding tone. "Tell me exactly what you saw." His patience with Piper was wearing thin. She had been sitting in her car crying for twenty minutes, begging to be left alone before finally joining Michael and Bobby in the sitting room at Betty's house.

"Michael, back off her for a minute. This hasn't been a very easy day," Bobby barked at Michael, as he rubbed Piper's back, supportively encouraging her to take her time.

Michael ignored Bobby's demand and pushed on. "No one said any of this was going to easy. We can't all curl up in a ball and cry when we realize how damn hard this is going to be. You planted the pictures, got the cameras up, all without getting caught. That seems like a victory to me." Michael knew Bobby was going to be the compassionate shoulder for Piper to cry on, and someone had to be the voice of reality.

Piper winced at the sharp edge of Michael's voice. She wasn't a crier—this wasn't at all like her—but as hard as she had tried she couldn't contain her sadness. She cleared her throat and stared away from both of them as she spoke. "The judge is using his charity to blackmail boys into keeping quiet about sexual abuse. When I went to put the pictures in his office I found a bunch of sick photographs and documents. They were from Legal Buddies, all with notes from the judge detailing his disgusting manipulation." Piper choked back tears, and her voice shook with emotion. "Michael, there were dozens of pictures of different boys in that box. I saw dates going back over ten years. If you had seen the pictures, the look in their eyes, you'd be feeling the same way."

"I see that stuff every day, Piper. It's hard, but you need to pull yourself together and we need to decide if this changes anything." Michael was unwavering in his lack of empathy. There was no time for that, no time for tears. If Piper wanted to play in the real world she'd need to act accordingly.

"Why are you being such an ass, Michael? If this was Jules you'd be bending over backward making sure she was all right." Bobby stood, feeling the only way to get Michael to listen would be to stare him straight in the eye.

Michael countered quickly. "Jules isn't trying to be some superhero. All I'm saying is, if this is what Piper wants, then she needs to shake it off. If something like this is going to rattle her, do you really think she's going to be fine when the judge turns up with a bullet in his brain? I know she's a tough kid, but we can't have any of this right now." Michael gestured at Piper's frazzled hair and puffy eyes.

"You're a real jerk sometimes, Michael. You think you know what's best for everyone." Bobby's voice grew from a frustrated tone to an aggressive shout.

"He's right," Piper cut in, standing to join the two men before a fight started. They towered over her, but she was certain she could break them apart if need be. She put her hand delicately on his chest, encouraging him to back down. "All this does is reaffirm what we're doing. The judge is worse than we thought he was. We keep going as planned and we make sure he can't hurt anyone else." She wanted to tuck herself under Bobby's warm

arm and bury her face in his chest, but she knew Michael needed to see her stand there, cheeks dry, lip not quivering, and continue with what needed to be done. "We watch the cameras this weekend and make sure the judge doesn't realize anything's going on. Then I call Christian on Monday morning when the judge's wife is out and get him over there." Piper cleared her throat and stood a little taller. "I'll take the first shift watching the cameras. You guys go kiss and make up."

CHAPTER 21

Monday had finally arrived. The weekend was uneventful, and the pictures had remained right where she had planted them. Piper sat in her car in Betty's driveway. She slouched down to avoid the penetrating stares from Bobby and Michael who were camped out on the porch. They had badgered her for hours about what the call to Christian should or shouldn't involve. When she'd finally had enough, she took the burn phone and retreated to her car, locking the doors.

She hadn't mapped out the entire conversation with Christian, but she knew what had to be said. More importantly, she knew how she needed to say it. Yes, she was nervous and rather than masking it, she planned to utilize it. Anyone calling Christian and expecting blind trust had better sound authentic. Coming across as calculated and unemotional would give him the idea this was all a setup.

She dialed the number she had scrawled into her notebook and drew in a deep, shaky breath. The phone rang twice, and then a man's voice came on the line.

"Hello," he answered, with an air of annoyance, probably at

the fact that the number was coming across as anonymous on his caller ID.

"Is this Christian Donavan?" Piper asked, starting off almost imperceptibly quiet and then letting her voice grow.

"Yes it is, but listen, I already know who I'm voting for, I've found Jesus, and my kid is probably already selling whatever your kid is. I'm a busy guy, and I'm not interested." The man paused waiting for the textbook *overcoming objections* rebuttal every new sales person was taught.

"I'm not a solicitor, Mr. Donavan. I'm very sorry to bother you, but I can assure you that this is important. It's about your son, Chris. I have some information that I think you need to know." Piper let her voice crack; she let the quietness of her tone reflect how terrified she was.

"What the hell is this, some kind of prank? If it is I'll tell you right now it isn't funny, and you'll regret this phone call. Tell me who this is." Christian's tone immediately grew fierce as he spoke through pursed lips.

"I'm sorry, I can't tell you who I am. I know who you are and what you do for a living, and I don't want to get mixed up in any of that. I'm an ordinary person who stumbled upon something about your son being in danger. I thought about minding my own business, but I don't want any more children to be hurt." She jumped at the shock of Christian's voice cutting in.

"You don't know shit about what I do for a living, and you certainly don't have any business talking about my son. This better not be bullshit. You've got thirty seconds to spit it out or I'm hanging up the phone, and if you think a blocked phone number can protect you, you're wrong." Christian's voice was now raised to a shout, and Piper could feel the phone shaking in her hand. This reaction had validated Christian's love for his son and his response to protect him.

"Please don't be upset with me. I'm trying to do the right thing here. You do business with a judge. If you go to his house, in his office above his bookshelf there is a loose board hiding some terrible secrets, secrets that pertain to your son. Please take this seriously. I know I've given you no reason to trust me, but for your son's sake, please go see for yourself." Piper pulled the phone from her ear, and disconnected, feeling a wave of nausea come over her. She had considered staying on the line long enough to get some kind of confirmation from Christian, but she didn't want to open herself up to any further questioning by him. The dramatic end to the conversation would have perhaps created an even greater sense of urgency.

She tucked the phone back into her bag and was climbing out of the car as Bobby and Michael approached. She knew there would be a barrage of questions, and she didn't want to participate.

"It's done," she said in a matter-of-fact way. "I'm sure he's heading over there now. Have we confirmed the judge's wife is gone for the morning?" She brushed past both of them and headed back toward the house. Betty and Jules had called in sick today at Michael's urging, wanting to keep them close.

"Yes," Michael said, jogging behind her trying to catch up. "She had a call with her girlfriend this morning about getting coffee and going jewelry shopping. We heard her leave twenty minutes ago."

"What a charmed life. Jewelry shopping, it only costs a few thousand dollars and your soul," Piper said as she turned the monitor of the laptop toward her and stared at the screen. She was convinced Christian would be there soon.

"We don't know that the judge's wife knows any of this. She could be as in the dark as the rest of the community," Bobby said, taking a seat next to Piper.

"You're not married to a man for that long without knowing what horrible things he's capable of. She's probably as sick and twisted as he is. I'm sure she covers for him all the time, hides his secrets." Piper knew Bobby could see she was drawing the connection between her mother and the judge's wife. Their eyes met and she shook her head. "Never mind, it doesn't matter anyway."

Thirty minutes passed and there was no sign of Christian at the judge's house. Doubt began to creep into Piper's mind about the effectiveness of her call. It didn't help that Bobby and Michael seemed to be thinking the same thing.

"Did you tell him to get over there this morning?" Michael asked. "Did he say where he was coming from? For all we know he could be out of town."

"Shut up, Michael, he's coming. I could hear it in his voice, he took it seriously and he's going to show up." Piper stood up and walked away from the laptop, hoping the old adage, a watched pot never boils, might be true.

"He may have been completely worried, but if he's not in town then he couldn't get to the judge's house even if he wanted to. You should have asked." Michael stopped talking at the sight of Bobby waving his hands for them to be quiet. Michael assumed it was another attempt to shield Piper from the harsh reality he was doling out.

"Someone's there," Bobby said, turning up the volume on the computer. "I heard the door open." Piper sat back down and crossed her fingers in a childish attempt at bringing them all some luck.

"It's Christian," Michael said as a man walked into the frame. Piper was surprised by Christian's appearance. He wasn't at all how she had pictured him. She had imagined he'd have a round beer belly crammed into a running suit, slicked back hair, and maybe even a thick cigar hanging from his lips. When she conjured up images of the head of a crime family she hadn't pictured a fit, shaggy haired, normally dressed man. His dark denim jeans, comfortably fitting cotton shirt, and tennis shoes were incredibly misleading. The picture coming through on her computer was grainy, but Piper could tell Christian shared the subtle yet dangerously handsome attributes of his brother Sean. They both had those rebellious eyes and an intentionally unkempt air about them that tended to drive women wild.

Christian crept skeptically around the office, still not certain if this was a trap. He looked up at the bookshelf and whispered, "Son of a bitch, this better be a joke."

The room was still as Piper, Bobby, and Michael all sat in anxious silence waiting for Christian to do something. Finally, he wheeled the office chair over to the bookshelf, as Piper had done a few days earlier. Bobby reached for Piper's hand. It felt so comforting to have him here with her as a moment she had long anticipated had finally arrived.

Christian's phone began ringing in his pocket before he could pull himself up onto the chair. He fished it out and read the caller ID. "Judge," he said with a devilish smile as he answered the phone, "you have incredible timing. I was just thinking about you."

"Holy shit, it's the judge," Michael said, slapping his hand to his forehead. "What if he tells him about the call? He could blow this whole thing up right now."

"He's not that stupid," said Piper. "If he genuinely thinks his son is in danger he's not going to show his hand to the judge. Sit down." She pointed to the couch and Michael obeyed.

Christian stood listening to the judge talk for a minute then finally cut in. "I'm not sure how many times I have to tell you, Judge. I'm not my father. I'm a businessman, not some hired gun to go cleaning up your messes. I've made you a lot of money, and you've gotten me and my crew out of countless jams, but I'm not your hitman. I don't go after innocent women because you're catching some heat from some rookie cop. Isn't this what your little puppy dog, Rylie, does for you?"

Christian used his shoulder to hold his phone pressed against his ear and hoisted himself up onto the chair. He felt around at the top of the bookshelf and finally found the loose board and lifted it free. "Holy shit," he said, pulling the photographs out of the hidden space and flipping through them, finally recognizing one as his son standing outside of his school.

"You know what, maybe you're right," Christian said, clearly trying to compose himself in the face of massive rage. "Maybe I am being shortsighted. Why don't we meet tonight at the mill and we can talk about some options. Say… seven o'clock?" Christian waited for the judge to reply then abruptly hung up the phone. He dismounted the chair and left the office.

"Where is he going?" asked Bobby, still in shock over what had just transpired. "He's not going to leave everything all messed up is he?"

Before full out panic could overtake the room, Christian reappeared holding a shoebox he had presumably gotten from the judge's closet. He climbed back onto the chair and filled the shoebox with the contents of the hidden space. When he was done he returned the loose board and the chair to their original positions. He reached in his pocket once more for his phone and dialed a number.

"Sean," he said his voice shaking with anger, "go pick up Chris at school, and take him back to your place. Don't stop anywhere, and don't screw around. Have a couple of the guys come by and watch the door. I don't want anyone coming or going besides me. Do you understand?" He waited as Sean replied and then punched his fist into the wall. "Sean, do what I tell you. Call me when you're back at your place. I'm going to be late tonight." He hung up his phone and returned it angrily to his pocket. He let out a long line of expletives that made even Michael blush slightly. He left the office and a minute later they heard the front door shut.

"I'm going to head over that way," said Bobby. "I think it's safe to say nothing is going to go down until the meeting tonight, but I'd like to have eyes on Christian until then. Can you track his cell phone and send me the information?" he asked, grabbing his coat and keys and heading for the door.

"Wait," Piper shouted. "I want to come with you." She had started this entire thing. She certainly wasn't ready to take a back seat now that it was getting serious.

"You'll meet me later. I'm going to hang back and watch to make sure nothing unexpected happens. Get in touch with me if anything comes up." Bobby hopped down the front steps and jogged to his truck, leaving no time for her to argue. In reality, he had some ideas rolling around in his mind about how to keep Christian from killing the judge while still being able to execute the important parts of the plan. Listening to Christian shirk the judge's requests to harm Betty and Jules had struck something inside of him. Christian was no saint, certainly a criminal, but he, unlike the judge and Rylie, had drawn a line in the sand when it came to harming innocent people. That meant something.

CHAPTER 22

The rest of the afternoon seemed to drag for everyone. Piper and Michael paced around Betty's house waiting for a call from Bobby. Betty and Jules felt the tension flood the house, so they decided to seek higher ground, retreating to their respective rooms upstairs. Bobby, at least, was keeping busy. He spent the afternoon hours tailing Christian who made multiple stops to different properties he owned. He was moving with purpose and incredible focus, not stopping to make small talk or exchange niceties with anyone.

When Christian finally seemed to settle into his house around four o'clock, Bobby picked up his phone to call Piper.

"It seems like he might be staying put for a little bit. This would be a good time to go set up the cameras at the mill and park somewhere to test all the equipment. I'll give you a heads-up once he's on the move again." He hated the idea of Piper going to the mill on her own in the middle of the afternoon when she could easily be spotted. He had, however, realized that there was little she thought she couldn't do, and trying to be the voice of reason or the knight in shining armor wouldn't get him anywhere.

"I'll head over there now." Piper grabbed the bag full of supplies that she had packed, double checked, and then repacked while waiting for the go ahead from Bobby. As she made her way to the door she heard footsteps tapping down the stairs behind her. Piper turned to see Jules standing there with a look of sadness on her face, her eyes red-rimmed and wet from tears.

"This is it, isn't it?" Jules mumbled in a quiet and concerned voice. "I could tell when Bobby ran out this morning, and now the look on your face says it all. I know you guys don't want me to be involved in this, and I can respect that. I want you to know that whoever killed my father robbed me and my mother of so many things, and in my eyes they deserve all the pain and punishment in the world. They don't deserve to live. I'm afraid if it comes down to it Bobby won't be able to face that, and might end up getting himself killed instead."

The tears started to roll again down Jules's cheeks, and Piper found herself, as usual, completely unprepared to cater to someone else's emotional needs. She assumed a hug was required, some kind of reassuring gesture that would stop the tears and ease her mind, but as she wracked her brain to find one she felt the pressure of wasted time bearing down on her. Piper had grown so much since meeting these wonderful people, but she still wasn't confident in her ability to comfort someone.

She looked past Jules with a flicker of panic in her eye. "Um, Michael… Jules needs you," she called out, and she turned away, heading again for the door. She knew that in the eyes of normal people she seemed cold-hearted and vacant. If they only understood that empathy and social skills were taught, not innately known, then perhaps they could forgive her ignorance.

As she tossed the bag into her car and put the key in the ignition she felt a slight weight lift from her chest at the sight of Jules wrapped safely in Michael's arms in the doorway of the house. At least if she couldn't give Jules what she needed she could get out of the way and let someone else do it.

The ride to the mill seemed to take an eternity. She knew she had a lot to do, all while trying not to be noticed. She pulled her car up two blocks from the entrance to the mill and walked casually toward the building, checking frequently to make sure no one was coming or going from its entrance. She quickly made her way to the back of the building where the barrel she had used to force her way in last time stood. She sighed with relief at the sight of the barrel, exactly as she had left it, below the window that she had needlessly broken. She pulled herself up and through the window and dropped, catlike, onto the ground below. Something about this felt easier than last time. Perhaps it was that she knew the layout of the mill or the players involved, or maybe it was that for the first time in her life she didn't feel alone.

It took nearly an hour to get everything set perfectly. As she walked back to her car she felt her phone vibrating in her pocket. She pulled it out and was relieved to see it was Bobby.

"He's heading that way now. Do you have everything set up?" There was no time for cordial greetings or casual chitchat. This was crunch time, and only vital communication of facts would work.

"Everything's set up. I'm heading back to my car now to make sure the cameras are working. I should know in a few minutes," she said, happy to hear Bobby's voice.

"I'll meet you at your car. I'm assuming Christian is trying to get there before the judge. He has a duffle bag with him, but I'm not sure what's in it or what he has planned." Bobby spoke quickly, and Piper could tell his anxiety was significantly higher than hers. She felt she had come to terms with the fact that Christian would kill the judge. But she knew Bobby was still searching for a solution, still holding out for an alternative. "I have an idea," Bobby added, stopping Piper in her tracks. She was afraid this would happen. "I need to run it by Michael. I'm going to give him a call and then fill you in as soon as I can. Send me a message when you know the cameras are operational." She heard the line disconnect and felt a knot in her stomach. She reconsidered the last thing Jules had said to her. Would Bobby really jeopardize his own life to avoid the bloodshed of criminals tonight? Were his ideals more of a liability than she had considered?

Piper sat tapping the steering wheel of her car, looking restlessly in her rearview mirror hoping to see Bobby either pulling up behind her or walking her way. In the fifteen minutes since they had spoken on the phone she had determined the cameras and microphones were working properly. She had watched Christian enter the side door of the mill and come into view of the cameras. He was moving some boxes and an old office chair around. She had tried twice to call Bobby, but she assumed he was still on the other line with Michael because he was not answering his phone.

Finally, she saw Bobby hustling up the street toward her car, his phone still to his ear. He pulled open her car door and flopped down into the passenger seat, bringing with him a gust of cold air. She wanted to interrogate him, scold him, and hold him all at once. Instead, she listened to the phone conversation as it continued.

"Yes, Michael, I think this could work." Bobby grabbed Piper's hand and squeezed it as a sign of excitement over the newly hashed plan.

"Bobby, wait," Piper heard Michael say on the other end of the line. "There's something I need to tell you first."

"Holy Shit," Bobby said, pointing at the screen televising the scene unfolding in the mill. "The judge is here. Whatever you have to tell me can wait. I've got to get in there." He hung up the phone and reached for the car door to leave.

"What are you doing? You can't go in there yet. That's not what we discussed!" Piper grabbed the sleeve of Bobby's jacket trying to pull him toward her.

"Michael and I think we've worked something out, but I have to get in there before Christian does anything, otherwise it's too late. I need you to trust me." He pulled her hand from his sleeve and held it, begging her with his eyes.

"No. I mean, I do trust you, but I think your judgment is clouded." The judge and Christian had begun talking, and the sound drew Piper's attention to the screen long enough for Bobby to hop out of the car.

"If anything happens to me, call the police. No matter what, stay in the car. Please trust me." He half closed the door and then pulled it back open and stuck his head in. "I think I might love you, Piper." He pulled his head back, closed the door, and ran toward the mill.

She held her breath, unable for a moment to process anything. Not the sudden changes to the plan, not the proclamation of maybe love, or the thought of something happening to Bobby that would warrant a call to the police. She turned her attention to the scene unfolding on the screen in front of her. She saw Christian sidle up to the judge and plunge something into his unsuspecting fat neck. The judge put his hand to his neck and looked puzzled before falling limp into Christian's waiting arms. Christian dragged his portly body toward a chair in the corner of the room and dropped him down onto it. She saw him pull a gun from his waistband and hold the barrel to the judge's forehead. Then she saw light from an opening door stream in and heard Bobby's familiar voice call out.

"Christian, stop." He put his hands up showing he had no weapon and moved farther into the room but not any closer to Christian.

Christian swung around and aimed the gun at Bobby who instinctively went to reach for his weapon. At the last second, Bobby seemed to remember he wasn't here for a shoot-out, but for a negotiation, and purposefully lifted his empty hands again. Piper felt her heart momentarily stop as she saw the large black gun pointing at the man who might love her.

"I'm here to save your life. I need you to hear me out. Can you put the gun down for a minute and let me talk to you?" Bobby kept his hands raised and voice steady. He hadn't had enough time to think through all his talking points, and now staring down the barrel of a gun, it seemed as though a little more preparation would have been beneficial.

"I'm not sure who you are, but there are only two people in this room whose lives are in danger, and I'm not one of them," Christian barked, clearly rattled by Bobby's sudden appearance.

"My name is Bobby, and I'm a cop. I'm not here to arrest you though. I'm here to help you. Lower your gun and give me a chance to explain. Please." Christian lowered his gun slightly, but gave no indication he'd be holstering it or handing it over. Bobby continued, "I know what this man has done, who he is, and I don't blame you for wanting to kill him. I have a plan that ensures he pays for his crimes and keeps you from spending the rest of your life in jail." Piper was as anxious to be let in on this plan as Christian was to, perhaps quite literally, shoot it down.

"There's no justice for a man like this other than a bullet in his brain, and even that doesn't seem like enough," Christian shouted, raising his gun, pointing it in the direction of the judge again.

"I know you think that, but there are dozens of other people—children—involved here and they deserve to see him pay for his crimes. They don't want him to just disappear, his body never to be seen again. If you pull that trigger now you'll be doing him a favor. When all of this comes out he's going to pray for death. I have a way to make sure he's held accountable and get you and your family a fresh start." Bobby signaled for Christian to lower his weapon again and tried to draw his attention away from the judge.

"I'm no rat. If that's what you're about to propose you can stop right there. I come from a long line of people who pride themselves on loyalty." Christian's eyes and gun were still fixed on the judge and Bobby knew he was running out of time. The judge was still motionless, but Bobby could see he was breathing. Whatever sedative Christian had injected into the judge's neck was certainly doing its job.

"You know when everything comes out about this guy, you won't be called a rat, you'll be a hero. There are certain lines you don't cross and even your crew would agree he's a monster. The people he's hurt deserve to see him pay, in the public eye. All I'm asking is you hear me out." Bobby felt the tightness in his chest fade slightly as Christian once again lowered his gun and turned toward him.

Bobby continued, "You know if I was to bring any evidence in against him, either me or the people I love would be dead before it ever came to light, and the evidence would be destroyed. You know exactly who is involved with the judge and you can give the evidence to people who you know don't have a relationship with him. I know you took a box from the judge's house, and I know it holds more than enough to ruin him, but you're the only one who can navigate the corruption and ensure it gets to the right people."

Christian's mind was spinning. This was supposed to be a quick and clean kill and now it was falling apart. This kid just didn't understand how things worked, so he'd thought he better set him straight. "They'll retry cases, and most of my guys won't stand a chance without having a judge in their corner. You might be right, they wouldn't stand for what this guy does to kids, but they wouldn't be willing to go to jail over it. They'd kill me." Christian's voice wasn't as harsh anymore. He wasn't barking and shouting, he seemed to be hoping for another solution.

"I know. That's why I've had a prosecutor friend of mine write up terms that would get you full immunity as well as relocation. You could take your money and your son and start a new life somewhere. I know you think this town is your legacy, the life your father led is all you're meant for, but this is the opportunity to give your son a whole new legacy." Bobby knew if this argument didn't sway him, if starting over wasn't appealing, then he was completely out of options and had no idea where to go from here.

Christian's eyes danced around the room as he thought over the proposal. He bit his lip and furrowed his brow, and Bobby took the hesitation as a positive sign—at least he wasn't immediately opposed to the idea.

He was so tired of this life, this chaos he was living. What this kid was proposing was something he had thought about every day since his son was born. This was the first time it lay before him, his for the taking. "I want my brother to come, too. If he's not included in the deal, then I'm not interested." Christian's stare was intensely boring holes through Bobby.

"Your brother has some serious problems. He tried to hurt someone I care about very much. You can't expect, with good conscience, we introduce him to a new community with no criminal record. He's a danger to women." Bobby wanted to tell Christian what his wonderful brother Sean had done to Piper but he didn't imagine it would do much to change his mind.

"It's the three of us or no dice. If I leave and give you the evidence you need about the judge, then dozens of cases will be retried. My friends *and* my enemies will all be facing possible jail time, and they'll no longer be able to buy their way out of it. If I leave my brother behind he'll be dead within a week. I know he's got some issues, and I'll get him some help. He needs to get out of here, get away from all this bullshit he thinks is our destiny." Christian's face suddenly softened, the sternness melting away and replaced with weariness. His eyes begged for compassion as he quietly uttered, "He's my little brother."

All of this was so counterintuitive to Bobby. There were good guys and bad guys, but now, standing here in front of someone he didn't think was capable of sincerity, he realized he might be wrong about the world. Maybe being a criminal didn't mean you didn't love your family. He'd never understood how someone could wake up every morning and break the law, but he knew what it meant to love someone enough to want to protect him. He never wanted to find common ground with a man like Christian, but that's what seemed to be happening. He cleared his throat and gritted his teeth and spoke in a tone, letting Christian know he was serious.

"If he goes with you, he registers as a sex offender under his new identity. He gets counseling, and I will personally come out there and hunt him down if he so much as grabs a woman's ass without her permission. He doesn't deserve a free pass as far as I'm concerned, but we've got the potential here to make a much larger impact." Bobby shook his head, disappointed with himself and the situation. Why did it always have to come down to compromising yourself to get things done?

Christian let out an audible sigh of relief. He wasn't ignorant to what a low-life moron his brother was, but he had an obligation to him. He was blood, and their father had completely failed Sean. It was a miracle he'd survived this long. Christian had personally beaten his brother senseless when he had found out about the horrific crime he had committed and the way he had tossed that girl out of his car like she was trash. He had saved his brother from prison by paying a hefty fee, but he had found other ways to punish him. Christian honestly believed he could save him, if he could only get him out of this town.

Christian couldn't believe what he was about to say. He couldn't believe he was about to sell out everything his father had taught him. When the doubt rose up in his stomach all he had to do was picture his son. There was no denying a new life, somewhere far from all this, would be the best gift he could ever give Chris. He closed his eyes and spoke quietly. "Judge Rosenthal. I won't meet with anyone else. If you can get her out tonight and get my family and me out of here by morning I'll give you whatever you want. I've got voicemails, loads of communications, and of course that box of filth I took from the judge's house sitting in my truck. You get Judge Rosenthal, and you've got a deal." Christian approached Bobby resignedly with his hand extended, ready to make a gentleman's agreement. As Christian and his loaded weapon came closer, it suddenly dawned on Bobby how dangerous this had all been, how close to death he'd been, and how furious Piper would be. At any point Christian could have, and maybe still would, lift his weapon and kill him.

Bobby took Christian's hand firmly and shook it. "I need your gun, Christian. You know we're not going to go sit with a judge while you have a weapon. We've both taken some risks here tonight. I need you to take one more." Bobby extended his hand and gestured toward Christian's weapon. Christian hesitated and looked over at the judge one last time.

"I want my kid to have a better life. I don't want him constantly in the crosshairs. I don't want him to be afraid of me the way I was of my father. I've tried to do things right by him, but at every turn I keep getting myself in deeper. This might be the first risk I take that actually makes him safer." Christian handed over his gun and wiped away the sweat that had gathered on his forehead. Christian asked, pointing over to the judge, "So what are we going to do with him? The stuff I gave him will keep him out for another eight hours or so."

"Do you have anything we can use to tie him up?" Bobby asked, deciding it was better to keep the judge in one spot to limit their liability of him either taking off or seeking retribution.

"I'm the head of the largest crime family in this state. I carry around rope like normal people carry a pack of gum. I never leave home without it," Christian said with a wry smile. Bobby wasn't quite ready to start cracking jokes with Christian, but he had to admit it was a pretty witty response. He bit his lip to hold back a smirk, and Christian patted him on the shoulder. "I get it *Officer*; I'm still the enemy here. I'm not trying to be best friends, but I have a feeling we're in for a long night so you might as well warm up to me now." Bobby and Christian headed outside as Bobby pulled out his cell phone.

"You can put comedian on your list of career options, since you'll be in the market for one. With any luck you'll get relocated somewhere real remote, maybe the Midwest. Can you milk a cow?" Bobby pushed open the door as he heard Christian mumble an expletive or two under his breath. It was clearly just dawning on Christian that he may not be picking his destination the way you would a vacation spot.

Bobby knew Piper would be bubbling over with questions and probably frustration. But she'd have to wait a little longer to scold him because Michael needed an update first.

CHAPTER 23

As Bobby drove down the quiet streets of Edenville, he tried to wrap his mind around the evening's events. He never would have imagined his passenger tonight would be Christian Donavan. He assumed, instead, the man would be handcuffed and riding in the back of his cruiser. He was equally surprised how well Piper had taken the direction he'd given regarding her heading back to Betty's and waiting for him to call. He had thought, for sure, she'd be furious for the sudden change of plans and her lack of involvement in the next few steps.

The quick conversation he'd had with her was still spinning around in his head. He had turned the words over and over in his mind trying to make sense of it. When he had sidled up to her car window and waited for her to roll it down, he was shocked by her smile. He'd immediately apologized but she barely let him finish his sentence. She had beamed gratefully up at him. "Don't apologize, Bobby. You didn't just save the judge's life tonight; you saved mine. I thought I wanted him dead. At first I was so angry that you put yourself in that situation, but when Christian finally lowered his gun and agreed to the terms you'd given him, I felt relieved. I've seen so much in my life I thought Christian killing the judge would somehow fix everything, but now I think it would have destroyed me. There you were again, rescuing me from something I didn't even realize was about to hurt me." She had leaned out of the car and kissed him, a short peck on the lips, and then she sped off to Betty's house. As usual, she had completely surprised him.

Christian's hands were shaking as he bit his already short fingernails. He wasn't sure why he felt compelled to speak, but he wanted someone to know this wasn't the life he had imagined for himself. "I don't think my son knows who I am yet. I think if we leave tonight and start somewhere fresh, some suburb with a gate and pool, he may actually never have to feel the way I did when I realized the kind of man my father was." He stared out the window, speaking more to the stars than to Bobby.

"How old were you when you figured it out?" Bobby asked, genuinely curious about what it must have been like to realize your father was a criminal. He now knew two people who had lived through that. Bobby thought maybe Christian could give him some perspective that would help him understand Piper better.

"I was twelve. I always thought my father was a foreman at a construction company even though, looking back, I realized he was never actually on a jobsite. He never had any tools, and he never came home dirty or anything. This particular Sunday, we were driving in his brand new red Cadillac Deville. I loved that car, and my father was so proud of it. He kept it immaculately clean. Suddenly, this old shit-box pickup truck with two guys in the cab pulled up ahead of us, and the driver started slamming on his brakes. I thought they were real jerks, maybe some kids messing around. My father was furious, and I remember him saying he couldn't believe they would do this with his kid in the car. Then they tossed their soda bottles out of their windows, and one made contact with the windshield and a crack spread across it. I could tell my father wanted to speed up and take care of this right then, but he looked over at me, patted my leg and said we'd head home. I remember memorizing the license plate in case my father wanted me to go with him to the police department to report the damage to his car. I thought I'd be such a hero when the detective would come over and I would say TS-1874. But I never had that chance. My father drove straight home, bypassing the ice cream shop, and told me to head into the house and tell my mother he'd be late." Christian cleared his throat, and Bobby could tell the story wasn't coming to a happy ending.

"The next morning I sat eating my cereal and watching the news with my mother. I heard a story come on that immediately got my attention. The reporter was standing in front of a burned out pickup truck surrounded by yellow police tape. Over his shoulder I could make out most of the license plate, and I felt myself getting lightheaded as I realized it was the truck that had harassed us the day before. The report stated that the two men in the truck had been shot in the head before someone torched the vehicle with a Molotov cocktail. I didn't want to believe that my father had anything to do with it. I convinced myself whoever was in the truck must have continued vandalizing vehicles and had crossed paths with the wrong person. It wasn't until I was on my way down our driveway to catch the bus and saw my father pulling in that I realized he was the wrong person they had crossed. He rolled down his window, and with a big smile on his face, told me how sorry he was we missed our ice cream cone the day before.

When I leaned in his window for a hug goodbye I saw his hand wrapped in white bandages, and the smell of gasoline stung my nose. When he saw me staring at his bandage he said not to worry he had burned his hand on the exhaust pipe of an excavator at work. That was the last time I hugged my father. For the next couple of years I watched everything he did. I had my antenna up and put together the puzzle that was my father, each piece revealing a more complex and immoral man. Then, as I got older, he pulled me into his life and made me a part of his world. After years of feeling so distant from him, I'd do almost anything to be close to him again. I know most of what I do looks like a choice, but you'd be amazed how quickly you can fall down the rabbit's hole and not know how to get yourself back out. I've tried everything to legitimize my family's business, but every time I get us out of one deal we get pulled into something else. I know it doesn't mean much to you, but I don't mess with the sex trafficking and prostitutes, I've stayed out of all the drug deals inside Edenville, and I was on the verge of ending our gunrunning. We dropped a shipment a few months ago, and it was the last one. We're still pretty deep in the gambling ring, and I know that's no more legal than anything else I mentioned, but I'd like to think it's a victimless crime." Christian wasn't sure why he was pouring his heart out to this kid. He had said more in the last five minutes to this practical stranger than he had said in the last year to people in his immediate circle.

"You aren't your father—you've got a great shot of putting all this behind you and sparing your son the things you went through. You're doing the right thing tonight." If there were any doubts swimming around in Christian's mind, Bobby was trying to proactively squash them. "This is the place. Michael asked me to come to his office first so he could talk with me privately about something, and then have you join us, but I'm thinking we should stick together," Bobby said, putting his truck in park outside Michael's office building.

"Let's get this over with." Christian swung open his door and huffed loudly, obviously dreading this moment even as he knew it was his best shot at a new life.

They entered through the back door of the office building Michael had suggested and boarded the staff elevator. It was a quick but quiet ride up to the ninth floor and as the elevator door split open Michael came into view.

"Are you kidding me!" Christian exclaimed, his eyes large and his face immediately turning red. He knew this was all too good to be true, deals like this never worked out. He reached his hand to his side where he would normally keep his gun and clenched his fist when he realized he no longer had his weapon. His only hope was there wasn't an army of the judge's men waiting just around the corner to torture or kill him. "This is the lawyer we're meeting with? You're dumber than I thought kid. He's on the judge's payroll, and I'm getting the hell out of here. The deal's off."

Bobby heard the words, but they didn't compute in his head quickly enough for him to even make an attempt at correcting Christian or to stop him from repeatedly hitting the close-door button on the elevator. Luckily, Michael had his wits about him and put his arm across the closing door, and it popped back open.

"Give me a chance to explain," Michael said hurriedly, imploring Bobby to step off the elevator and into his office so they could talk. If Michael was trying to calm Bobby with his demeanor he was doing a terrible job considering his forehead was covered with sweat and he was almost breathless. "This is why I wanted to meet with you first. This is what I wanted to tell you on the phone earlier."

"You wanted to tell me that you're on the judge's payroll?" Bobby asked incredulously, his brow furrowed and his stomach turning in knots. He had prepared himself to be surprised by how deep this conspiracy would run, but he never assumed how close to home it would hit.

"No. Well, not exactly, it's a long story, but if you don't get off the elevator I'm not going to be able to tell you any of it." Michael said, gesturing for him to step through the doors and give him the opportunity to explain.

Christian crossed his arms over his chest and glared at Bobby, refusing to address Michael. "I'm not getting off this elevator. If you want to chitchat with your buddy here, you can get off and let me go or he can get on and start talking." With that, Michael acquiesced and joined them on the elevator. "Listen Bobby, it's not what you think. Not everything is black and white, good guys and bad guys. If you hear my side of the story I know you'll understand."

"I can't believe I let you get close to Jules," Bobby yelled, his fists clenched and ready to strike his betrayer. "How could you screw all of us like this? What exactly have you been doing, losing cases on purpose or something?"

"Yes," chimed in Christian, "that's exactly what he did. It was with one of Duke Cheval's guys who caught a case for possession with the intent to distribute. Your buddy here sandbagged the case on purpose." Christian's voice was angry, and his finger was pointing accusingly at Michael.

"That isn't true, how about you tell the whole story, Christian?" Michael sighed somewhat dejectedly, and launched into his explanation. "Some people approached me about making some evidence in the case disappear, and I told them to go to hell. They came back and threatened me, so I threatened them right back, letting them know they didn't scare me. I told them I intended to have them charged with tampering and intimidation. A week later I got a package in the mail loaded with pictures of my baby sister who was away at college. There were photos of her in class, out in the campus courtyard, and sitting in the local coffee house. Then finally there was a picture of one of Cheval's guys talking to her in front of her dorm. A note read, 'You might not be afraid but you can bet she will be.' I had my sister leave school immediately and sent her to stay with our uncle. I tried the case and brought forth all evidence I had available. I still lost, but it wasn't for a lack of trying, I can promise you that." Michael choked out, his voice catching as he stared hard at Bobby. "I could have brought the evidence to the judge but, just like you, I had no idea who I could trust. I did my job without hesitation, and my conscience is clean. I'm sorry that I didn't tell you that I'd been approached by these idiots. I was trying to put it all behind me. The moment I heard you and Piper had a plausible plan to do something about it, I got on board."

Bobby turned from Michael to Christian who was now noticeably silent and staring at the floor of the stopped elevator. "I don't know the details," he mumbled, sounding much less confident than he had moments earlier. "I remember hearing chatter that he wasn't really playing ball and that they were going to pay a visit to someone in his family. When I heard the guy got off, I just assumed their threats had worked and Michael had thrown the case."

"You know what they say about assuming," Michael barked. "Only assholes do it."

"I'm pretty sure that isn't the saying," Christian replied, shooting a dirty look back at Michael.

Bobby waved his hands, cutting through their childish attacks. "You should have told me," he said, his mind bouncing between anger and pity. Michael was right, he'd have certainly done the same thing if he thought Jules, Betty, or Piper was in imminent danger. Look at how many concessions he had already made since starting out on this. It wasn't like Michael had lost the case intentionally or destroyed important evidence. Should he have blown the whistle? Maybe, but as Bobby was starting to find out not everything was quite so cut and dry.

"Judge Rosenthal is going to be here any minute." Michael said impatiently. "She's probably down there right now wondering what the hell is wrong with the elevator. We've got one shot at this, and if she thinks for a minute we aren't all calibrated then she'll pull the plug. You won't get your protection and relocation," Michael said pointing at Christian, "and you, Bobby, won't get your justice."

Bobby turned to Christian and tried to put this whole thing in perspective. "You remember earlier tonight when you told me you wanted your brother to be included in your relocation? It goes against everything I believe, but I am going out on a limb, because I trust you'll get him help. You know him better than I do, and if you really believe you can help him then I have to default to you in order to make the rest of this work. I'm asking you to do the same. I know Michael, and I believe him. Without him we can't pull this off."

Christian didn't speak. He only nodded and rolled his eyes. Michael released the stop button on the elevator and they all stepped out as the door opened back up.

CHAPTER 24

"Judge Rosenthal, I can't thank you enough for coming out this time of night. I know it's a little unorthodox, but I can assure you it will be worth your while," Michael said in his work voice, which was a bit softer and more polished.

"Mr. Cooper, until I came in and saw Mr. Donavan sitting there I was prepared to give you quite the tongue-lashing regarding after hours calls to a judge. Now I must admit I am a little intrigued," Judge Rosenthal said. She was a tiny woman with frail hands and wispy brittle hair. Her pointed nose nearly took up half her face and her thin lips seemed to be permanently pursed. She appeared meek, but as Michael had seen firsthand in the courtroom, one should never mistake her stature as a weakness. There was nothing weak about Judge Rosenthal.

"I've always known you to be a highly ethical and unbiased judicator. I've enjoyed every opportunity I've had to try a case in your court." As Michael attempted to continue, the tiny judge cut in.

"Don't let me give you the wrong idea, Mr. Cooper, just because I am intrigued doesn't mean I want to sit here all night while you blow smoke up my ass. I still have hopes of getting to bed at a decent hour, so get to it."

"Mr. Donavan has long been aware of judicial misconduct by Judge Lions." Michael cleared his throat and continued, "He has been privy to and part of multiple counts of bribery, extortion, and intimidation all spearheaded or supported by Judge Lions. He has ample evidence of this and is here tonight to give a sworn statement regarding his information," Michael explained curtly, knowing that Judge Rosenthal was not in the mood for fluff.

Judge Rosenthal looked wary. "And I suppose he's doing this because of a sudden spell of conscience? Or should I assume that he is looking for full immunity and most likely some kind of witness protection?" The judge pushed her glasses up tighter to her face from the bridge of her nose. She had done her job long enough to realize nothing this size came without costs.

Michael knew this was a game of chess and he was playing against an expert. "Mr. Donavan feels when he provides this information he will be at great risk as will his brother and son. In return for his testimony he would like—" The judge huffed loudly and cut in.

"Michael, for goodness sake, it's late and this isn't court, can we please cut the bull? How serious is this? I've had my concerns about Judge Lions for a long time, and I've been waiting for the right opportunity to end the ridiculous circus he considers a courtroom. Are you telling me this is it? Is this credible?" Judge Rosenthal pursed her lips together. She would have gladly driven Christian to the airport herself if it meant removing a corrupt judge from his seat.

"Judge Rosenthal," Christian said quietly, "it's more than all the legal stuff that brings me here today. I've known about his deals for years. I've given him buckets of money in return for favors." Christian reached into his breast pocket and pulled out an envelope. "I found these in his home," he said, sliding the pictures across the table to her. "I've been a part of some pretty heinous things in my life, but I won't spend another minute dealing with a man capable of that."

Judge Rosenthal pulled open the envelope and, in her composed fashion, thumbed through the pictures of Judge Lions and his victims. She didn't gasp, or even wince, because, unfortunately, she had seen her share of these kinds of things.

"Mr. Donavan, I despised your father. He was a brutal man with no moral compass. I've had numerous people cross my path who were damaged by him in so many ways." The three men all sat stone-faced, unsure what correlation she was trying to draw. "But I adored you. I saw you often around town, and you have the sweetest spirit and kindest eyes. I would often pray for you, that you might have a chance to forge your own path and not fall prey to the legacy of your father. As time went on I saw you being sucked into his world. I thought perhaps when your own son was born or when your father died you would take those as opportunities to change your ways. I want you to know that what you are doing here tonight separates you from your father. There would have been no pictures awful enough, no crime vile enough, for your father to put aside a mutually beneficial relationship and do the right thing." Judge Rosenthal reached her hand across the table and patted Christian's arm. "Michael," she asked, getting back to business, "what are you proposing we do next?"

"I'd like for Christian to document everything he can and compile the evidence against Judge Lions. Then he writes up his statement and coordinates with a witness protection team to get him out of here first thing in the morning. Judge Lions is currently indisposed at a designated location where he can be picked up anytime a warrant is issued." Michael could feel the wheels spinning in his mind. There would be so many steps once this was put into motion.

"Your Honor," Bobby said quietly, "there is a police officer who has been a right-hand man to Judge Lions for years. He conspired to, or possibly did, kill an Edenville police officer ten years ago."

"Stan?" Judge Rosenthal questioned. This time, there was unmistakable emotion in the judge's voice. Bobby nodded his head, and she continued, "I knew Stan well, we went to school together. Do you have any proof that they were involved in his murder?" The Judge sat up a little straighter in her chair.

"I don't, and I'm not sure we ever will. I thought it was important for you to know when we go through this process. Christian can give you enough evidence and important information to implicate Officer Rylie in plenty and ensure he spends the rest of his life in jail. I just wanted someone else to know, even if we couldn't do anything about it now.

Bobby knew it wasn't of any legal significance to a judge to know about crimes someone may have committed if there was no proof, but he came here to say his piece, and he wasn't going to let this opportunity pass by.

"I'm glad you told me. If we can't find the evidence to incriminate them for the murder, we'll make sure they never see the light of day again. It might not be exactly what you were hoping for, but it's certainly better than what they have right now." Judge Rosenthal's smile was warm. It was amazing how quickly she could transition from the stern, disciplined judge to a warm and comforting maternal figure.

"There is one more thing, Your Honor," Michael said clearing his throat nervously. "Bobby was an essential part of bringing all this together. Without him we never would have been able to pull it off." Michael paused, surprised by the look of annoyance spreading across the judge's face.

"I can assure you, Michael, you'll all get your time in the spotlight. I'm sure they can get someone very famous to play you in the movie version of this epic adventure you've been on." The judge rolled her eyes, never surprised by the size of men's egos.

"You're misunderstanding me. No matter how many of the

people we put in jail, there'll always be someone seeking retribution for what we are about to do. Bobby has lived here his whole life. He has people he loves dearly who would be in jeopardy if his name was in any way associated with this. He's not looking for notoriety. On the contrary, I'm asking for anonymity for him. I know we're not in the business of removing people's names completely from something like this, but I was hoping, considering the circumstances, you would make an exception. Allow Christian to write his statement without mentioning his interactions with Bobby." Michael wasn't speaking now as a lawyer, his shoulders weren't back, his chin wasn't up and his eyes were notably avoiding everyone in the room. Michael had turned off his confident boisterous persona and was now only asking a favor for his friend.

"I genuinely hate putting my foot in my mouth, it really annoys me. I'm sorry I misread your request for confidentiality. Under these very unique circumstances I think we can find a way to leave Bobby out of the written statement. I would imagine, Michael, that you, too, have people you would like to protect. Is your desire for fame outweighing your concern?" She raised an eyebrow at him and smirked. She assumed there was another reason for him not including himself in his request and she wanted to hear it.

"I don't intend to leave you standing alone in this," Michael responded. "Christian is going to be getting relocation and protection, Bobby has more people here in town who deserve to be protected. I know there will be some blowback, and I know what I signed up for." Michael had returned to his courtroom posture and tone.

"That's all quite laughable, Michael. I appreciate your concern, but I can assure you these men don't frighten me. I never married. I have no children, no family, and ample protection for myself. What you have both done is extraordinary, and while you deserve the accolades of your community you are far more likely to get the retaliation of the many scorned people who will be losing either their freedom or their paycheck. I suggest that before Mr. Donavan takes pen to paper and starts telling this story you make your decision. You have an opportunity to wake up tomorrow morning and act as surprised as everyone else when you hear the news." Judge Rosenthal pulled her phone from her purse and began typing a message on it. She was trying to minimize this moment by not giving it her full attention. She appreciated the gesture on Michael's part, but the fewer people involved the less likely the collateral damage.

"As long as you're sure, your honor, I would greatly appreciate it." Michael felt a weight lift off his shoulders as the thought of his sister flashed through his mind.

"Yes, hurry up then. I'm already out much later than I had hoped to be. Mr. Donavan, let's get this straight then, you found these pictures while you were a welcomed guest in the Lion's home. You felt it was your duty to ensure the judge is held accountable for his deplorable actions, and you therefore contacted me directly. We met, drafted a plan for the relocation of yourself, your brother, and your son with the conditions that you turn over any and all evidence you have that pertains to Judge Lions and any of his associates. Are we all clear on that?" Judge Rosenthal barely looked up from her phone as she spoke. There was an opportunity here for anyone in this room to recant, to get cold feet, and she wouldn't be a part of making this moment feel profound, even though it was.

The three men shook their heads in agreement as they looked at each other. The room was quiet now, and they fixed their eyes on the judge, waiting for their next direction, and she was happy to oblige.

"Mr. Cooper, I've just sent a message and there are two men on their way up. They escorted me here tonight and will now be in charge of getting Mr. Donavan and his family on a chartered plane tonight." She turned her attention over to Christian.

"Mr. Donavan, please draft your written statement and then contact your brother to ensure everyone is ready to leave within the hour." The Judge stood, and, out of sheer habit, all three men stood as well. "There is one last thing I'd like to say to the three of you. This is a clean slate, Mr. Donavan, not a free pass. There is a difference. I will not be privy to where you have settled. This is both for your protection and my own, but these two men," she said pointing to Bobby and Michael, "will be informed. If you or your brother step one toe out of line I will personally have you dragged back here and deliver you to whoever is offering the highest bounty for your head. You haven't made good choices up until this point, but that doesn't mean you aren't capable. I won't be around to give your brother the same warning, so I hope you will convey this to him. When people are seeking revenge for this, I'm sure your brother will make a suitable substitute for you. You don't want him shipped back here because he can't keep his hands to himself." The judge moved toward the conference room door and flagged down two large men and waved them over. "Michael and Bobby, it was a pleasure meeting with you this evening. We have it all under control from here. I'd tune in to the morning news tomorrow, I plan to send them one hell of a story to run." She shook both of their hands and smiled widely at them.

"Bobby," Christian said, reaching his hand out. "Thank you for stopping me tonight. If you ever need anything don't hesitate to ask." Bobby nodded his head and shook Christian's hand, amazed how this night had turned out.

The elevator ride was silent as Michael and Bobby attempted to process what had happened—what they had just accomplished. As the elevator doors opened and they stepped out, Michael finally found his voice through the thoughts swimming in his head.

"We've got quite the story to go tell the girls, don't we?" Even though everything had come together, there was still one thing that terrified Michael. "Bobby, I'm really sorry for not telling you about that case. I should have trusted you enough to tell you, I should have believed you'd understand. If you want me to head home and not come back to Betty's with you, let me know."

Michael held his breath, not wanting to hop in his car and drive to his cold loft apartment and sit alone on a night like tonight, but he would if it was what Bobby wanted.

"I wish you had told me, but there's no rulebook for things like this. Even if I was still mad at you I wouldn't be crazy enough to keep you from Jules tonight. I had one near-death experience already, I don't need another." Bobby slapped Michael on the shoulder. It wouldn't have been so long ago that an infraction like Michael's would have been enough for Bobby to lose all respect and cut all ties with him. The last few months had taught him the only thing that mattered was surrounding himself with people who cared—friends who cared about each other, about the world around them, and doing the right thing. No one was perfect, but people can be perfect for each other.

"You think she'd miss me if I wasn't there tonight? I thought maybe it was all this commotion and when this settled down she'd toss me aside," Michael said, relieved at the forgiveness and the invitation.

"She still might, but I doubt it. She really seems to like you. I know your reputation though. Don't confuse my ability to get over the withholding of a part of your past with how I might act if you hurt her. You won't survive that." Bobby raised his eyebrows and wiped any sign of humor away from his face, he was serious.

"I like her Bobby, she's special. I don't know where it's going to lead but I can assure you my reputation is grossly exaggerated, and I won't hurt her. I guess I should give you the same speech about Piper. I'm the closest thing she has to family as far as I can tell, and I don't want to see her hurt either." Michael pushed through the front door and stepped out onto the sidewalk pressing the button to unlock his car.

"I don't intend to hurt her. You might not be sure where things with you and Jules are going, but I have no doubts where Piper and I are headed. I love her," Bobby laughed, not able to contain his happiness. He had thought for years that he was in love with Jules, but now, in contrast to how he felt about Piper, he realized his affection for Jules was one of family.

"What? Man, that's fantastic," Michael shouted. "Just be careful, Piper is like a bird, you don't want to spook her. She's always ready to fly away. I think if anyone can figure out how to love her, it's you." Bobby put his hand out expecting Michael's firm grip but instead Michael pulled him in for a hug. "I'll meet you at Betty's."

CHAPTER 25

As Bobby drove his truck up Betty's long dirt driveway he tried to make this night about the victory they had all achieved. He tried to direct his mind to the joy and relief Jules would feel or the vindication Betty would experience. Instead all he could think about was Piper. She brought him to this place in his life, this crazy moment he never imagined he'd experience. He tried to force himself to think of Stan tonight, but instead the thought of holding Piper superseded everything.

Every lamp in the house was on, like a lighthouse calling the men home. Bobby waited a moment while Michael pulled in, and they exchanged a knowing look as they stepped onto the driveway. They knew they were about to be greeted with a whirlwind of questions and commotion. They both took a deep breath as the porch door swung open and Jules came sprinting out.

Bobby felt a pang of sadness when he saw only Jules running toward them. For the first time, she wasn't the person he was hoping to hold. Judging by the familiar but quick hug he shared with her, it was clear she was thinking the same thing. He had hoped to be embracing Piper by now, and she couldn't get to Michael fast enough.

Jules moved past Bobby and, staring up into Michaels green eyes, she asked, "It's good news, isn't it?" She held her hands over her heart, protecting it.

"It's great news," Michael said, laughing as Jules jumped up toward him, throwing her arms around his neck and her legs around his waist. Bobby was relieved to see Betty coming toward him, a good distraction from the passionate kissing he could see out of his peripheral vision.

Betty put her warm hands on Bobby's cold cheeks and smiled. "Well done, son. He'd be so very proud of you." She patted his cheeks and looked away before the tears gathering in her eyes spilled over. "For the love of Pete, Julie Marie, dismount that man before you hurt him. Act like you got raised right." Jules rolled her eyes and slid her way down Michael. "Plus I want to hug him," Betty said opening her arms wide to Michael.

Bobby could do nothing but stare at the screen door as Piper's shadow appeared behind it. He wondered why she wasn't racing down to him. Was she angry? Hurt?

"That girl is crazy about you, Bobby," Jules whispered from behind him. "She's a hard nut to crack, but she's got eyes for you something fierce. Whatever you do, don't blow it."

"I'm wondering if I already have," he said quietly, his heart aching for her to join them. Feeling out of options, he waved at her awkwardly, and could see the brightness of her smile against the darkness of the night. The weight on his chest finally floated away.

"Let's all get up in the house and have something warm to drink. I'm sure you've got lots to tell us, and it's colder than a cast iron commode out here." Betty shooed them all toward the porch as Piper opened the door. She patted Michael on the shoulder as he passed by and attempted to do the same to Bobby. He caught her hand before she could, and pulled her out onto the porch, letting the door shut noisily behind her. He didn't care if that drew the attention of everyone who was now inside—he wanted this moment.

"I've got a lot to say to you, Piper." He pushed the loose hair off her face, tucking it behind her ear, and lowered himself slightly to meet her eyes.

Piper was trying desperately to play it cool. "You've got an anxious crowd in there waiting for details. I'll be here when it's all over. We'll get a chance to talk." She hadn't expected how overwhelmed she'd be at the sight of Bobby, safe and standing in the doorway. If life up to this point had taught her anything it was that loving something too much was dangerous. Her feelings for Bobby scared her. The amount of willpower it took to suppress her innermost thoughts of what she wanted for her life was stifling.

"I think I can deal with that. We'll talk later. But we'll kiss right now." Bobby leaned in and kissed Piper with such urgency that she almost stepped backward. It only took a second for the sweet taste of his lips and the smell of his clean skin to make her fall toward him. His cold hand running over her cheek and through her hair sent chills through her whole body.

As he let her go he knew it may not be easy to love Piper, or to help her to let go of her past and believe in him, but it would be worth it.

Bobby heard Betty clearing her throat, and though his eyes were locked on Piper's he knew they had an audience.

"I'm happier than a puppy with two tails that y'all are getting on so well, but I've been wearing a hole in the floor pacing and waiting. There'll be plenty of time for pawing at each other later." Betty took the liberty of opening the screen door and waving them both in.

The group gathered in the familiar sitting room, and Bobby began to tell Betty and Jules the details of what had transpired. Both sat with eyes wide and occasionally cursing at the realization of who was involved. Piper was pleased as she heard him recount the details of the events between Judge Rosenthal and Christian Donavan. She was so relieved to hear that not only would they see justice served, but they would be safe from any retaliation as well. When Bobby finally finished, he asked if they had any questions for him.

"So they won't actually get charged with Daddy's murder? They're going to jail and getting punished, but no one will ever know they killed him?" Jules didn't want to sound ungrateful for all that had happened, for the risks that everyone had taken, but she wanted her father's story told.

Michael felt the need to step in and answer. "No, I don't think they'll be able to charge them with it, but we won't know until more of this gets sorted out. I know it's disappointing, but I can assure you that I'll follow it closely, and if there is any opportunity to do so, we'll pursue it."

"I'll tell you what," Betty said, sitting up straighter in her chair, "the best thing you've ever done is not tell me about any of this until it was over. I'd've cut that judge's throat and let him bleed all over his runny eggs without a second thought about spending my life in jail. I know y'all took some big risks, and I want you to know I'm eternally grateful. I can't tell you what knowing the truth has done for me. It's a debt I'll never be able to repay." Betty wiped tears from her cheeks.

"Well, I'll take my payment in pot roast," said Michael, trying to lighten the mood. "Or fried chicken. Really, I'm pretty flexible."

"I'll put a big meal out for breakfast tomorrow. You kids are all staying over, aren't you?" Betty asked, looking hopeful for the company.

"Of course," said Bobby, ignoring the urge to grab Piper by the hand and drive her somewhere, anywhere they could be alone. "Judge Rosenthal assured us all this would be the headline story tomorrow, so we should all be together to watch it."

Betty nodded, looking exhausted. "I'm turning in. My heart is tired. You kids stay up and help yourselves to anything in the kitchen. I'll see y'all in the morning." Betty went around and kissed each of them on the forehead then slowly dragged her tired body upstairs.

"We've got to go celebrate," Jules said in an excited whisper. "Let's go out for a drink and dancing. I can't sit in this house all night, I'll go mad." She was standing now and practically jumping out of her skin.

"I think I'll hang back here. My adrenaline has been on overdrive, and I need to unwind for a little bit. You and Michael should go," Bobby said, stretching as if he were completely exhausted, even though he had never felt so awake.

"Come on, Michael, let's go out. I'm so excited. I want to have some drinks and laugh and have a good time," Jules said, pulling Michael up by his arms.

They all moved to the porch as Michael and Jules pulled on their coats to leave. They couldn't keep their hands off each other, and every other sentence was punctuated by a kiss and a smile. As they stepped off the porch, Michael turned back toward Piper who hadn't said more than a handful of words since they had returned. "You good?" he asked, winking at her, knowing that maybe he should stay, but he really didn't want to.

She nodded yes and waved them off. She couldn't fight the feelings that had followed her throughout her life, the melancholy in the face of everyone else's joy. She didn't know why she felt worse in this moment than she had through all the turmoil of the last few months.

As Michael's headlights disappeared from view, darkness fell back over the front yard. Bobby had begun loading wood into the firepit and searching around for the matches.

Piper sat on the familiar porch swing and pulled a blanket over her legs. She watched Bobby building a fire to keep her warm and realized that really was who he'd be to her. Maybe she didn't know how to keep herself cozy and balanced on the inside, but he would keep lighting her fires to make up for it.

He sat down beside her, reminding Piper of the first time they had sat there together. It was funny how wrong their perceptions of each other were then—how far from the truth. Now it was like they were sitting down together for the first time as they really were.

"I know that I might have spooked you earlier when I said I thought I love you. We haven't known each other long, and there has been so much going on you probably think I'm crazy. That's why I want to take it back," Bobby said, pulling the blanket up.

Piper didn't think she was ready to be loved, but that wasn't at all where she thought the conversation was going. "I understand," she said, trying to mask her shock.

"I was wrong when I said I think I love you. What I meant to say… what I *should* have said… is I *do* love you. There's no hesitation here. I know how I feel about you. I won't rush you or pressure you to be something you aren't or to feel something you don't, but I'm not foolish enough to lie to myself or to you. I didn't want to make some big proclamation tonight, but sitting out here with you right now, I'm having a hard time not blurting out some very corny stuff." Bobby reached over and laced his fingers with hers. "Will you sit and listen to me professing my love?"

"We've been through a lot, Bobby, and I'm sure emotions are running high for everyone. Part of me wants to get lost in your eyes and let you say sweet things to me all night, but a bigger part of me has no idea how to deal with all of that." Piper felt her anxiety rising. She'd prepared herself for all kinds of heartbreak in her life, all forms of disappointment, but falling in love was not something she'd readied herself for. "I have some fundamental flaws, Bobby. Like tonight when everyone was smiling and celebrating, that's not at all how I felt. These moments when most people are overjoyed, I'm completely out of sorts. I'm anxious and sick to my stomach, because for me these happy moments are fleeting. When I let myself indulge in the idea of something even remotely positive, reality comes flooding back in to knock me down. I'm not built to enjoy life; I'm built to endure it. I don't understand why you would love someone like that." Piper felt the tears as they moved down her cheeks, but she didn't care. She wasn't self-conscious or afraid to look weak. Bobby had seen more of her than anyone, and somehow he was still sitting here begging for the chance to love her.

"Piper there are so many things in this world to be afraid of. Don't let happiness be one of them. You don't understand why I would love you? I love you because you are tenacious in the face of reality. I love that you have no idea how incredible you are, because that means I get to be here when you finally figure it out. There's a good chance that one of these days you're going to wake up and see yourself the way I see you, and I can't wait to be a part of that. Whatever loving you brings my way, I'm ready for it." Bobby brushed the tears from her cheeks and pulled her into a powerful hug. She felt a little afraid of how tight it was, but when she let herself melt into him she realized this is what loving him would be like. Maybe she'd feel squeezed, maybe she'd worry about not getting enough air, but it was the warmest, safest place she'd ever been and she didn't want him to ever let go.

"You must be pretty jealous of Michael and Jules then, aren't you?" Piper settled her herself onto his chest and he rested his chin gently on the top of her head. She hadn't really cuddled much before, but now she sure understood why people did it.

"Why in the world would I be jealous of the two of them? I'm glad they are hitting it off, but I don't feel the least bit of envy." Bobby gazed off into the fire. He knew Piper didn't profess her love in deep terms of endearment, but she had let him hold her, and he took that as a small pledge of love for now.

"Hitting it off? Where do you think they're going? I imagine they went to have a few drinks, and soon they'll be having shameless passionate sex back at his place. And you are sitting on a porch, watching a fire, holding my hand. It doesn't seem like you planned this out quite right." Piper smiled up at him and waited for another kiss, which he gladly gave.

"I wouldn't want to be anywhere else right now. When I make love to you, I don't want to think about this day and everything that happened. I don't want to share the day we make love with anything else. I don't want to be clouded by adrenaline or cramped up in the cab of my truck like a couple of high school kids. Tonight is about holding you and kissing you and showing you that it's safe to celebrate. I've got the rest of my life to love you. We'll have our moment, and it will be incredible." Bobby squeezed Piper tighter, and while he really did mean what he was saying, there was part of him that wanted to ignore his own advice and find a quiet place to show her how he felt.

"Doesn't Betty have a bottle of strawberry moonshine up in her pantry?" Piper asked, sitting up and smiling mischievously. "She did say we could help ourselves to whatever we wanted, right?" She hopped up and tiptoed her way into the kitchen, lifting herself onto the counter and pulling down the mason jar of moonshine Betty had shown her months earlier. She decided to forgo the glasses and take turns with Bobby, sipping the sweet and potent concoction until she had no choice but to be content.

CHAPTER 26

Sometime during the night the fire burned down, but the moonshine had kept them warm. Bobby and Piper had fallen asleep, awkwardly curled up on the porch swing, completely tangled in each other.

Bobby was startled awake by the sound of an approaching car, and he rubbed the sleep from his eyes. The engine sounded rougher than Michael's car, and the shape of the headlights cutting through the night were unfamiliar. His job required him to take notice of these types of things. The lights were square, the car boxy, and there was a dim light on top of it. In his sleepy stupor, it didn't make any sense.

"Wake up, Piper," he said, shaking her gently. She heard the concern in his voice and immediately shot up, regretting the combination of the moonshine and the sudden movement. "There's a strange car pulling in. I think you should head in the house." Bobby remembered his service weapon was hanging by his coat just inside the door.

"It's a cab," Piper said, squinting to see who its passenger might be. "I can see the light on top of it." Piper had seen more cabs in her lifetime than the average person. She recognized it in an instant.

As Bobby stood, he pulled Piper up and behind him and inched slowly for the door. He planned to quickly push Piper into the house and grab his gun. But before he could pull the screen door open he heard the familiar bubbly laugh of Jules as she spilled out of the cab, losing her balance and rolling into the dirt. Michael was a step behind, laughing too hard to help her up. He handed the fare to the driver who abruptly backed out of the long driveway. As the headlights disappeared, Bobby headed down the porch steps to retrieve the two drunken idiots before they hurt themselves.

"Really?" Bobby asked, looking down at Jules, who still couldn't contain her laughter or regain her footing. "I guess I should be glad you guys took a cab."

"Well we know the cops around here are real tight-asses. We didn't want to take any chances," Michael said as he pulled Jules up to a standing position. "Help me get her in the house," he muttered, half stumbling over his own feet. Bobby took notice of the buttons on Michael's shirt that were misaligned, clearly fastened hastily. He turned to look back at Piper who was probably right about how Michael and Jules had spent their night of celebration, but Bobby still had no regrets.

"You're on your own buddy. I've done my share of holding that big mop of red hair while she hugs the toilet. The only help I'll give you is a little advice. When she says she's feeling better and she's ready to go to bed, she's wrong. Toss a pillow in the bathroom for her or you'll be changing sheets and scrubbing carpets the rest of the night." Bobby turned on his heels and headed back to the porch and rejoined Piper who had settled back on the swing. She smirked at him and found her warm, comfortable spot and pressed up against him.

They slept on and off for the next couple of hours until they heard the recognizable sounds of Betty preparing a meal in the kitchen. Her steady humming and the clanking of dishes were soon followed by the most comforting smells of cinnamon and bacon.

Bobby stood and stretched. His arm that had been propping up Piper's head for hours was completely numb, but it was absolutely worth it. He pulled the reluctant Piper to her feet and kissed her face gently. "Let's go watch the news," he said with a smile.

Betty greeted them in the kitchen and said, "Good Morning. I'm sure hoping you are in better shape than the two lushes asleep on my bathroom floor. I've got breakfast almost ready. Bobby, go wake them for me, and Piper, turn on the television there." Betty looked noticeably relieved this morning. Piper knew it wasn't actually possible for her to have slept off a few worry lines, but Betty certainly looked more at peace.

As the whole group settled into the kitchen around the table, Betty spun the small television to face them. "Don't be making a mess, either. My broom has never been as busy as it has since you kids moved in," she said, handing them each a napkin.

"Don't look at me," Michael said defensively. "I'm not a slob, it's these guys." He pointed to each of them, placing the blame.

Betty wasn't buying it. She raised a skeptical brow and shook her head. "I suppose it's someone else dropping the food you eat, under the chair you sit in. I was born at night, but not last night, my boy."

He waved his hand at her playfully. It certainly wouldn't be an issue today. Jules and Michael could hardly glance over at the large stack of pancakes and bacon, as they recovered from their celebration last night.

Betty hushed them all, quieting their complaining and jokes. She loved the noise that surrounded her table this morning, but the news was about to start, and she didn't want to miss a moment of it.

"It's a new day here in Edenville and we're happy to have you with us this morning," the white-haired anchorman said. Bobby had never been so happy to see his silly combed-over hair and busy, colorful tie. The man was goofy, but he had been the anchor on the local news program since Bobby had moved here. It was easy to take him for granted, but today, on a day when they anxiously awaited the news, it felt comforting that it would be coming from a familiar face. "We've got a breaking story that you'll hear exclusively here at WNC4. Late last night Judge Randall Lions was arrested on charges of sexual crimes against children, judicial misconduct, and a host of other crimes that we're told are still being assessed. Judge Lions has been presiding over cases in Edenville for over twenty years. He is the head of a popular non-profit organization that helps children of currently incarcerated parents gain an appreciation for the justice system. Our sources tell us that this charity, Legal Buddies, was in some way associated with the charges brought forth this morning. Judge Lions and his office could not be reached for comment, but we did hear from Judge Samantha Rosenthal who is helping spearhead the investigation. Here is a clip from our interview with her." The screen switched over to Judge Rosenthal sitting in front of a large microphone.

"Lord Acton, a historian and moralist, said, 'Power tends to corrupt, and absolute power corrupts absolutely.' There are checks and balances in our society for a reason. This corruption has gone on far too long, and I will personally work to ensure that everyone involved is held accountable. The positive news is this case has an unprecedented amount of evidence and a strong corroborating witness. This will be tried in a court of law, but I am incredibly confident that we have taken a very corrupt and perfidious man off the bench, and, more importantly, off the streets of Edenville." At the end of her statement she looked directly into the camera and nodded her head, almost like a thank you. Michael smiled, feeling like in part it was meant for him.

The show cut back to the quirky anchor. "We thank Judge Rosenthal for making time to talk to us. In other news, a long-time police officer of Edenville, Officer Aaron Rylie, was found dead in his home this morning of an apparent self-inflicted gunshot wound. We have not been able to confirm yet if the events surrounding the arrest of Judge Lions and the alleged suicide of Officer Rylie are in any way linked. We'll continue to investigate this rapidly unfolding story, and, as always, keep you informed." The show broke to commercial, and Bobby leaned across and turned the television off as an uncomfortable silence filled the room.

They had expected to be whooping and hollering at the headline story this morning, but the news about Rylie had thrown them all into a tailspin. Bobby thought perhaps he should speak, but couldn't find any words. Luckily Michael was able to weigh in.

"He had the same opportunity as anyone to be tried and plead his case in court. He made the choice to kill himself. That isn't on any of us." He looked around the room trying to read everyone's expression, but just found darting eyes and uncomfortable fidgeting, until he glanced at Betty.

She had her chin up and a look of defiance on her face. "That's no skin off my back, I say let God sort it all out." She stood up and dropped her napkin onto her plate. "The sun is just starting to come up; we should all go out and enjoy it. It's going to be a beautiful day."

No one had finished eating, nor did they really feel like filing outside to watch the sun come up, but there were so few things they wouldn't do for Betty.

And as usual, Betty's idea was right on. The sunrise was the perfect way to start this day fresh. Watching the streams of light cut through the trees that lined the front yard was therapeutic. The clouds were bright red—it looked as though someone had set fire to them.

Jules sidled up to Michael who was standing against the porch railing, and he wrapped his arm around her. Betty hummed quietly on the squeaky wooden rocker. Bobby and Piper were right back where they had just left, cuddled comfortably on the porch swing.

Jules rested her tired head on Michael's chest and took in the beauty of the morning sky. "It's so colorful, but you know what they say, red sky at morning, sailor take warning. I bet there will be a fierce storm tonight."

"Not always," Bobby said, looking down into Piper's sweet face, "sometimes a magnificent sunrise is just that. You don't always have to be waiting for the storm; you can just enjoy the colors."

Piper got the message, and she didn't think she'd ever grow tired of hearing it. If Bobby wanted to be the man who reminded her it was safe to enjoy the moment, then she'd let him. She smiled up at him seductively as he slipped his hand under the back of her shirt and let his fingers dip slightly under the top of her jeans. Everyone else seemed to be so mesmerized by the beautiful morning sky that Bobby felt perfectly comfortable leaning in toward Piper and nibbling her ear. They had both been patient and responsible. They had committed themselves to following through on what they had started, and now it was done. The only thing left to do was give in to their desires.

Piper's body was craving more of him. If the fire she felt when they kissed was any indication of what making love to him would be like, she wasn't sure she'd survive. Then again, it wouldn't be a bad way to go. She pulled away from him as she saw Jules turning back toward them, grinning like a school girl with a secret.

"I'm exhausted," Bobby said, hopping out of the chair like he'd just been stuck with a needle in the backside. "I think I'm going to head home. Piper, I'll give you a ride."

It didn't seem possible, but Jules's grin grew even larger. "Yes

Piper, enjoy the ride Bobby is about to give you. Don't forget to buckle up." She and Michael leaned into each other, giggling.

Piper's face was crimson with embarrassment as Bobby pulled her from the swing to her feet. He wrapped his arms around her for a hug and whispered through her hair, "I might even let you drive."

She shook him off and dug her elbow into his side, pretending to be annoyed. In reality she was desperate to get somewhere alone with Bobby. She wanted to be on him, under him, she wanted him in a way she had never imagined possible.

Bobby put his arm over her shoulder, and they were about to head into the house to get their things when Bobby's ringing cell phone drew everyone's attention. It was early for a phone call, especially since everyone he normally talked to was standing there with him.

"Good morning Captain Baines," Bobby said, trying to keep his cool even though his instincts were telling him something might be wrong. At first Piper thought little of the call until she saw the blood drain from Bobby's face as he dropped his voice lower and stepped into the house and out of earshot.

A knot formed in Piper's stomach, and judging by the worried looks passing between all of them, she wasn't alone. Perhaps something had already gone wrong with the judge's case. What if Christian and his family hadn't made it safely out of town yet? Maybe Judge Rosenthal's promise of anonymity for the group hadn't panned out.

Bobby was pulling on his duty belt as he stepped back onto the porch. He could feel the pressure of nervous stares weighing down on him. They all had reason to worry, but only one of them, beside himself, would know why.

"A girl was attacked on campus early this morning. Due to everything going on with the judge and the scene at Rylie's house, they need all available hands on deck to secure the evidence at the college." Bobby pulled on his coat and tried to think quickly about how to proceed. How, he wondered, could he tell them all the truth yet not break the trust Piper had placed in him?

"Is the girl going to be all right?" Jules asked, leaning into Michael. All this drama was making her weary. Hopefully this story would have a happy ending.

"She was beaten badly and is in critical condition. Betty, it's going to be a long day, do you have anything I can take with me to eat?" Betty shot up and hustled into the house, happy to oblige. "And Jules, I left my shaving kit up in the bathroom – can you grab it for me and bring it down? I can't go to work looking like this. I'll have to hit the precinct first." Jules hurried into the house to gather Bobby's forgotten things. She hadn't always been so accommodating, but Bobby could feel the direction of their relationship finally changing for the better. He owed it all to Piper.

The moment they were gone, Bobby spun toward Piper and crouched down in front of her. "The girl who was attacked this morning," he started in a no-nonsense tone, "had the number twenty-three carved into her thigh. I'm going down there to get more information, but this can't be a coincidence."

Piper brought her hands up, covering her mouth as she gasped. Her eyes immediately filled with tears and her body started to tremble. Her worst nightmare was becoming a reality – her father was back for her. Bobby leaned in and squeezed her tightly. As he pulled away, he whispered to her, "you're not alone anymore, Piper. We're in this together."

"Why the number twenty-three?" Piper asked, clinging to Bobby's arm, not ready for him to let go. "It doesn't make sense. Delanie was his twenty-fourth victim. If it really is him, why use the number twenty-three again? It has to be a copy-cat. It can't be him." Piper knew she sounded manic, she could hear her voice rattling with fear. She needed Bobby to look her in the eye and tell her it wasn't her father. She needed him to tell her she was right, that it didn't make sense and there had to be some other explanation.

Instead, he was already connecting the dots in his mind. "It could be, but if he knows you're alive now, if he's found you, then he's likely sending you a message. When he killed Delanie, he thought you were dead. I'd imagine he'll want to try to draw you out and finish what he started. I don't have all the answers yet, but that's what my gut is telling me."

He hated to loosen his grip on her while she was still shaking, but time was of the essence. "Michael, we have a little trouble." Bobby couldn't find the right words, and he knew he didn't have the time to explain, but luckily he didn't need to. He and Michael had learned to trust each other over the last few weeks and along with that came the ability to read between the lines. "The attack at the school hits close to home for Piper. It might be nothing, but we can't take that chance. I need the girls to go to your house. I know I've already asked so much of you, but I swear, once my shift ends at nine, you're off the hook."

"I'm not looking to get off the hook here," Michael said in a low voice, glancing over Bobby's shoulder at Piper who was clearly shaken. "I've got your back, man, we'll talk more tonight. Until then I won't let any of them out of my sight."

Jules and Betty rejoined them on the porch, both obediently holding the items Bobby had requested. Piper had managed to compose herself and stood to wave Bobby off. Michael read this as a sign that Piper was not about to make her concerns about the attack public knowledge.

As Bobby hopped down the porch stairs, he looked back over his shoulder at Piper. He was fairly certain the brief moment of calm they had all just experienced was about to be snuffed out. Odds were that Piper's father had found her, and everything they had hoped to start would once again have to wait. They were about to come face to face with the darkest parts of Piper's past, but they were going to do it together.

The End

Including Chasing Justice(Book 1 in the Piper Anderson series), Danielle Stewart has 7 free books to kick off a new series. Start one for free today with any of these books below:

Chasing Justice
Flowers in the Snow
Three Seconds To Rush
Hearts of Clover
Facing Home
The Goodbye Storm
Fierce Love

EXCERPT FROM BOOK 2, CUTTING TIES

Bobby:

When I became a police officer I swore an oath. "On my honor, I, Robert Murphy Wright, will never betray my badge, my integrity, my character, or the public trust. I will always have the courage to hold myself and others accountable for our actions. I will uphold the constitution, my community, and the agency I serve. So help me God." As I run that last phrase through my mind, I realize it has morphed from an affirmation to a plea. *Help me, God.*

I pledged to tell the truth, to execute the law, because the law is the only thing that separates us from living in a state of anarchy. We are not meant to be judge, jury, and executioner. Falling in love was not supposed to challenge that. They were mutually exclusive ideas. You should be able to love someone and honor your responsibilities at the same time. That is, unless the person you love has been failed by the system so many times she can't trust it. If I'm constantly searching for ways to stand behind the words I swore that day, and she is forever looking for channels that undermine them—can we truly find happiness together?

Meeting Piper, the daughter of a serial murderer, was like winning the worst kind of lottery. No matter how much I try to rationalize it, try to convince myself loving her is dangerous, I can't stop. I watch her battle herself, wondering if the wickedest parts of him are somehow a part of her. She rubs her hand over that scar he left on her leg, the number twenty-three carved so precisely, and I know she fractures a little more. Something broke me the same way it broke her, we just pieced ourselves back together differently.

Witness protection was supposed to be the answer for her. Edenville was supposed to be her fresh start. Watching her accept the unreserved affection of my friends, Betty and Jules, gave me a hope that maybe she could find peace. Maybe we could find a way to love each other.

But I didn't plan for the fact that her past wasn't quite as buried as she hoped. When I got the call that a girl on campus had been attacked, the number twenty-three carved into her leg, I knew the trajectory of our lives was about to shift. But something doesn't fit. Too many facts don't align with the normal methods of her father, the Railway Killer. Has he found her or is someone emulating his evil? Why use the same number again? Especially considering Piper was not his last victim. Her mother was number twenty-two, and the unfortunate girl killed after Piper's attack was twenty-four. This discrepancy is the small glimmer of hope I'm clinging to.

Yes, I fell in love with a fragmented and damaged girl, but she isn't the only one with a dark past. I have my own secrets, my own history. I begged and fought to know hers with no intention of ever revealing my own. Not to her, not to anyone. With every second that ticks by, every inch closer we get to her past, I'm afraid we'll end up unearthing my own. Life isn't supposed to be this hard, love isn't meant to be this complicated. So why don't I walk away? Those eyes. Those big, brown, old-soul eyes of hers just keep calling out to me. One run of my fingers through her silky, dark hair, one brush of my lips on her skin, and I get dangerously distracted from what I believe.

EXCERPT FROM BOOK 2, CUTTING TIES - CHAPTER ONE

"I heard it was a crazy scene over at the university. Did you get a peek at that girl's leg? Creepy," Officer Lindsey LaVoie said as she squatted down next to Bobby and laced her boots. He still hadn't gotten used to seeing her in the precinct locker room. It was pretty clear none of the male officers had. Prior to her being allowed in there, many of them had often strutted around naked with their chests puffed out proudly. Now they scurried from the shower to the stalls wrapped in robes or towels. Bobby actually appreciated the change. As far as he was concerned no one should have to look at that many hairy asses before breakfast.

It had been a long battle, Lindsey against the whole department, but she'd finally won. All it took was threats of legal action. Bobby could understand. She just wanted to be treated as an equal, like anyone else on the force. But that was still a far cry from reality. She'd been granted the right to ready herself in the locker room, but her peers found other ways of punishing her for not being a man. They responded just a little slower than normal when she radioed for back up. Partner assignments were like a revolving door after each officer inevitably complained to the captain. Bobby knew when it was his turn to partner with her he'd make it work. Lindsey was as effective as any of the officers he'd worked with, and he trusted she always had his back. They'd formed a casual friendship primarily built on the fact that he didn't treat her like garbage—a low standard but a welcomed change for her.

He watched as she pulled her blond hair into a tight bun with quick precision. It was a good representation of her overall performance on the force. She was incredibly efficient, quick, and reliable. Bobby thought she had a nice face, but her body was built stronger than he preferred. She had a sturdy frame that she worked tirelessly to keep solid and competitive. He had made a point to refrain from deciding if she was attractive or not. To him she was a colleague, and just like Bill Thomly with the buckteeth or Micah Chilling with the handlebar mustache, the way she looked didn't determine how she did her job. The problem was part of him kept wishing he were attracted to her. Wouldn't it be easier to love someone like Lindsey? Knowing that you both believed in doing things the right way, knowing you'd both sworn the same oath. He didn't want to stop loving Piper, his feelings for her were stronger than anything he'd ever felt. The spark when he touched her and the chemistry and bond between them was something he'd waited for his whole life. But as he watched Lindsey he let the stray corners of his mind admit that loving her would be easier, and probably much smarter.

"I didn't see the cut on her leg, but I heard the girl was a wreck," Bobby replied, fighting off his inner voice and reminding himself it was Piper he'd been thinking about all day. She was the one he was counting the minutes until he could hold.

"What do you think? An angry ex-boyfriend or something? It seems kind of sadistic." It wasn't uncommon for Lindsey and Bobby to chat about a crime that had occurred, to brainstorm, but this was different. He did have an idea who it was and why it happened, but he couldn't bring himself to say it.

It had been a long shift, and as late afternoon set in he was ready to get out of there. "I've got to head out. If you hear anything will you give my cell a call? I'd like to stay up to date on it." Bobby slapped her on the shoulder like he would any other officer, but he awkwardly pulled his hand away slowly. Nope, that didn't feel right. Was that too hard, he wondered? Did I make her feel uncomfortable? She read his face and laughed.

"Come on, Bobby, I'm not made of porcelain. Get over yourself." She punched his shoulder and he stumbled back with the force. No, he thought, she was certainly not fragile. "I'll call you if I hear anything," she chuckled. "Have a good one."

Piper hadn't slept in far too long. After hearing about the campus attack that was eerily similar to the attacks her father had committed, Bobby had insisted Piper, Betty, and Jules spend the day at Michael's house. She wanted to say they didn't need a babysitter, but having Michael around did put her mind at ease. They'd be safer there, and though she had faced plenty of danger in her life, this felt different. Piper kept fighting the gnawing feeling that once again she'd roped innocent people into her mess of a life. Betty and Jules had welcomed Piper into their lives so willingly, and all she'd done so far was muddy it up. Michael, the lawyer she suckered into helping take down Judge Lions, kept getting pulled further into her wake of troubles. At some point she expected them all to realize loving her was more trouble than it was worth, and that scared her.

Piper spent the day counting the minutes until Bobby's shift would be over and he could tell her what he'd found out about the campus assault. Did they know who did it? Was it her father? She had wanted to fight sleep and stare out the window until she saw him pulling up, but her eyes grew heavy as lead, her head too weary to hold up. She finally took Michael up on his offer to crash in his bed. It took only a minute before she fell into a fitful sleep.

She'd been haunted by nightmares most of her life, but since she'd moved to Edenville, they'd subsided. With the possibility of her father finding her, that dry spell seemed to be over. Her mind clouded over with a familiar scene. This was a nightmare she'd had before. It wasn't soft around the edges like a dream sequence in a movie. It was sharp, and the way it took her senses hostage made her feel like the prisoner. She couldn't just see the scene, she could smell her father's musk, feel the wobble in her chair. Her sleeping body was helpless now as it overtook her mind.

"This tastes like shit! I swear to God, Coco, you can't cook a meal to save your life. This isn't what I wanted!" her father shouted across their lopsided thrift store kitchen table.

Piper, a smaller version of herself in this dream world, shrank down into her seat. Her father's raised, sharp voice had that effect on her. She was twelve years old. Her father had insisted they sit down for Christmas dinner, something they had never done before. The entire holiday season really meant nothing to her family. There were never presents, special traditions, or family gatherings. The only thing Christmas brought was a more glaring contrast between them and happy families. It was the perfect time of year to realize how little you had.

Her father spoke again, and now he was manic, desperately trying to recreate a scene he'd seen on television. He'd wanted them all to play a part, and so far it wasn't going according to plan. He was spiraling out of control. He'd wanted the house decorated, but her mother couldn't come down from her high long enough to hang the stockings properly. He'd wanted a nice meal, a true holiday dinner, but cooking was something her mother was not capable of. Everything was burnt, or soggy, or cold.

"I told you I wanted this to be like the movie," he hissed, beating his hand on the table. Piper knew what came next. Her father's emotional escalation was the same almost every time he beat them. First he'd bang

his fist on a table, a wall, a car. Then he'd throw something. This particular time it was a plateful of freezing-cold instant mashed potatoes. The way they landed with a squishy thud on the floor almost caused Piper to laugh, but she knew it would enrage her father more. Finally, he would toss a few more inanimate objects before moving on to her mother.

It was by no means a one-sided fight. Her mother would defend herself, sometimes even initiate the violence. It was a relationship Piper never understood. They were two toxic people who brought out the worst in each other, but just couldn't bear to be apart. When one escalated, or spun out of control it seemed to fan the fire in the other.

There were days Piper could slip away, be forgotten, and escape the wrath. This was not one of those days. Her father's rage was bubbling over as the Christmas scene he had tried to orchestrate fell miles short of his expectation. Now they would pay the price.

Piper shot up in bed, sweating and panting. She heard her own voice whimpering just as she had that day, the Christmas that never was. She looked around the room, trying to get her bearings. Michael's bedroom, she reminded herself. Safe.

She thought back through the dream for a moment, reliving it through the eyes of her younger self, but now processing it as an adult. Piper hadn't known her mother's real name wasn't Coco until she was nineteen years old. She watched her mother fill out a job application and scribble down the name, Caroline Murphy. She often wanted to ask her mother where the nickname came from, how long she had been called Coco, but she never found the right moment. That could sum up much of her relationship with her mother, never quite the right moment to talk, to understand each other, to say the words that sat heavily on their minds.

"You good?" she heard Michael ask, his large frame leaning in the doorway. He had heard her struggling and saw her awaken startled and upset. She drew in a deep, centering breath and nodded her head. Michael was a very calming presence in her life now, and she felt better just seeing him. His sandy blond hair had gotten long in the last few weeks, and he was in need of some gel and a comb. But Michael was one of those men who would have to try really hard not to be attractive. Even as he lost focus on his grooming during this chaotic time, he still looked better than most men who'd put hours of work into their appearance. You couldn't do much to dim the brightness of his emerald eyes or take away from the strength of his boxy, distinguished jaw. He belonged on the cover of a romance novel, his muscular arms lifting the luscious blonde woman with a heaving bosom. His shirt torn open, the skin of his perfectly smooth chest would be a glowing bronze. Yes, Piper thought to herself, if Michael's career as a lawyer was ever to fall apart, he could certainly make some money in other ways.

It took another few minutes after Michael returned to his living room for Piper to gather herself. She smoothed her wild dark hair down and rubbed the rest of the sleep out of her eyes. She glanced over at Michael's sleek alarm clock and realized time had gotten away from her. She leaped from the bed and headed through the apartment toward the window. Without a word, she skipped right by Betty and Jules who were sipping tea around Michael's glass dining room table. Bobby should be here, she thought. He should know what's going on by now. As she peeked out the window, she saw his red pickup pulling in. She ran down the old industrial stairs of Michael's apartment building and burst through the heavy rusted door to greet him.

She felt the knot in her stomach tighten as she read Bobby's grim expression. He stepped out of his truck with heavy shoulders. His dark brown eyes were filled with worry and his jaw was clenched. She couldn't imagine the news would be good, not with that look on his face.

"What did you find out?" she asked, her voice shaking with emotion. The cold air sent a shiver through her. Her thin cotton shirt was no match for the late fall air.

He walked hesitantly toward her, hating to see her sad, wanting to save and warm her all at once. "It's still early in the investigation. The girl is in stable condition. She told detectives she was attacked from behind, and no other witnesses have come forward. It's too soon to know, really. The forensics team is just starting to go over the evidence now. I don't know much more than I did when I left this morning." Bobby opened his arms and she fell wearily into them, letting the muscles of his biceps tighten and curl around her. They were both so tired, physically and emotionally.

She reached up and ran her hand through his short dark hair, and down his neck. It was funny to her that even though they hadn't loved each other long, she seemed to have figured out small yet important things about him. When he was stressed out he stopped shaving, as if the energy to slide the razor down his cheek was too much for him. Or maybe the time spent looking in the mirror made his mind turn over and twist in ways he didn't like. It seemed to change the whole dynamic of his face, but the beginnings of a beard looked good on him. She loved the scratchy sensation it gave against the softness of her palm.

Even in the midst of all this chaos she had to fight the urge to get lost in a passionate moment with him. His touch made this entire thing feel like a distant worry rather than the looming danger it truly was.

"I guess we wait and see what they come up with," Piper murmured, talking into his shoulder as she squeezed him tighter, feeling safe in his arms.

"I think we need to go down to the precinct and tell them what we know. They haven't tied this back to your father at all. No one is even considering the fact that it might be bigger than just some campus crime. It's important they know you're here." Bobby rested his chin on Piper's head and closed his eyes. He knew she wouldn't want to rehash her history, but in his heart he assumed she'd do what was right, even if she did it reluctantly.

"No," she said sharply as she pulled away from him. His chin fell suddenly, sending his teeth into his tongue. It was equally as jarring to Piper. Leaving his arms felt like the shock of a windy day—your hat blowing off your head before you could even raise your arms to try to stop it. She was the one backing up, but it still felt like he was the one being pulled away.

"We have no idea if this is my father or not. Someone could have easily searched the Internet for serial killers and decided they wanted to play lunatic for the day. I'm not going to go shout from the rooftops that I'm here in Edenville only to find out this had nothing to do with me."

Bobby was stunned by her steely tone and met her frustration with his own. "I'm not asking you to go on the ten o'clock news. I'm asking you to come down and talk to the captain. Tell him what you know, who you are. You have a responsibility here."

"Do you think I went on the ten o'clock news back in New York? No. But somehow information was leaked. My father found out I survived and now here I am. If this attack wasn't my father, if it was someone else, I can kiss Edenville goodbye. You can kiss me goodbye. All I have is this new identity. Please don't take it from me. I can't start over again." She stared up at him, letting her eyes speak.

She had powerful eyes that seemed to have the ability to express things that words couldn't. They were the eyes of a broken-hearted person, and anyone with an ounce of empathy couldn't resist their pull. She didn't flash them often, she never wanted them to become too familiar or to lose their effect, but right now they were necessary. She could tell her stare was creating small fractures in the shield Bobby had placed between them, but it had yet to shatter.

"I'm a police officer, Piper. You can't ask me to withhold information about an active case. There's a massive internal investigation going on right now. People are being linked to Judge Lions, and everyone is on edge. Edenville has been completely turned on its head, and we need to be as forthcoming as possible with any information we have. Heads are rolling, jobs are being lost, and people are going to jail. We need to stay on the right side of this. I know when you sat in your living room and told me who you really were you didn't imagine it would ever come to this. You told me because you love me, and now I'm asking you to trust me."

"Bobby, honestly, what's your hang up? You love me. That should come first. I get the good guy thing. I even understand the sense of duty, but does that really trump how you feel about me?" Piper didn't want to appear hurt, but she couldn't understand why he towed this line with so much damn conviction. What was really keeping him from putting her first?

He wanted to shout that she *didn't* understand, that maybe she never would. His own history had created that black and white definition of the world. Just as hers had made her jaded and skeptical, his past had made him this way. All he had to do was keep walking the straight and narrow to keep his demons stuffed away. The rules were the rules for a reason, and as long as he followed them he'd never find himself back in that terrible place he'd escaped. He was convinced Piper didn't need to know why he was so inflexible and law-abiding. She just needed to know and accept that he was.

When he didn't answer she continued her plea. "All I'm asking is for you to let the investigation play out for a couple of days. Let the forensic team do its job." She moved back toward him and wrapped her arms around his waist, begging him again with her eyes. "Please, promise me you'll give it a couple of days."

Bobby couldn't do that. The conflict raging inside his body kept his mouth from agreeing to her terms. He wouldn't make that promise. It was far too similar to one he'd made before, one that ended so badly he still couldn't forgive himself. "And what about everyone upstairs?" he asked as he deflected her request. "Do you plan to keep them cut out of all this? Do you want to go back to hiding everything about yourself from people who care about you?"

Piper assumed she'd need to make some kind of concession. She was asking a lot of Bobby, likely too much. It was only fair to expect she would have to give something in return. "I'm going to tell them the truth. I trust them, and I know they care about me. They deserve to know who I am." She stood on her tiptoes and held Bobby's face in her hands. "I'm sorry I'm not normal. I hate that I come with all this baggage. Please, stand by me on this."

He leaned down and kissed her, instantly calming every jagged nerve and untying all the knots in her stomach. The effect on Bobby was slightly different. The kiss didn't calm him, it scared him. Loving her scared him. She made him walk a fine line he'd always avoided. He was afraid loving her would be his undoing.

Their bodies however didn't seemed to be as conflicted as their minds. They leaned into each other, Bobby's hand grasping firmly to Piper's lower back and pulling her in tighter. There were some things that weren't impacted by the reality of a situation, and their physical attraction hadn't tapered off at all. On the contrary, the tension between their bodies, the desperate hunger to finally come together, had grown to an almost unmanageable level. She let her body grind slightly into his and a low moan passed from his mouth to hers. The passing of a rumbling motorcycle broke them from each other, reminding them that no matter how badly they wanted to give in to their desires, once again they would have to wait. Understanding the attack today would need to come first. Just like they had put the task of taking down the judge before their passion. It felt like the right thing to do at the time, but now as their bodies ached for each other and more problems stood in their way, they were both wondering if waiting had been the right choice.

Continue reading Book 2: Cutting Ties

ALSO BY DANIELLE STEWART

Piper Anderson Series:

Book 1: Chasing Justice

Book 2: Cutting Ties

Book 3: Changing Fate

Book 4: Finding Freedom

Book 5: Settling Scores

Book 6: Battling Destiny

Book 7: Unearthing Truth

Book 8: Defending Innocence (Pre-Order)

Piper Anderson Bonus Material:

Chris & Sydney Collection – Choosing Christmas & Saving Love

Betty's Journal - Bonus Material (suggested to be read after Book 4 to avoid spoilers)

Edenville Series – A Piper Anderson Spin Off:

Book 1: Flowers in the Snow

Book 2: Kiss in the Wind

Book 3: Stars in a Bottle

Book 4: Fire in the Heart

Piper Anderson Legacy Mystery Series:

Book 1: Three Seconds To Rush

Book 2: Just for a Heartbeat

Book 3: Not Just an Echo

The Clover Series:

Hearts of Clover - Novella & Book 2: (Half My Heart & Change My Heart)

Book 3: All My Heart

Over the Edge Series:

Book 1: Facing Home

Book 2: Crashing Down (Winter 2018)

Midnight Magic Series:

Amelia

Rough Waters Series:

Book 1: The Goodbye Storm

Book 2: The Runaway Storm

Book 3: The Rising Storm

Stand Alones:

Running From Shadows

Yours for the Taking

****

Multi-Author Series including books by Danielle Stewart

All are stand alone reads and can be enjoyed in any order.

Indigo Bay Series:

A multi-author sweet romance series

Sweet Dreams - Stacy Claflin

Sweet Matchmaker - Jean Oram

Sweet Sunrise - Kay Correll

Sweet Illusions - Jeanette Lewis

Sweet Regrets - Jennifer Peel

Sweet Rendezvous - Danielle Stewart

Short Holiday Stories in Indigo Bay:

A multi-author sweet romance series

Sweet Holiday Wishes - Melissa McClone

Sweet Holiday Surprise - Jean Oram

Sweet Holiday Memories - Kay Correll

Sweet Holiday Traditions - Danielle Stewart

Return to Christmas Falls Series:

A multi-author sweet romance series

Homecoming in Christmas Falls: Ciara Knight

Honeymoon for One in Christmas Falls: Jennifer Peel

Once Again in Christmas Falls: Becky Monson

Rumor has it in Christmas Falls: Melinda Curtis

Forever Yours in Christmas Falls: Susan Hatler

Love Notes in Christmas Falls: Beth Labonte

Finding the Truth in Christmas Falls: Danielle Stewart

****

BOOKS IN THE BARRINGTON BILLIONAIRE SYNCHRONIZED WORLD

By Ruth Cardello:

Always Mine

Stolen Kisses

Trade It All

Let It Burn

More Than Love

By Jeannette Winters:

One White Lie

Table For Two

You & Me Make Three

Virgin For The Fourth Time

His For Five Nights

After Six

By Danielle Stewart:

Fierce Love

Wild Eyes

Crazy Nights

Loyal Hearts

Untamed Devotion

Stormy Attraction

Foolish Temptations

You can now download all Barrington Billionaire books by Danielle Stewart in a "Sweet" version. Enjoy the clean and wholesome version, same story without the spice. If you prefer the hotter version be sure to download the original. The Sweet version still contains adult situations and relationships.

Fierce Love - Sweet Version

Wild Eyes - Sweet Version

Crazy Nights - Sweet Version

Loyal Hearts - Sweet Version

Untamed Devotion - Sweet Version

Stormy Attraction - Sweet Version - Coming Soon

Foolish Temptations - Sweet Version - Coming Soon

NEWSLETTER SIGN-UP

If you'd like to stay up to date on the latest Danielle Stewart news visit www.authordaniellestewart.com and sign up for my newsletter.

One random newsletter subscriber will be chosen every month this year. The chosen subscriber will receive a $25 eGift Card! Sign up today.

AUTHOR CONTACT:

Website: AuthorDanielleStewart.com
Email: AuthorDanielleStewart@Gmail.com
Facebook: Author Danielle Stewart
Twitter: @DStewartAuthor

30261787R00168

Made in the USA
Middletown, DE
24 December 2018